12 MEN
for

PHILLIPA
ASHLEY

sourcebooks
casablanca

Published by Sourcebooks Casablanca, an imprint of Sourcebooks
P.O. Box 4410, Naperville, Illinois 60567-4410
(630) 961-3900
sourcebooks.com

Originally published as *Decent Exposure* in 2006 in Great Britain by Little Black
Dress, an imprint of Headline Publishing Group, London. This edition issued based
on the paperback edition published as *Dating Mr. December* in 2010 in the United
States of America by Sourcebooks Landmark, an imprint of Sourcebooks.

Library of Congress Cataloging-in-Publication Data
Names: Ashley, Phillipa, author.
Title: 12 men for Christmas / Phillipa Ashley.
Other titles: Decent exposure | Twelve men for Christmas
Description: Naperville, Illinois : Sourcebooks Casablanca, [2020] |
   "Originally published as Decent Exposure in 2006 in Great Britain by
   Little Black Dress, an imprint of Headline Publishing Group, London.
   This edition issued based on the paperback edition published as Dating
   Mr. December in 2010 in the United States of America by Sourcebooks
   Landmark, an imprint of Sourcebooks"--Title page verso. | Summary: "This
   smart, sassy contemporary romantic women's fiction won the Romantic
   Novelists Association New Writers Award and is the basis for a Lifetime
   television movie starring Kristin Chenoweth that reruns every year. Emma
   Tremayne moves to the Lake District looking for peace, quiet-and
   celibacy. So perhaps it's not the best idea to help the local mountain
   rescue team put together a "tasteful" nude fundraiser calendar.
   Especially since quite a lot of the community is poking their noses into
   what she's up to-and most have gotten the completely wrong impression
   about Emma's intentions"-- Provided by publisher.
Identifiers: LCCN 2020023566
Subjects: GSAFD: Love stories.
Classification: LCC PR6101.S547 D43 2020 | DDC 823/.92--dc23
LC record available at https://lccn.loc.gov/2020023566

Printed and bound in Canada.
MBP 10 9 8 7 6 5 4 3 2 1

Praise for Phillipa Ashley

"Lovely books filled with warm and likeable characters. Great fun!"
—Bestselling Author Jill Mansell for *Wish You Were Here*

"Fulfills all the best fantasies, including a gorgeous, humanitarian hero and a camper van!"
—Bestselling Author Katie Forde for *Carrie Goes Off the Map*

"Excellent characters and an exciting romance guaranteed to make you quickly turn the pages."
—*Romance Reviews Today* for *12 Men for Christmas*

"Ashley's fun contemporary romance is crafted with humor, a sexy premise, and the intriguing backdrop of the picturesque Lake District."
—*Booklist* for *12 Men for Christmas*

"A delightfully witty and sensual contemporary romance."
—*Romance Junkies* for *12 Men for Christmas*

"Funny, lighthearted romance… Enjoyable, enlightening, and fun. The author creates believable characters that the reader will love."
—*Long and Short Reviews* for *Carrie Goes Off the Map*

"[Ashley] uses humor in a winsome, wicked way to shepherd the characters past their flaws and foibles to propel them to a happy-ever-after with a sizzle… Sparkling entertainment!"
—*Long and Short Reviews* for *Just Say Yes*

For John and Charlotte
with all my love

Chapter 1

"Excuse me, love," said the bearded man in the front row, ever so politely, "did you say *naked?*"

Emma Tremayne clutched her folder of proposals tighter and smiled a smile that went no further than her cherry-scented lip gloss. "That's right, Bob. Naked."

Bob, bald, ruddy-faced, and fiftysomething, nodded as if she'd just confirmed the price of a cheese scone in the local café.

"You mean without any clothes on?" murmured a whippet-like lad whom Emma recognized as a local builder.

"That's the general idea of a nude calendar, Jason, yes." Smiling sweetly, she fixed her eyes on him, then regretted it as a blush spread to the roots of his hair, competing with his red curls for color.

Now that was odd, she thought as a dozen faces tried terribly hard not to look in her direction. If she'd known how easy it was to turn a roomful of hard-bitten men into quivering jellies, she'd have tried it years ago. Unfortunately, right now, it was exactly what she *didn't* want.

In front of her, leaning against fading walls, perched on rickety chairs and peeling Formica tables, were some of the most macho men in England. Tall and short, green and vintage, each of them looked like a nervous schoolboy hauled up before a particularly bossy headmistress. You'd certainly never have known they were a mountain rescue team from the look of them. Or that they'd saved over fifty lives in the past twelve months alone and were expert at rappelling and belaying and all kinds of skills that weren't needed among the sushi bars and coffeehouses and mirror-windowed tower blocks of the city life Emma was used to.

They didn't look extraordinary at all. In fact, they could just as easily have been part of a church choir or, admittedly, a rather fit darts team. Which was exactly why this project was going to be such a huge success. It was a good thing, Emma told herself, that as a seasoned PR person, she had already run through this scenario in her head a dozen times. If she didn't believe in her idea 100 percent, how on earth could she expect them to?

She smiled even more broadly at Bob Jeavons as he slouched on a broken chair. As team leader of the Bannerdale Mountain Rescue Team, he had the power to crush her project with a single word. Emma wanted to take her jacket off, but she didn't dare.

Bob placed his chipped mug, still half-full of tea that by now must have grown cold, on the floor tiles and folded his arms. He studied her for a moment, oblivious to the bead of tea trickling down his beard. "Correct me if I'm wrong, love, but doesn't that mean everyone in Bannerdale will see us with our kit off?"

"Oh, I do hope so," she said airily, ignoring the gasp of horror from Jason. "I really hope so, in fact, because if everyone in Cumbria sees you with your kit off, it will mean that I've done my job properly. It will mean," she carried on, warming to her theme, "that everyone will want to buy the calendar and that we'll raise heaps of money for a new base. Which, if you don't mind me saying," she added, eyeing the paint peeling off the window frame, "you do actually need quite badly."

"Not *that* badly," said a new voice.

Emma peered into the gloom of the room. It was difficult to see where exactly the voice had come from, as the late March evening was drawing in and the strip light had flickered and died shortly after they'd come in.

She looked at a dark figure standing in the doorframe. "Did someone else have a contribution to make?"

This time, the response was easier to locate. It was a cross between a snort and a harrumph, rather like a rhino in heat—not that she'd ever met one.

"I'm sorry, but does someone have a cold?" she asked, with more than a trace of irony.

"No. But someone needs their head examined if they think this is a good idea."

The owner of the voice stepped into the room, and her heart seemed to stop. Will Tennant. She might have known. She'd only met him once before, a few weeks ago when she'd suggested the team get some rather funky promotional merchandise to sell at festivals and open nights. He hadn't been amused then and he certainly didn't look amused now.

As he rested his six-foot-plus, nearly two-hundred-pound frame against a spare patch of wall, Emma felt herself grow even warmer. That superstrength antiperspirant might be good for trekking through a steamy jungle, but it was no protection at all against a man who had all the charm of a grizzly bear.

"I know it seems a bit…radical," said Emma defiantly, trying not to be intimidated. She couldn't quite see Will's face in the dimness, and anyway, she'd forgotten her contacts, but she knew what his expression would be. Patronizing, sarcastic, or hostile, possibly all three.

"Radical?" said Will, crossing his arms.

God, that man was massive, thought Emma, momentarily distracted by the muscles in his forearms.

"Is that what you call it? I'd have said bloody ridiculous. We'll be the laughingstock of all the teams, you know."

"*You* might, mate," laughed Jason, giving Emma a small victory. *Hmm…*she thought, *a little phallic competition might not be a bad thing. With all this testosterone around, it could be a very good thing.*

"You need the funds for a new base, and you need them quickly," Emma explained patiently. "Donation cans and stalls at the village festival are all very well, but you need to do something really dramatic these days to attract attention."

"We don't need that kind of attention," growled Will. "There are other ways of getting the money without fancy PR gimmicks."

Emma's blood approached boiling point. At this rate, the idea of a nude calendar would be thrown out without a meaningful debate, and she'd worked so hard on the proposals—for nothing too. Helping the local mountain rescue team with their fundraising wasn't exactly in the description for her new job with the tourist board. She was here out of the goodness of her heart and, she might have added, was offering them a free consultancy that back in London would have cost them hundreds of pounds.

. As the water tank on the old slate roof gave a temperamental shudder, she sighed.

She definitely wasn't in London now.

"It would all be very tasteful, of course," she went on breezily, feeling very exposed herself. "No one would actually see anything." She halted, not quite knowing how to put it. "Well, I mean, you'd have things to cover your decency, of course."

"What things?" asked Phil, a wiry-looking guy with a ponytail.

"Well…props. You know, tools of the trade. Helmets…"

Emma didn't get any further. As the room erupted, she caught the eye of the only other woman in the room and wished she hadn't. Suzanne Harley, the squad doctor, was visibly shaking, and Emma could see her trying to stop herself from spluttering cookie crumbs all over Bob. Emma frowned hard at her. She needed all the allies she could get, and if even Suzanne wouldn't take her seriously, there was no hope.

"It's entirely up to you, of course, but I have put together some proposals. Here's the design we did for an air ambulance charity," she said, holding up a glossy calendar. The cover had a shot of twelve men posing in front of a helicopter. Granted, they didn't leave much to the imagination, but it was all very classy and stylish. In fact, she was rather proud of it.

Suzanne giggled. Jason's mouth drooped cavernously. Will shook his head in despair.

Emma ignored them and held up an Excel spreadsheet. "Actually, I've also brought a detailed breakdown of the money we raised. With the calendar sales, corporate sponsorship, fees from magazine interviews, and the extra cash from the ensuing publicity, it came to over fifty-six thousand pounds. That should make up the difference between the donations you've already accrued and the total required for the new base."

Suddenly, people sat up straighter in their seats. Eyebrows were raised. Someone let out a low whistle. Only Will looked unmoved.

"And you're sure about this?" asked Bob after a pause. "You're sure people will want to look at a bunch of hairy blokes? I mean, some of us are well past our sell-by dates."

"Speak for yourself, Bob," said Jason.

Emma wanted to hug him and mentally put him down for Mr. January. She handed him a calendar to look at. "Believe me, every woman in Bannerdale would love to find you in her stocking on Christmas morning," she said, crossing her fingers.

Emma knew she sounded far more confident than she looked. Even though her charity campaign for the helicopter medics had been a huge success, she had to admit that her recent track record had been…well, barely short of disastrous. Which was why she was up here, working as public relations officer for the tourist board, not directing a glitzy campaign from the lofty heights of Rogue Communications, the London PR consultancy.

Not that anyone knew that. Not yet anyway.

Someone passed Will a calendar. He rifled through it for a nanosecond and shook his head. "So it's come to this. A serious organization made a mockery of."

Emma felt all trembly and terribly close to hating him. Which wasn't good. She'd hated quite a few people recently, and it was getting to be a habit.

"Actually, I respect a man who speaks his mind, so perhaps you should discuss it among yourselves and then put it to a vote," she said, keeping her voice neutral. "You might feel less inhibited with me out of the way and"—she stared right at Will, whose designer stubble made him look more like a grizzly than ever—"more able to say what you really feel."

He stared back at her, his brown eyes cold. "*Actually*, Emma," he said sarcastically, "I think you'll find we've always been able to speak our minds up here. In fact, we were managing perfectly well before you came."

"Now, Will. I know I'm one for plain talking, lad, but that's a bit much. I think it's a cracking idea, lass. It's just a bit of a shock, that's all," cut in Bob, smiling at Emma. "You need to give us a bit more time to get used to it. Ignore Will. He's just a miserable bugger."

Emma would very much have liked to ignore Will, but right now, he was making it pretty difficult. "I'll leave this stuff with you, and you can let me know your decision later," she said, picking up her untouched mug from the table. "Now, shall we all have another cup of tea? I'll make it."

———

Alone in the tiny kitchen, Emma poured out the last of the tea into a cup with no handle, wincing at the sight and smell of the rusty liquid. This was only her second visit to the base, but she already knew they liked their tea as up front and plainly spoken as everything else. She'd been terribly careful not to talk too much about spin and profiles and target audiences. She'd even wondered if she should have turned up in something more casual than her work suit, but that would have been going too far. She liked looking smart, even if everyone else lived in a fleece. Besides, she could no longer afford a whole new wardrobe, so sticking out like a sore thumb would have to do for now.

"They'll come around, you know."

Looking up from her undrinkable tea, she found Suzanne Harley carrying a tray of empty mugs.

"Well done, Emma. You've really got them going. That joke about the tools and helmets was a masterstroke."

Emma thought of admitting it was a slip of the tongue but decided against it. Didn't she look like enough of an idiot already?

"Thanks for the vote of confidence, but I think some of them are going to take a lot more persuading before they buy into the idea."

She handed Suzanne her cup, but the doctor shook her head and wrinkled her freckled nose.

"Thanks, but no thanks, Emma. And I shouldn't think you have anything too serious to worry about, given the reaction from young Jason. In fact, he seems worryingly enthusiastic about getting his clothes off. And you have Bob on your side, which counts for a lot."

"What about Will Tennant? He seemed unreasonably annoyed at the whole idea of a calendar. Somehow, I feel like I've wronged him in a previous life." And why should he bulldoze her idea when the others seemed almost ready to come around, she thought. Just who did he think he was?

Suzanne sighed. "Will is always happiest when he has something to be angry about. He's not that bad, really, Emma, underneath the sarcasm and the rudeness and the bloody-mindedness..."

"You make him sound so charming."

Suzanne let out a laugh of derision. "No one in their right mind could ever describe Will as charming—though he doesn't seem to have any problems with the opposite sex. Look, give him time to come around. Don't try and persuade or push him. Just leave him to stew for a while. You never know. He might be more receptive than you think."

Emma pulled a tissue from her bag and blew her nose. The dust really was terrible in here, and she didn't believe Suzanne for a moment. "I don't think he'll ever be receptive to a fancy PR guru from the evil fleshpots of the metropolis," she sniffed.

"Hmm. It must be a bit of a shock for you, moving up here," said Suzanne with a wry smile. "There's hardly much action beyond the local pubs and the Conservative club."

"It's not too bad," said Emma. "There's a talk by the Herdwick Sheep Society next week, and the community hall is showing old Bond films on Saturday nights as long as there isn't a Young Farmers' event. It says so in the parish magazine."

Suzanne feigned shock. "The parish magazine, eh? Well, even though I'm supposed to be a pillar of the community, I haven't resorted to that for entertainment. What on earth made you leave your job and move to Bannerdale?"

It was the question Emma had been dreading. And one that, in the past few months, she'd been lucky to avoid. Fortunately, like the professional she was—correction, *once* was—she had her answer prepared.

"It was a fantastic opportunity, a unique environment, new challenge..."

Suzanne raised her eyebrows. Emma took a deep breath and made a decision. It was no use, she told herself. From what she'd seen from their few meetings so far, Suzanne seemed like a genuine person, and unlike some people, she also had a sense of humor. Emma decided she deserved the truth. Besides, she felt she'd tasted enough deception and spin over the past few months to last a lifetime. Most of it from her ex, Jeremy Forbes.

"My boss was shagging my boyfriend. I threw something at her, and she sacked me," she said, straight-faced.

Suzanne laughed out loud. "Sounds like a perfectly good reason to me."

Emma realized with a start that Suzanne thought she was joking. Maybe it was just as well, after all. Maybe her new friends weren't quite ready for the whole truth just yet.

"Don't feel you have to resort to the parish mag again," said Suzanne, leaning back against the countertop. "Why don't you come out for a drink after the meeting? I doubt the Black Dog could produce a mojito, but they do have a half-decent glass of red wine. And if you're very lucky, you might get chatted up by Silas from the dominoes league."

"Is he hot?"

"In 1947, I'm sure he was."

Emma grinned. "Then I'll definitely come."

Just then, a swell of voices drifted in, signaling the door of the meeting room had opened.

"Ah. The moment of truth. I believe my vote is required. Are you coming, Emma?"

"I think I'll stay here. It might be less embarrassing. Tell them I'm washing up and come and fetch me when you know the result."

"OK. But I wouldn't worry. They'll go for it. Money always talks."

As Suzanne was half out the door, Emma had a sudden thought.

"Suzanne, if we can't get enough guys to agree, is there any chance you would pose for one of the shots?"

The doctor stopped, turned, and smiled. "Emma, I know how much the rescue team needs a new base, and I'm willing to help you in any way I can. But pose naked on a calendar with that bunch? Not unless I was drugged, tied down, and certified insane. You've got more chance of getting Will to do it."

Well, that was plain enough. But she didn't blame Suzanne. Being the only woman made things a bit awkward, and being a local GP probably made it much worse. It was no use moping; she'd better get on and do something while the team was discussing her idea and putting it to a vote.

She turned on the tap, hoping the heater might produce enough warm water to at least give the dirty mugs a cursory rinse. If she could only find a drop of dishwashing liquid, that would be a big help. She smiled. Back in London, they'd never dreamed of making their own tea. Her boss, Phaedra, had very few virtues, but indulging herself was one of them. If there wasn't a pot of Blue Mountain bubbling somewhere in the office, there was always some assistant willing to fetch a Starbucks coffee or a smoothie. Emma shivered. That last beverage was now off the menu. In fact, she hoped she'd never see one as long as she lived. Not after what had happened on that fateful day with Rogue.

She opened a cupboard under the sink, hunting for the dish soap and finding only a half-empty bottle of some dubious-looking solution in between the bleach and an old mousetrap. Emma tried not to notice the small black droppings next to the trap. This was the country, after all, and she didn't want to be a wimp. And what was that they said? You were only ever six feet away from a rat in London. Urban myth or not, she knew where most of them hung out.

Pulling off her jacket and longing for some dishwashing gloves, she set to work on the mugs. With only her bare hands and no detergent, it wasn't very effective, but she was doing her best. Most important, she was being useful.

"Here. Try this."

Emma turned around. It was that voice again. Deep and distinctive, the soft Cumbrian accent taking the edge—a tiny bit—off the gruffness. A big hand, sprinkled with hair, reached above her head to a shelf and pulled down a bottle of green liquid.

She ought to have said thanks, but after the reception she'd gotten from Will earlier, the words seemed to stick in her throat. She took the bottle from his hand ungraciously.

"Shouldn't you be in the meeting room, making the case for the prosecution?"

He leaned against the counter. It had warmed up in there, next to the boiler, and Emma again felt herself grow uncomfortably hot in her suit. "Aren't you going to vote against me?"

"I abstained."

"Oh."

Squirting a splotch of liquid into the sink, she wondered why she felt so self-conscious. She kept her eyes on the sink and her hands busy, whipping up the foam with her fingers, feeling a bit shaky.

"And if I had voted, it wouldn't have been against you."

She plonked a wet mug on the drainer. Will picked up a tea towel and started drying the mugs.

"Do you mean that?" she asked.

He placed the cup on the counter, shining and clean. "I wouldn't have voted against you personally. Only against your idea."

"Thanks a lot," she managed, dropping a plate in the sink and succeeding in splashing his trousers.

"You're welcome," he said without a trace of irony.

Emma had never known that washing a few cups and plates could be so excruciating—or complicated. She felt confused. Was he holding out the olive branch by helping her? Or was he here to let her know he meant business and wouldn't be denied his say? His directness about the calendar was irritating in one way, unnerving even, but at least he'd laid his cards on the table, which was more than some men did.

Will also wasn't giving her any clues. He didn't say anything else, just carried on drying crockery and placing it on a shelf above the sink. Occasionally, he waited, a trifle impatiently perhaps, if she couldn't keep up with his drying.

She also found herself trying hard not to touch him in any way, which was difficult given the smallness of the room. Once, she brushed against his arm and felt the hairs on it touch her bare wrist. He didn't seem to notice, but Emma felt the tickle go on after they'd lost contact. As she scrubbed at a plate hard enough to wear a hole in it, debating whether to try and make conversation, Suzanne poked her head around the door again.

She was good, Emma gave her that. Her face barely registered her surprise at finding them in apparent domestic harmony at a kitchen sink.

"Keeping busy?" she asked mischievously.

"Team building," said Will, startling Emma.

"See—he does have a sense of humor lurking somewhere," laughed Suzanne.

Will threw the tea towel down on the countertop without smiling. "For some things," he said and strode off toward the meeting room.

Emma stood with her mouth open, and Suzanne shook her head. Emma hardly dared to ask the outcome of the vote, but as they trooped back to the room, she was soon put out of her misery.

"There. Told you, you had nothing to worry about," Suzanne hissed as Bob's voice rang out, confirming that the motion to take part in a nude calendar had been carried unanimously.

"Where's Will gone?" Emma whispered, searching for him among the other men.

Suzanne rolled her eyes. "I think he's sorting out some gear. Anything to get away, probably. What was he doing in the kitchen?"

"He wanted me to know he only hates my fundraising methods, not me personally."

"That's something, I suppose. I told you he's not that bad."

Emma was saved from replying by Bob.

"So that's eleven in favor and one abstention," he declared to the group. "It looks like that's it, lads—and Sue. There's no going back. Get yourselves in training, and stock up on the fake tan."

Predictably, groans filled the room.

"That won't be necessary," reassured Emma. "It would be better if you went for the natural look. Although I'll volunteer to do a spot of waxing if anyone needs it."

Leafing through a calendar, Suzanne frowned. "Wait a minute. You said that eleven people had volunteered. That means we're one short."

Jason put up his hand. "We could have a group shot," he suggested. He was so sweet, Emma thought, picturing him au naturel, cuddling one of the rescue dogs.

"It would be better if we had a guy for each month. You know, Mr. January, Mr. February, Mr. March, et cetera. You can all put your name down for one," she offered, handing out a pad and pen. What difference it made, she really couldn't see; they were all going to be starkers, but it was always good to give people the illusion that they had a choice. "Maybe choose your birthday month? That would be appropriate. Jason, you go first as you seem to be so keen."

"I only want to help the team," he said, turning strawberry again. Poor lad, Emma thought. He couldn't have been more than twenty. She wondered what his mum would think.

Ten minutes later, the pad came back, with more crossings out than her old math book. Two of them had wanted October, having creative visions involving Halloween pumpkins, and one man couldn't decide between his wedding anniversary and his wife's birthday, but things had been arranged, somehow, to most people's satisfaction.

"Only Mr. December vacant, then?" asked Emma, feeling relieved and far happier than she knew she deserved. "No one fancy being the Christmas cracker?"

Jason laughed. "More like a turkey."

"We're going to have to find someone else," said Bob.

Phil, the ponytailed man, gave Emma her pen back. "Yes, but who?" he asked. "We can hardly go around asking for contributions from friends and relatives, and it *is* meant to be a team project."

"What about asking Wardale MRT to put someone forward?" suggested Suzanne.

"I don't think so," said Bob.

"No way!" cried Jason.

"What's wrong with Wardale?" whispered Emma to Suzanne.

"Penis envy," replied Suzanne, forcing Emma to stifle a giggle.

"There's a bit of a history there. They got a lottery grant for their new base, and we missed out."

"But don't they help you out on rescues?" asked Emma. "I mean, I'm sure Bob told me the teams often work together."

"Of course we do, and quite often if there's a major incident. It's all strictly professional on a callout, naturally. But afterward"—Suzanne gave a sharp intake of breath—"never the twain shall meet."

"Oh dear."

"I suppose," said Bob, scratching his beard thoughtfully. "We might have to, if we're desperate…"

"What about Harry Caversham?" offered Suzanne.

Bob nodded. "Hmm. I did wonder. He may be one of them now, but he was a member for five years until he moved house."

"I'll do it."

Emma stared at the door where Will had managed to creep back in without her noticing again. He moved quietly for a grumpy giant. "But only if I *absolutely* have to," he added, eyeing Emma.

"Don't feel obliged on my account," said Emma primly.

"I don't," he said, smiling at her now with what looked like a flash of amusement in his eyes. It was gone before she had time to register it, and his trademark glower was back on his face. "But it's a damn sight better than dragging outsiders into this bloody charade."

Bob laughed. "Very gracious, Will. Don't put yourself out, mate."

Will didn't laugh back but just shrugged his shoulders. "The offer's there."

Emma was trying desperately not to look too smug or too surprised. She picked up the pad, wrote down his name, and gave him a brief professional smile.

"Thank you, Will. It looks like you're Mr. December."

He narrowed his eyes at her and stalked off again as the meeting broke up, leaving Emma exhausted and a bit shell-shocked, with a sticky blouse and a mouse dropping stuck to her cuff.

———

"Well, I have to admit, I never thought I'd see that," said Suzanne as they walked out of the base later, en route to the Black Dog. "Will agreeing to take his clothes off in public."

"It was a surprise," agreed Emma, wondering for the umpteenth time just what she had let herself in for.

"Then again," said Suzanne mischievously, jangling her car keys, "I didn't think he'd want Wardale getting involved. And you have to admit, miserable bugger though he is, he is going to look rather aesthetic…"

"Sue, you're married!" giggled Emma, realizing how Will had been backed into a corner. And Suzanne was absolutely right. Emma had to concede, even though it went against all her principles, that at six foot three, dark-haired, and disgustingly handsome in a rugged, rough-edged kind of way, Will Tennant was the only one she'd have paid good money to see naked.

Chapter 2

SIX MONTHS EARLIER, AS A SECURITY GUARD HAD GUIDED HER onto a London street, Emma Tremayne had vowed that henceforth, she would live the life of a PR nun. She'd leave her city life behind her and find a quiet little corner of England where nothing humiliating or painful was ever going to happen.

Now, as she dragged her aching legs up six hundred meters of hillside a few weeks after the rescue meeting, she was having doubts. A tiny voice in her head was hinting that maybe—just maybe—volunteering to help the Bannerdale Mountain Rescue Team hadn't been such a good idea.

To be fair, Emma told herself as she stepped over a pile of sheep droppings, her diary entry for that Saturday afternoon hadn't read *ogle naked guy on top of mountain*. It had said *finish unpacking*. Even now, there were still boxes blocking the way to the closet in her lakeside flat.

She'd actually had her hand in one box when she'd gotten the call to "supervise" the photo shoot for the calendar. Her new boss, James Marshall, had sounded even more fraught than usual. And how could any woman refuse a man whose wife had gone into labor early?

"Oh, James, I can hardly go along and stare at twelve naked guys," she'd protested. "It's strictly an all-male affair...we promised them!"

"Emma, I wouldn't ask you, but I'm desperate. They're waiting for me in the delivery suite now."

She had a sudden vision of James, his suit trousers rolled up, wading into a birthing pool. "If you really can't get anyone else, I—"

"Fantastic! I knew I could rely on you. Besides, it's only one man today—Will. The main shoot was last week, but he was away on business."

"Will? *Will Tennant?*"

"Yes. Him. Why? Is there a problem?"

"No. No problem at all," she lied as her pulse accelerated. "Apart from the fact he'll be in his birthday suit, I'm sure he'll relish the prospect of me staring at him. Where's it happening?"

"At the summit cairn on top of Black Fell. Make sure you take your walking boots, and make sure they do something creative with Mr. December!"

"Give my best wishes to your wife…" she'd begun, but the line was already dead.

Will. Emma sighed. It would have to be him, wouldn't it? She knew how much he hated the idea of the calendar, and she hadn't seen him since the meeting where he'd decided, albeit reluctantly, to go ahead with it. Now she'd been sent to "supervise" him while he took his clothes off…

Emma was nearly at the summit now. Just a few more yards and she'd be upon him. She stumbled on some loose stones before hauling herself over the last ridge as a trail of moisture trickled down the small of her back. Then she saw him. Standing behind the cairn—self-conscious and with his usual scowl, but every bit as magnificent as the view.

Mr. December.

One glance was enough to take in the full glory of the naked Will. Dark-brown hair tousled by the breeze, designer stubble, and the kind of lean yet muscular body you only got from lots of healthy activity. His light golden tan, while not all over, had clearly not been acquired in Northern England. She would like to have focused on the color of his eyes. Liked to have, but currently they were concealed by a pair of wraparound shades.

"Sorry!" she heard herself shout above the noise of the wind whistling across the fell top. "It's Emma Tremayne. I came to help supervise the photos…but I can see I'm a bit late." She cringed even as the words left her lips. What a stupid thing to say—and she simply had to stop staring at him.

"It's OK. I'm not looking," she said, hoping that holding her hands over her eyes would make him feel more comfortable with the situation.

It didn't.

A deep voice, as icy as the frost crystals on the rocks, snapped her back to reality. "You've seen me now, and we're all adults, so you may as well come over here. We've nearly finished, haven't we?"

The photographer obviously knew when it was time to quit, and he began to fold up his tripod and equipment. So she'd come all this way for nothing. OK. Fine.

Mr. December shivered and hugged himself. "Any chance whatsoever of me having my coat?" he demanded. "It's right next to you."

"Well...are you sure it's OK?"

"Just get me my coat...please."

There was a note of desperation in his voice. It really was *very* chilly up here.

Picking up his red high-tech jacket, she approached him, eyes firmly fixed on the rocks at her feet. The second she was within range, she held it at arm's length. A moment later, he was standing there, almost respectable.

"It's safe to look now," he said.

Hmm...safe...not sure about that. She lifted her eyes and found they ended up somewhere about the middle of his broad chest. From behind his dark glasses, he was gazing down at her glowing cheeks with a wicked grin that did nothing to cool them down.

"So, Emma, how did you wangle your way into being here?" he asked, a teasing note creeping into his voice. "I thought we'd all agreed that James Marshall would direct the photo shoots."

"His wife's in the hospital having a baby, and no one else could come. Believe me, it's not a job I would have volunteered for—actually."

"So it's *actually* that bad, eh?"

"Oh, no. I mean it was you I was thinking of...me being a woman... though now you come to mention it, I should really ask for danger money."

"Charming!" he exclaimed. "In that case, maybe I shouldn't be Mr. December after all."

But as he took off his shades, she could see there was a definite glint in his dark-brown eyes.

"What I meant to say was…it's probably wholly inappropriate for me to be here in the circumstances. We did promise that it would be a men-only project. Just to save any awkwardness."

"Well, it only goes to prove one thing," said Will, pulling his mountain rescue jacket tighter. "Never believe a word PR people say. Now, do you mind if I put the rest of my clothes on? You can supervise if you like."

"That won't be necessary! I'll wait over here until you're decent," she cried hastily and walked back to the rock. Keeping her gaze fixed on the horizon, she tried to fathom out why he'd been so resistant to the calendar. It was ridiculous. No one else had objected to the idea. Certainly not when they'd heard how much money the air ambulance had made from the one she'd produced for her old PR firm.

How could Will not want the squad to raise funds for a new base? Frankly, she'd been shocked when she'd seen their present base, a ramshackle affair cobbled together out of some old farm buildings. They deserved so much better. And she knew she was good at her job.

Now that she had a chance to put the carefully honed PR skills she'd brought from her senior position at Rogue—now that her ideas and enthusiasm were helping to achieve so much more than coverage for a new brand of smoothie or the latest electronic gadget—she'd begun to believe in herself again. Working for the tourist board, volunteering to help the mountain rescue, her skills could actually help people.

She had to admit it felt good. For the first time in months, she felt good about herself.

Perhaps Will was embarrassed at having to take his clothes off. Well, she had news for him—he shouldn't be! With a body like that? Fit and hard and lean muscled. A swirl of desire stirred in her stomach.

Oh…

Emma swallowed a tiny lump in her throat, wondering where that swirl—which was unexpected but admittedly rather nice—had come from. This was Will, she reminded herself, grateful that the pink stealing into her cheeks could be put down to the effort of climbing up here. Will, who'd made no secret of the fact that he hated her idea and seemed to resent her presence. Will, who thought far too much of his own opinions and seemed to think everyone else should follow his lead. Besides, it was completely unprofessional to be thinking of a client in this way, especially one who needed more convincing than most that she was every bit as good at her job as he was.

And even if he hadn't been Will but some other gorgeous naked bloke, she still couldn't risk having a crush on any man these days. It was too soon after Jeremy. Maybe it always would be.

Emma snatched a lungful of cold mountain air, glad to feel the icy wind sting her cheeks. In a moment, she told herself, Will would be back in his clothes, and she'd be back in control.

———

While he got dressed, Will took the opportunity to size her up. Hmm, he thought, here she was again: Emma Tremayne, the squad's new PR "guru," on loan from the local tourist board. They were very fortunate to have her services, or so he'd been told.

Against his will, he had to admit he'd been impressed by the professional way she'd pitched the calendar concept to the team. Impressed by her powers of persuasion—but not by the idea. He was still adamant that it was a gimmick, a publicity stunt that would only bring the squad into disrepute and make them the laughingstock of other teams.

But her PR skills weren't the only thing he'd taken notice of. Back then, she'd been wearing a short but businesslike black skirt and the kind of heels rarely seen in a mountain rescue base. Even today in her new fleece and walking boots, flustered and windswept, she was stunning. Suddenly, he was thankful he was back in the safety of his combat trousers.

He fastened up his jacket and gave himself a mental shake. This wasn't a good time or place to start thinking about the PR girl in that way, no matter how sweet or hot she was. In fact, Will reminded himself, there was never a good time or place to think about a woman like that.

Not now.

For nearly two years, he'd sworn off love the way other members of the team swore off alcohol and junk food. Unlike them, he had stuck to his pledge. It hadn't been difficult to keep, considering the catastrophe that had prompted it. Two years ago, he'd gotten his fingers burned so badly he'd vowed he would never let a woman under his skin again. He wasn't averse to letting the odd one near his bed, but closer than that?

No way. Not after Kate.

Yet he had to admit that there was a lot about Emma that was mouthwateringly attractive. Totally impractical, of course, but undeniably sexy. Although her long, dark hair needed tying back, he liked the way it kept flying away in the breeze and getting into her eyes. How her tight jeans, completely unsuitable for walking, clung to her pert bottom. The trace of makeup she was wearing wasn't necessary, but it did set off her eyes—the exact shade of jade he'd seen on a temple idol in Thailand.

Oh yes, thought Will, turning up his jacket collar against the wind, Emma was definitely one of the few women who might make it as far as the four-poster in his cottage. But first she looked like she needed a drink. He saw no sign of a rucksack—no sign of a map either, and somehow he knew that a compass and whistle were out of the question. She probably had a phone, though, and he suspected it would be a state-of-the-art, dinky little one with every feature possible except a signal.

"It's OK. I'm decent now," he called to her, delving into his sack for some water and energy bars.

He threw a bottle of water and one of the bars to Pete, the photographer, who was about to set off ahead of them. Then he unscrewed the top of a second bottle, walked over, and handed it to Emma.

"Thanks," she murmured in relief, drinking half straight down before ripping open the energy bar.

He opened a third bottle, and as he sipped his drink, Will watched her munching the snack. She looked cold now. That much was obvious from the way her nipples were pressing against the soft cotton of her cute pink T-shirt. In his opinion, Emma Tremayne needed an intensive course in mountain survival. If only he'd brought the bivvy tent with him or a sleeping bag to snuggle under while he taught her the best way to keep warm in an emergency situation.

"You shouldn't have come up here on your own," he said gruffly, trying to tame his unruly thoughts. He reached into his rucksack for another bottle. "And you'd better put your fleece back on now that you've cooled down a bit."

She shook her head as he passed the water to her.

"Take it," he insisted. "You look a bit dehydrated."

"I'm fine," she blurted out, spraying crumbs over him from the last of the bar.

Will dropped the bottle and her fleece in her lap anyway.

"James shouldn't have sent you up here alone. You've got no proper gear, no map, and no experience hiking by the look of it. You've been helping us out for a few weeks. You should know better by now."

"I've survived, haven't I?"

"Today," he said grimly. "You'd be surprised what might happen if the weather closes in. See that bank of clouds over there?" He pointed at the western horizon. "That's a weather front. You won't be able to see a thing up here but mist in a couple of hours."

"Don't exaggerate. I've got my phone, and this isn't the Himalayas, and before you ask, I have got a signal. Absolutely nothing could go wrong."

"The times I've heard people say that. If only it were true, Emma, we'd all be out of a job. I just don't want you to find out the hard way. Come on, then. Time to get back."

She was probably right. He was being a bit self-righteous. It was a busy route, and it was unlikely she'd have come to any harm. But he'd never been able to turn down a challenge, be it a playground skirmish, a difficult rescue, or a bright and sexy woman.

———

Emma handed him her empty bottle as he packed the trash away. *It's OK. I'm decent now*—that was what he'd said. His words had zinged her from head to toe. *Decent* was the last adjective she'd have used in connection with Will.

Strong, surprisingly warm fingers closed around hers as he hauled her up from the ground. They were rough—toughened by rocks and ropes, she supposed. Unlike Jeremy's, soft and smooth from life at a laptop. She preferred Will's. They felt…safe and dangerous all at the same time.

She tugged herself free of his grip and, for a brief moment, caught a flicker of something in his eyes. But it was gone just as quickly as Will simply shrugged and concentrated on buckling up his rucksack.

He was unfathomable, she thought. No doubt he was totally dedicated to his work with the squad, but on the few occasions they'd come across each other, he seemed to have taken particular exception to her. Well, so what if her idea of a "route" was finding the shortest way from the tube station to a skinny latté? She might not know anything about rappelling down a cliff, but she did know a lot about the power of publicity. At the end of the day, her help and ideas might get them a new base—even Mr. know-it-all December couldn't deny her that.

"You really don't approve of this calendar, do you?" she asked as they set off down the path. She had to say something; his silence was more annoying than his caustic remarks.

"Do you want me to be *absolutely* honest?"

"I do consider it a desirable trait in a man."

Will halted on the stony path. "If you really want a straight answer, then no—I don't like the idea at all. Frankly, I think it makes a mockery of a serious organization."

"Don't sit on the fence, Will. Speak your mind."

"You did ask me for a truthful answer."

She was determined not to give up. This idea was her brainchild, and she was going to defend it to the hilt.

"Come on now. Even you have to admit it will raise the squad's profile and, more important, raise money for the redevelopment of the base. The facilities are hopelessly inadequate."

"They are indeed—hopelessly. And we desperately need to sort them out. But I'm not sure this is the way to go about it." Will couldn't bring himself to tell her the real story. That he had already put up half the funds for the new base. That, actually, he had offered the whole amount, but the committee had flatly refused to allow one team member to pay for the lot.

Besides, it wasn't as if he had no sense of humor. He needed it when he was out on a rain-lashed hillside, sometimes on a wild-goose chase. And, he reflected grimly, black humor was a way of coping with some of the awful things they saw. In fact, it was his only way of dealing with it. But he did not like being ridiculed. And if people thought he was the bad guy for expressing his opinions, that was their problem. He refused to be made a fool of by anyone—ever.

Still, Emma was persistent, he'd give her that. In fact, she was so sweetly persuasive that his heart almost melted a fraction of a degree.

"Will, the calendar is bound to generate a lot of helpful publicity— and that's in addition to the sales. At my London agency—"

"You're forgetting something, Emma. We're not in London now. This is Cumbria, or haven't you noticed?" he said, dismissing her low-slung jeans and shiny new walking boots with a sweep of his hand.

"Then if you're so absolutely against it, why on earth did you agree to be Mr. December?" she replied, exasperated at last.

"Once it was agreed by the committee, I had no choice. After all, I am one of the team leaders. We all stick together. You know that, Emma. I had to set an example, no matter how bad an idea I think it is."

They reached a ladder stile, and Will went over first, then put down the rucksack to help her over. "Not going too fast for you, am I?" he asked.

"No, I'm fine—and I don't need helping over the stile. Thanks," she replied, climbing down the steps and ignoring his offered hand.

He shrugged, suddenly adding, "Look, I may have been a bit unfair. I know you meant well in suggesting the calendar, but I'm not one for smooth talking. What you see is what you get with me."

Hmm…and that is *something to shout about*, she thought to herself, but as for his apology? It was a nice try, but he hadn't eaten nearly enough humble pie. Several yards in front, his red rucksack was bobbing up and down as she descended the path. She felt tired. She'd spent the past few evenings unpacking the last of her stuff, and she'd been up late on the internet, emailing her brother and nieces who lived in New Zealand.

Too hot again in her jacket, she was still struggling to keep up. It went against the grain, but she was going to have to ask him to slow down. Then she glimpsed heaven: the parking lot was visible just a few hundred feet below. She heaved a sigh of relief and quickened her step to catch up with him, knowing there wasn't far to go. It was just as well, as her thighs were burning now and her calf muscles were starting to shake and cramp as she tried to keep pace with the long, long stride of those never-ending legs...

It was inevitable, really—unavoidable that her world would suddenly turn upside down.

One moment, she'd been trying hard *not* to concentrate on Will's admittedly fit backside as she followed him down the path. The next, she was making a close acquaintance with the mud and something that looked suspiciously like sheep droppings. As she lay on the ground, she felt her heart pounding like a pneumatic drill and heard a loud thudding in her ears.

"Emma! Are you all right?"

A pair of oversized muddy boots had stopped inches away from her nose. She opened her mouth to reply but seemed to have been robbed of the power of speech.

"Can you get up? Are you hurt?"

"I'm OK," she heard herself croak as she tried to struggle to her knees. "Just a bit shaken up."

This time, she didn't hesitate in taking his offered hand.

"Ow!"

"What's the matter?"

He helped her to her feet and turned over her hand with surprising gentleness. Livid grazes glistened red across her palms, tiny chips of gravel adhering to the raw skin.

"Just a few abrasions...nasty though," he remarked and pointed to the knees of her jeans, now appliquéd with mud. "What about the rest of you?"

"The grass and bracken saved my legs, I think..."

"You're lucky not to have broken your wrists," he observed—rather harshly, in Emma's view. She hadn't done it deliberately, and if he hadn't been going so fast, it might never have happened.

"You need to get those hands cleaned up," he ordered. "Come on. I've got a first aid kit in the Land Rover."

"No really, I'm fine."

"You'll never drive home in that state. Don't be silly. Unless you don't trust me?" he challenged, narrowing his eyes.

"Of course I do! I just don't want to make a fuss, that's all." But that was the trouble. She didn't trust him. She didn't trust any man these days. Not even to do something as innocent as clean her sore hands.

"It's no bother," he replied in such an unexpectedly gentle tone that her stomach flipped. "Now can you get down to the parking lot in one piece on your own, or do I have to carry you?"

"You'd never manage it—not with all that gear too."

Will's mouth twisted in a smile. "I was joking, actually, but if you really want me to, I'm more than happy to oblige."

"No!"

Damn. She'd never hear the last of it if he did have to carry her down a mountainside. City girl Emma can't even walk off a hill without something going wrong. They'd love that, especially the way Will would paint it.

Minutes later, to Emma's immense relief, they'd reached the little graveled parking lot, almost deserted now as the afternoon drew to a close. She thought of marching straight back to her car, but she had to admit her hands *were* hurting, and if she was brutally honest, she was in dire need of some TLC. It was too late anyway; Will was already striding purposefully toward her, cutting off any chance of escape.

"Over here," he said, indicating the Rescue Land Rover parked on the shoulder. Opening the back doors, he flipped open the lid of a professional first aid kit and brought out a pack of antiseptic wipes.

———

"Sit down, then, so I can look at you. Let's get your jacket off," he said, feeling unaccountably self-conscious. He helped her slide the jacket sleeves down her arms, carefully easing them over her sore hands. As he did so, he couldn't help but notice the lush fullness of her breasts, the slight beading against her thin T-shirt.

The desire suddenly running rampant through him was playing havoc with his bedside manner. Brisk cheerfulness, that was his aim with injuries, but Emma was starting to make him feel very unprofessional indeed. He wanted to sweep her into his arms and kiss her better. Kiss all of her better, in fact—maybe even use his mouth and tongue to make her better too.

For some reason, she'd got him behaving like a teenager, and yet he hardly knew her. He tried hard to focus on doing his job, to stay on safe ground rather than venture any deeper into the unfamiliar territory that was Emma.

Clearing his throat, he took her hands in his as if he were examining a piece of porcelain. "These grazes need washing thoroughly as soon as you get home, *and* you need to get every bit of grit out of them, but I'll do my best to make it more comfortable until then," he said curtly. Returning her hands to her lap, he ripped open the antiseptic pack and debated whether or not to warn her before he started.

"This might sting a bit."

As he touched the raw skin on one of her hands and she nearly jumped ten feet in the air, he realized he'd just made the understatement of the year. She winced and tried to take her hand away.

"Don't be a baby," he said brusquely, imprisoning her fingers in his. "It's not that bad."

"You sit here and say that."

"I'm only trying to help, but if you don't want me to…"

"No, I'm grateful. Really. It's just…so sore."

"I know it's tender, Emma, and I'll be as careful as I possibly can." He crossed his heart solemnly. "Promise."

He could see she didn't believe him, and she was right not to. He saw her bite her lip, her eyes glistening as he cleaned her hand, and he reflected on how this would be the perfect time to ask her out on a date. And if she'd been any other woman, he would have.

But Emma? Now? It just didn't seem, well, ethical.

A horrible thought darted into his mind; maybe his conscience was coming home to roost. She looked so gorgeous, sitting there, her feet scraping the ground, her new boots muddy, a smudge of mud on her face. Trusting him. That last observation made his stomach flip and caused an unprofessional response lower down. He rubbed her hand harder than he meant, and she twitched in discomfort.

———

As soon as he'd finished sticking a dressing on her hand, Emma was ready to make her escape. That dark and sexy gaze met hers, and for a nanosecond, she thought she glimpsed something more tender than irritation or his professional manner. It might even have been tenderness, but it was so fleeting, she was already wondering if she'd imagined it. Whatever it was, Emma suddenly felt a strange pricking at the back of her eyes that made her want to get to the haven of her car right away.

"Thanks so much, Will. Bye then," she muttered and had already gotten three paces from the Land Rover when she heard him calling her, not unkindly but with a distinct tinge of amusement.

"Emma—hold on a moment, please."

She turned around to face him. What on earth could he want now?

"I hate to tell you this, but actually, I need to do your other hand…"

———

An hour or so later, both hands protected by attractive white dressings, Emma was nearly back at her apartment. The cuts were hurting but nowhere near enough to warrant the tears threatening to put in an appearance at any moment. She realized it wasn't the fall that had caused them but Will's unexpected care for her.

His gentleness, however grudging, had reminded her how vulnerable she had become since Jeremy. Charming, handsome, shallow Jeremy had reduced her to this state when he'd laid her heart open six months before. Now it seemed that any man had the power to reduce her to jelly with a simple act of kindness, she chided herself. Any man, that was, whom she just happened to meet, minus his clothes, on top of a mountain. Especially one in a rescue team, with a body to die for, demanding she sit down and let him tend to her wounds.

She was climbing the staircase to her flat now and scraping the key in the lock. Pulling off her boots and taking off her coat, she collapsed onto the sofa. She curled up and hugged the huge purple, star-shaped cushion that had been a flat-warming present from Jules and Sarah, two of the London friends who'd stuck by her after she'd been given the boot from Rogue and Jeremy all in the same day.

Emma let out a little sob as she remembered how her friends had handed out the wine, the sympathy, and the tissues and helped her trawl the internet looking for a new job. They'd even driven all the way up to the Lakes to help her move in to the flat. But after a weekend helping her settle in, they'd had to go back, of course. She could see them now, jumping into Jules's bloke's van before heading home to London with promises of wild weekends to come and dire warnings about sheep shagging.

Emma had smiled and waved and reassured them that the local sheep weren't her type. And then she'd hauled herself up the stairs to the flat and done just what she was going to do now—have a bloody good cry.

To her shame, the tears had soaked the cushion before she fell asleep, exhausted, as the afternoon reached its close. When she awoke, the purple star was still clutched to her like a favorite doll, the sun was starting to set over the lake, and the flat was still in disarray. As she dragged a tissue from the pocket of her jeans and wiped her sticky eyes, she decided to put the kettle on and give herself a motivational talk.

She was a strong, independent woman who was getting her life back in order. Starting with her small flat, one of the few aspects of the whole sorry mess of her life that had turned out well over the past few months. OK, so it didn't have a view over a buzzing main street bristling with the scent of coffee and ethnic food. It wasn't six tube stops away from Jeremy's favorite teppanyaki restaurant or three from the deli where the old woman ordered in his favorite pastrami because "he was so polite and *so* handsome."

This little flat, she reminded herself, was twenty minutes' walk from a bottle of milk and several hours from a bowl of miso soup. Yet it had its own advantages. It had a view over the lake that made your soul soar, and most of all, it was as far as she could get from the glittering offices of Rogue Communications.

Emma sighed as steam filled her tiny kitchen. Her new job as the tourist board PR officer was busy and steady rather than manic and thrusting. The people were just what she'd needed. Like a nice cup of afternoon tea, they were strong and warm and comforting.

And Will?

She'd only met him a few times, but her reaction to him was disturbing. He certainly wasn't like a nice cup of tea. No, Will was more like a double espresso with sugar, unstirred. A mouth-searing caffeine jolt, laced with sweetness *if* you were lucky enough to get to the bottom of him. Once tasted, he'd be difficult not to crave. She would have to stick to tea.

She certainly didn't want to be jolted by anyone these days. Jeremy had done enough of that for a lifetime. Just because Will had made her feel unsettled and turned on and very confused didn't mean anything. In fact, considering what had gone on today, a microwaved dinner, a glass of Shiraz, and her favorite feel-good DVD were just about all she could cope with. That and the chance to collapse into bed, her hands duly and painfully de-gritted as Will had ordered.

Under normal circumstances, the film would have absorbed her until the credits rolled and her eyes rebelled. Until tonight. Tonight, her mind kept returning to the fellside, to Will. To his dark hair ruffled by the breeze and his hard body as she handed him his jacket, to his tough tenderness as he held her grazed hands in his. As she drifted off to sleep, she was in his arms on Black Fell as he laid his jacket on the grassy hillside, stripped her naked, and made powerful, mind-blowing love to her.

Chapter 3

"I HOPE YOU'RE NOT LOOKING FOR A HERO, EMMA. BECAUSE WILL Tennant most definitely isn't one."

Emma glanced up from the newspaper that was spread over her desk at the tourist office. Jan Edwards, the office admin manager, was standing in front of her with a cookie packet in one hand and a plastic cup in the other. At twenty-nine, she already had one divorce, six cats, and a shameful collection of cheesy rock CDs that she'd proudly shown Emma when they'd shared a curry and a bottle of wine one night after work. After just a few weeks, Emma had already realized that what Jan didn't know about the Bannerdale social scene wasn't worth knowing— although she also had to admit some of it was pretty dodgy.

"Hi, Jan. Just doing the press cuttings."

"Oh really?" asked Jan innocently as Emma peered again at the article she'd been reading: "Outside Edge Reaches New Heights." There on page three, appropriately enough, was a photograph of Mr. December, wearing a rather different kind of suit, Emma noted, from the one on the mountain top. A sharp business suit, shirt, and tie, to be precise.

His designer stubble was nowhere to be seen, and his hair had been tamed into some kind of submission. He wouldn't have looked out of place on a city trading floor—if it hadn't been for the climbing ropes and harnesses slung over his shoulder.

Jan plonked her plastic cup on top of Mr. December's head. Brown liquid slopped onto his designer suit, wrinkling his shirt and tie.

"You did hear what I said, didn't you, Em? Will's no hero—if you're thinking what I think you're thinking…"

"I'm in no danger, Jan, and I've absolutely no desire to meet a hero or a villain—not after recent experiences. You know that," she declared as Jan decapitated the cookie packet with her fingernail.

Emma's eye wandered back to Will's photo. She had to admit he did tick all the usual boxes. Tall, dark, gorgeous, fit…and, according to Jan, single. What woman wouldn't have him on their hit list? If they were looking, which she wasn't.

She peeled the cup off Will's face and braved a sip. "How do you know so much about him, Jan?" she asked as the coffee made her shudder. "And thanks for the…er…what is it exactly?"

"It says cappuccino next to the button," supplied her colleague, pulling a face. "But they all taste like washing-up water to me. As for Will, I don't know him that well personally…but I've heard plenty from his conquests."

OK. Fine. Emma's mental pen was hovering above an extra box on the list. The one she didn't want to tick. The one marked "philandering love rat."

"Con*quests*? Have there been many?"

"Oh, dozens," said Jan airily. "Well, three that I can actually swear to—since he finished with Kate Danvers, that is."

Emma braved the cappuccino again and cringed. "Who's Kate Danvers?"

"His ex-fiancée—a local solicitor. He dumped her a couple of years ago. The morning of their wedding, to be precise."

"Bloody hell!"

"I know," said Jan, clearly delighted with the dramatic effect.

"And he actually jilted her? On the day?" Emma was stunned. Will was definitely cynical, maybe a bit of a lad, but dumping his bride almost at the altar? It was the stuff of Victorian melodrama, with him as archvillain.

"Oh yes," Jan continued airily. "Everyone round here knows that Will wanted to graze in pastures new." Noticing their boss look up from his computer in his glass-walled office, she lowered her voice a decibel.

Emma glanced at James and smiled. James looked like he couldn't decide whether to smile back or come out and tell them to keep the noise down. She felt a bit sorry for him. He'd slunk into the office sporting red eyes and crumpled trousers that looked like he'd slept in them.

"James looks a bit grumpy for a new father," murmured Emma, torn between guilt and a desperate desire to hear more gossip about Will.

Jan gave their boss a friendly wave, then turned her attention straight back to Emma. "He's off on paternity leave tomorrow, so we'll get a bit of peace for a week. Now, where were we?"

"Will, I think," said Emma as casually as she could manage.

"Oh yes. The git. He must have done the dirty on Kate. Why else would she have rushed off down south so suddenly? He's never denied it either."

Emma's stomach lurched. So this was the man she'd almost developed a crush on. What a pig. And what a lucky escape, not that he'd made a move on her or anything. Well, one thing was for sure. The love-rat box had a thick black check mark.

Jan offered her a cookie and added conspiratorially, "I'm not one to gossip, but if you had any ambitions in that direction, it's only fair to warn you what he's like."

"Believe me, I do not and never will have any ambitions of the kind."

Jan was almost level with Emma's ear now, one huge hoop earring brushing against her face. "It's when he asks you to his cottage that you really have to worry…"

"I can't think what you mean."

"This is purely hearsay, mind," Jan whispered, "but he's got a massive four-poster bed, *and* he isn't lacking in the other department either. Though you've already seen everything he's got to offer, haven't you?"

"Jan!" Emma hissed. "You're absolutely outrageous!"

"I'm only going by what the girls in question said." She straightened up. "Seriously, Em, I'd watch him. He's a woman-hater. Takes you out a few times, gets you back to the cottage, then 'wham, bam, thank you, ma'am,' and you won't hear from him ever again. You'll just be another notch on his impressive bedpost."

"There is absolutely no way I will ever be a notch on anyone's bedpost, least of all Will's," cried Emma. She caught Jan's raised eyebrows. "Stop looking at me like that! I mean it. I don't do commitment-phobes or jilting love rats, no matter how well provided for, financially or otherwise."

"Methinks the lady doth object too much."

"Protest. It's 'methinks the lady doth protest too much.'"

"Protest? Hmm. I'd like to see you doing that faced with the gorgeous Will... Anyway, I must get back to the budget spreadsheets." Jan snatched up the cookies giving Emma a glimpse of an amazing design on one of her nail extensions.

As she tried to concentrate on her press release on the village's new Wordsworth Center, all she could think of was Will. What an absolute pig. Still—there were a lot of them about, and she'd just met her second, by all accounts. What kind of a guy jilted his fiancée on their wedding day?

Fortunately, Emma reflected, he hadn't so much as asked her for her phone number, let alone tried to lure her to his cottage. All she'd had was a businesslike, "Goodbye. See you around," as she'd left him packing the first aid kit away. He obviously didn't fancy her, so there was no chance of her name ever being etched on his four-poster.

Or ending up like Kate Danvers—cast aside like a piece of trash on the fellside when he became bored. Well, if he ever did try anything, she knew exactly what she was going to say to him, and it wouldn't concern the size of his boots.

At lunchtime, she drew the newspaper out of her desk drawer again:

The driving force behind Outside Edge is local businessman Will Tennant. The 34-year-old entrepreneur has built up the company from scratch into one of the fastest growing chains of outdoor stores in the country. Now he's planning to branch out into a lucrative new area—property development.

It's become Bannerdale's worst-kept secret that Tennant has his eye on the former Lakeshore House. The man himself won't be drawn on any possible plans for turning the building into luxury apartments, but any plans like that are bound to be met with strong opposition.

"No comment"—but no denial either, was the best

response the *Gazette* could get from Tennant when asked about his interest in Lakeshore House.

Local folk will be watching this space...

———

Checking that no one was looking, Emma snipped out the article and stuffed it in her handbag.

———

"OK, Max, what do you think? Is it viable?"

Two weeks after his photo shoot, Will was giving Lakeshore House an appraisal with his friend Max Coleridge. He noticed the wisteria and ivy were already threatening to smother the building and smiled ruefully. Two years of neglect could take its toll on any structure—heart or home.

"*If* you can get planning permission and the finance, then yes—I think Lakeshore House would make a great outdoor center," offered Max.

"Finance won't be a problem." Will had laughed at the article in the *Gazette*. "Planning to branch out into property development," the reporter had "revealed." Well, he'd branched out into that area some years ago and long before the market had gone ballistic, and his best deal had been his home, Ghyllside Cottage.

He turned his attention back to Max. He'd liked him ever since they'd first met or, rather, beaten each other up in the playground of Bannerdale primary school. Fighting over a girl as he recalled. By the end of the bout, they were swapping football cards, the nine-year-old siren forgotten. Twenty-five years down the line, Max was a successful architect, and they were still sparring.

They'd spent two hours going over the whole building, looking at its potential. Bedrooms, seminar rooms, kitchen facilities, parking: every aspect had been weighed up coolly and critically.

With his contacts from his teaching days, Will knew he could provide a really great place for youngsters whose idea of the great outdoors was the parking lot outside a fast-food place. Taking off his hard hat, he wiped away a trickle of sweat from his forehead with his arm. It was humid for mid-April, and as his eyes rested on the mountains, he could tell a storm was threatening.

"So it's not a pie-in-the-sky idea?" he repeated.

"How many times have you asked me that?" Max grinned.

"Only a few," Will conceded. "Most of my mad ideas have actually turned out rather well—eventually."

He smiled to himself. He'd had many mad ideas in his time. Like managing to pass his A levels and get a place at university even though he'd spent most of his study leave climbing. Like training to be a teacher, then leaving immediately afterward to get Outside Edge off the ground.

Will cast his eye over Lakeshore House one last time. Through the trees and overgrown shrubs in the grounds, he could just glimpse the lake in the distance. It would be perfect if he could fend off any property developers. The planners *should* be on his side, but one never knew, not when so much money was involved. He never took anything for granted in business or otherwise these days.

"Are you up for it, then?" asked Max.

"What? Buying this pile?"

"No. Our next mission. Can you cope with it?"

Will slapped his friend hard on the back. "It's a deal. Off you go then—get me a double orange juice. I'll be along in a minute."

Max didn't need asking twice and set off in his Porsche, unnecessarily spinning the wheels and sending the gravel flying. Will guided the Range Rover up the drive at a more leisurely pace. At the top of the drive, he pulled on the handbrake and got out. He was visualizing the stone pillars at the entrance with a new sign for the center.

The keys to the car were in his hand when an exotic bird glided past the gates—one with a very pretty tail he'd have recognized anywhere. Today, encased in a long, fitted skirt that clung in all the vital places, the effect on him was instant and alarming. However, this time, he was in no danger of giving himself away.

Emma had made it a few feet past the hood of his car before he called out, "Ms. Tremayne. For a moment there, I thought you hadn't recognized me with my…"

"Clothes on? Why even bother saying it, Mr. Tennant?"

The bird had paused, deciding whether this particular insect was worth her time. Then she turned, and Will felt the full effect of her jade gaze. He felt like blinking in the glare even though the mist was already descending below the mountaintops.

"We must stop bumping into each other like this. People will talk."

"You're the master of the original chat-up line," replied Emma.

"A chat-up line?" he echoed. "Was that what it sounded like? If you want to make assumptions…"

"At least you're properly dressed today," she countered, obviously taking in his suit and tie.

"You too—if, dare I say it, rather posh for Bannerdale. Where are you off to? A corporate presentation? Or the mini-mart?"

Emma glanced down at her linen suit, gauzy scarf, and suede document case. Yes, she did stand out a bit among the hikers in their windbreakers and walking boots.

"The launch of the new Wordsworth Center, actually. Anyway, what's your excuse for having a shave? Not your birthday, I take it?"

Will's hand moved to his chin, and he wanted to kick himself for rising to the bait. Instead, he folded his arms casually across his chest.

"Does that mean you object to a bit of rough then? Or do you think I'm a wolf in sheep's clothing?"

A wolf, eh? thought Emma. A dangerous predator with a civilized face. Heavens, he looked even more intimidating in a designer suit than he did stripped bare. She could almost see him, eyes blazing, licking his lips as he moved in on her for the kill. And the most frightening thing of all was that part of her wanted to be devoured.

She stood up, clutching the folder tighter to protect herself.

"You've got me wrong, Will. I don't mind a 'bit of rough,' as you call it. I don't judge anyone on appearances, even though I may be from the sophisticated south."

His lazy smile as he listened to this, arms folded, was incredibly infuriating.

"But sometimes a wolf is a wolf, whatever his disguise—or lack of it," she said.

"And just how does a woman spot this wolf?" asked Will. "By his stubble? His brand of sunglasses? Or can she actually read his mind?"

"By his arrogance and lack of respect for other people's ideas."

"Ah, we're back to the calendar now."

"No. You're entitled to your opinion on that. As a matter of fact," she said, tapping the folder in her arms with her fingertips, "I've got the proofs in here."

A direct hit for me, she thought as his arms and smile slipped.

"Have you now? Have you been examining the pictures closely?"

"Actually," she said coolly, "I'm going to present them at the next team meeting. Will you be gracing it with your presence?"

"I wouldn't miss it for the world. Now can I give you a lift to your launch party? It's started to rain, or hadn't you noticed?"

She hadn't, but the first drops were already splashing onto the linen sleeve of her suit, soaking into the weave. She didn't think she'd ever get used to the weather up here, it changed so quickly. When she'd set off, there'd been blue skies over the hills. Now she could barely make out even the lower peaks.

"Will you dare step inside my lair, or do you want to turn up to your do looking like you've dived into the lake?" he asked.

She had no choice. Taking a step toward the gleaming black four-by-four, he opened the door and held out his hand to help her in. She didn't want to accept it, truly didn't want to, but it was too late, and she felt the firm grip of his fingers on hers as he helped her up into the plush interior.

Getting into the driver's side, he put the keys in the ignition, then turned to her.

"How are your hands? Better? Let me take a look."

"This really isn't necessary, you know…" But he was already holding them lightly but confidently in his long, strong fingers. Once again, his touch made her tingle all over, and she cursed herself for her reaction.

"Hmm…two weeks makes a big difference," he commented, then abruptly put her hands back in her lap. The engine purred into life at his touch. "Better be off. I promised to meet up with a mate, and he'll be wondering what I've been up to."

And probably won't believe it if I tell him, thought Will as he negotiated the village one-way system. *Won't believe that I've been flirting unsuccessfully with the most stunning woman in Bannerdale. The one who thinks she's a tough, sophisticated babe but can't see that she's sweet and vulnerable.*

Thinking of Emma like that made him wonder again why he wasn't asking her out while he had the chance. He braked sharply and told himself to keep his mind on his driving before he squashed a tourist. The traffic was backed up in the village as walkers hurried down off the fells and sought shelter from the rain in the cafés and shops. The sidewalks were heaving, some people spilling out onto the road. They were going to be here awhile more than he'd anticipated, and with Emma now cool and silent, it could seem like a very long drive.

"Busy at work?" he asked, desperate for something neutral to say.

"Naturally. It's the start of the tourist season."

"Of course. Stupid question."

The diesel engine ticked over, and the wipers swished monotonously as they waited in the traffic. Will debated whether to turn on the CD player, then remembered that he had Meat Loaf's *Greatest Hits* in it. He casually turned up the air-conditioning as the windows began to mist.

"Outdoor Pursuits business good?" she asked, startling him.

Under normal circumstances, Will would have had a ready answer to a question like this. He wasn't nearly as averse to a bit of spin as he'd made out when it came to his company.

"It's, um…OK. Good, actually. Why do you ask?"

"I saw your business feature in the *Gazette*. It was on page three, wasn't it?"

The amused edge to her voice left him in no doubt she was winding him up. "Their reporter badgered me to do it, and our marketing people thought it would…"

"Be good PR?" she teased.

"Well, yeah."

Will changed gear, thankful the traffic had started shunting forward again, albeit far too slowly. At this rate, Max would have given up on him.

"They look intriguing, your development plans for the hotel," said Emma.

He smiled inwardly and also felt a tug of surprise. She was definitely interested in him. Maybe just in a professional sense, as the tourist board would be in a project that affected the community. Maybe in more than that. He wasn't sure which, but he was going to play his cards close to his chest anyway.

"I think they're interesting, but it's very early days yet. The *Gazette* is making a mountain out of a molehill, as it usually does. There's not a lot of exciting news around here, as you've probably found out."

"I wouldn't be too sure about that," she said, turning to him as they queued at the village's only set of traffic lights. "Some of it is absolutely fascinating."

"Even my business strategy?"

"Depends what it is. Who's going to benefit? If your plans contribute to the community and might bring more visitors here, then of course I'd be interested—from a professional point of view, that is. That was Lakeshore House you picked me up outside, wasn't it?" asked Emma.

Picked her up? Will saw the irony of it but let the remark lie.

"Yes. I was taking a look at it with the architect," he said easily, suspecting exactly where the conversation was leading.

"And what did you think? Did it suit your big plan?"

"Maybe. Maybe not. We'll have to see how it goes when I get the surveyor's and architect's reports."

"I expect it's none of my business, but you'll be treading on a few toes if you're planning to develop it for residential use—unless you mean to provide affordable homes, that is. That would be different."

Will felt himself simmering. "So you feel qualified to comment, do you, having been up here five minutes?"

Emma turned to him, and their eyes locked. "It's an important local issue, I'm entitled to my opinion, and I know most of the local people would agree with me. I must admit I was rather surprised when I read the report. I mean, I'd have thought it wouldn't do your image any good to get their backs up. Is it really worth alienating people just to make a fast buck?"

"Perhaps you'd know more about making a fast buck than me, Emma. Hanging round with all those city types with their massive bonuses," snapped Will, then regretted it. He tried to keep his voice steady. "Look, I didn't mean to be rude, but things don't work like that up here. Fast bucks aren't that easy to come by."

"I can assure you I've never seen anyone's massive bonus—and I wasn't interfering, merely giving my opinion," snapped Emma.

Will gripped the wheel tighter, feeling very annoyed. He could, if he wanted to, tell her his plans for the outdoor center, but damn it, why the hell should he? It wasn't that he didn't trust her; it was the principle of it. He thought it best to keep his business tactics private for now, and after being hectored by her on a subject that was dear to his heart, he didn't see why he should enlighten her.

An impatient hoot from the car behind made him swear.

"The lights have changed," said Emma.

"I can see that."

He thrust the car into first gear, and it roared forward. He pressed his lips together and said no more, though now he was not only irritated with Emma but also angry at losing his cool.

On the other side of the lights, the traffic began to thin. She didn't ask him anything else. He put his foot down as much as he dared with so many walkers about, and within minutes, he was steering the Range Rover up the steep drive to the Wordsworth Center. He parked as close as he could to the front doors. The rain thundered down on the roof of the car, and Will was glad he wasn't on rescue duty.

"Thanks for the lift," said Emma, fiddling with the seat belt.

He hesitated a second before popping the button for her and jumping out of the driver's seat. She'd made it halfway out of the passenger door before he got there and wrenched it fully open, leaving him standing like a chauffeur holding the door back. He barely heard her muttered "cheers" as her back view disappeared like quicksilver into the

center, the rain coming in torrents now, soaking his shirt until it clung
to his chest.

———

As she stepped through the doors into the Wordsworth Center, Emma
heaved a sigh of relief. Whew. Ten minutes in a confined space with Will
Tennant was more than enough for any woman.

How dare he pop the seat belt for her! Or think she needed him to
open the car door. She almost snorted out loud. As for taking her hands in
his like that, it made her shiver at the thought, a shiver that was so like a
tingle of desire it had her shaking her head in disgust at her own weakness.

Will, she told herself firmly, wasn't worth wasting any time on. He
had been so defensive about the newspaper story, probably because he
was going to make a fortune out of turning the place into luxury flats.
That would be another hotel gone and used as second homes by wealthy
people from…well, from places like London. It was a huge issue up here,
the way house prices had sky-rocketed until local people couldn't afford
to live and work in the place where they were born. Will was going to
be very unpopular indeed if that was what he had in mind. Not that she
cared, of course. It was just one more reason to keep her distance.

"Emma, you haven't forgotten your speech, have you?"

"Of course not, James," she replied, smiling, as her boss greeted her
at the door. The usually immaculate James had a smear of baby milk on
his unironed shirt. She accepted a glass of orange juice from a waitress as
he ushered her into a quiet corner.

"Emma, I meant to email you a list of the center's benefactors from
home, but I've been so busy. Can you believe how little sleep a newborn
baby needs?" He rolled his eyes. "Now for goodness' sake, don't forget to
mention the sponsors, or there'll be hell to pay. Most of them are here to
bask in the glory and to see their names on the plaque." He indicated a
red curtain, waiting to be unveiled by the mayor.

Reaching into his pocket, James pulled out a crumpled printout and
handed it to her. Emma scanned it quickly. She recognized the owner of
a hotel group, a local supermarket, and some government department.

There, at the bottom, was the name of the managing director of a large chain of outdoor equipment stores.

Mr. Will Tennant—Outside Edge.

Her heart sank. Had he been deliberately put on this earth to torment her?

"Profuse and heartfelt thanks will do nicely," James was saying with a grin. "Major groveling to benefactors always goes down well, but you don't need me to tell you that."

"Do I really need to mention them all by name?" she asked, the list drooping from her fingertips.

"Each and every one, I'm afraid." With what she thought was a particularly cruel twist, he added, "Especially Tennant. He's put up the biggest share, although he doesn't seem to be here. Not his kind of thing, I suppose. Probably climbing a cliff somewhere." He looked at his watch. "Oops. I must go. I'm supposed to be on paternity leave, and now I've shown my face, it's back to the breastfeeding. I make the tea," he added—unnecessarily, in Emma's opinion.

"James, wait—"

He'd gone. Leaving her holding the baby. *Thanks, James,* she thought crossly. *Grovel to Will?* She didn't think she could do it without choking, but at least he wasn't there to see her do it, she consoled herself as she buttoned up her jacket and headed over to the podium.

Five minutes later, she was stepping up onto the little stage and taking the microphone, feeling cool, calm, and almost confident.

Oh no. Please, no. Please, ground, open up and swallow me.

There at the back of the room, head and shoulders above most of the audience, was a figure she couldn't mistake. Dark and ruggedly handsome and more than a little damp. She just managed to stop her jaw from dropping as a hush descended on the room and a very small sea of expectant faces gazed up at her.

———

Groveling hurt. It hurt a lot, and when it was all over, the ripple of applause was started by the tall, dark-haired man who was now smiling despite his soggy shirt. And who was now making straight for her, a glass of wine in his hand.

"Nice speech," Will murmured as he brushed past her.

"Nice shirt," she hissed as she noticed the steam rising from the damp cotton.

"Nice ass."

No. He couldn't have said that. Not even Will would have dared be so sexist. She must have misheard or imagined it. Risking a glance behind her, she saw he was already talking to a slight man with a pink shirt and a goatee. Emma recognized him as Max Coleridge, the center's architect. They were laughing out loud at some shared joke.

Will deserved a slap on the face, and if they hadn't been in public, she'd have been tempted to give him one. She grabbed a glass of juice and took a deep breath. Bother, she couldn't see his face from here, just his broad shoulders and the shirt clinging to the muscles in his back.

"I didn't know you were a friend of Will Tennant's?"

Emma tore her eyes away from Will's broad shoulders to see Annette Croft, the center director, beaming at her.

"I'm not. I mean, I've met him once or twice. I help out with the mountain rescue PR," she added neutrally.

"He's one of our main benefactors. Very generous."

"I'm sure he is."

"We're very lucky to get a commitment like that from the business community. It's not easy, as you might think, but Outside Edge have always been supportive. Will and Kate always tried to help us if they could."

"Really?" asked Emma, toying with her glass, her fingers feeling clammy against the stem.

"Oh yes. Kate Danvers was a local solicitor. Will's fiancée. Ex-fiancée, I should say." Annette lowered her voice. "Although I shouldn't say anything at all about her, really. Nice girl. Such a shame it all went so wrong."

Emma was tempted to do the second most unprofessional thing she had ever done. But the words *It was hardly her fault she was left at the altar* stayed inside her head and didn't make it out of her mouth. Mainly because she was sipping her juice at the time.

Annette had no such scruples. "Everyone was very surprised when it all fell through." She glanced at Will. "Shocked even. Who would have thought it?" Her eyes traveled back to Emma, and she smiled ruefully. "Still, we can't let it affect our professional relationships, can we? Whatever he may have done in his private life, he's still a much-needed sponsor. Would you like another drink, dear?"

"I have to be getting back to the office, actually," replied Emma. *And right now*, she thought, *I can't spend another minute in Will's company*. As she walked out of the building, grateful to find the rain had stopped, she thought back to the day's events. Will's defensiveness about the hotel development, his appearance on the sponsor's list at the center, and Annette Croft's comment about the community needing his support whatever he chose to do— all these things added up, and the balance was not in Will's favor.

An idea suddenly struck her that made her feel even more annoyed. Maybe he wouldn't have to face much opposition to his plans. He was, after all, a rather big fish in a small pond—perhaps he got away with all kinds of things because of that. Money talks, as Suzanne had pointed out at the base. People would put up with a lot when hard cash was involved.

But later that evening, as she sat in the window seat of her flat, Emma's mind was focused on a very different aspect of Will. She'd also told him a little white lie earlier that day. She hadn't exactly had the proofs of the calendar photos in her folder. She'd had only one of them.

His to be precise. The others were safely locked away in her desk drawer at work, but she just couldn't resist sneaking Mr. December home. Just for the occasional peep, mind. Mainly for the purposes of research. Research into spotting wolves in sheep's clothing. Six-foot-three-inch wolves with broad shoulders, a taut stomach, and a dark trail of hair that went all the way from his navel to his... She couldn't confirm exactly where the trail ended, because the photographer had hidden Mr. December behind the cairn.

She shoved the proof back into the envelope with disgust.

Had it come to this? Sneaking home a risqué photograph in a brown envelope like someone hiding naughty magazines? She had turned into a dirty old woman—although twenty-eight wasn't *that* old…

Her fingers went to the envelope and withdrew the picture one last time. Just to study her enemy. Just to find out if he really did have the most magnificent pair of thighs she'd ever seen. It took half an hour of close scrutiny to convince her that yes, he really did.

———

On the opposite side of the lake, Will was pulling up outside his house. After the launch, he'd spent until seven o'clock in the office. He was ready for another quiet night in at Ghyllside Cottage, and he couldn't think of anywhere better suited to peace and tranquility. At times, he had to admit, it was almost too peaceful. It might have seven bedrooms, but only one of them was ever used—and almost exclusively by him.

Will stopped short on his way up the gravel drive to the front door and instead turned and headed over the lawns to the jetty that pointed, like a finger, at the village on the opposite shore. Peering at the sunlit buildings straggling up the hillside, he could just make out the flat where Emma lived. He wondered what she was doing. Maybe she wasn't even there. Maybe she was out on a date. Someone might be with her now, in her bed…and why should he care? Their encounters had been few, but all of them had left him feeling frustrated and sometimes, as it had today, pretty pissed off.

After all, he told himself as he turned his back on the lake and walked back along the jetty, he knew very little about her background or her past. Nothing at all about why a bright and confident woman like her had moved up here to what must be the back of beyond, career-wise. Will knew he was as much a part of the Lakes as the rocks and hills that towered above the house.

He pushed open the door to the cottage, dropped his keys on the hall table, and flicked on the table lamp. The old longcase clock ticked slowly, sounding unduly loud in the silent house. Will sighed. He'd known for a long time he would never share Ghyllside Cottage with Kate Danvers. After the reception he'd had earlier, it didn't look like Emma would be tasting his hospitality for even one night.

Chapter 4

No WHITEBOARD, NO AUDIOVISUAL KIT, AND ABSOLUTELY NO mineral water. Emma had to smile as she helped Dr. Suzanne Harley carry an old table to the front of the meeting room at the mountain rescue base. How far she'd come from the boardroom of Rogue Communications. They'd been legendary in the marketing world for their lavish entertaining and innovative product launches. The base, on the other hand, was legendary for drafty toilets and a temperamental boiler.

The two-hundred-year-old building had once been a barn, and while it was in the ideal spot for reaching the fells, the team had out-grown it several years before. The gear was stowed away in perfect order, but it was absolutely everywhere, filling every nook and cranny. There was no private place where relatives could sit quietly and wait for news or, worse, comfort each other when, as inevitably happened, there were fatal accidents. They needed a bigger, better-equipped HQ, and Emma felt proud that her idea was going to help them get it.

She was on her way to collect a chair from the stack when Will appeared. "Let me take that," he offered, and before she could protest, he was placing it behind the table. She noticed his designer stubble was back, and his sunglasses were now perched unnecessarily on top of his head. His close-fitting T-shirt gave just a hint of the taut body underneath—a body she knew so well by now it could have been her specialist subject on *Mastermind*.

Unpacking her briefcase, she watched him put out chairs as the other team members drifted in one by one. Her eyes rested on the large board-backed envelope on the table that contained the proofs for the calendar.

Twelve arty shots in stark monochrome, save for a shocking splash of scarlet in each. The designer had picked out the distinctive red Rescue logo in every shot: the sign on a Land Rover, a badge on a bag, a jacket slung over a shoulder.

A glance at her watch told her it was time to get proceedings underway. She wondered if there was time to go to the ladies' to redo her lipstick. Naturally, it didn't matter what she looked like, not up here anyway. Still, a final check might not do any harm…

"Nervous?" Suddenly, Will was standing beside her as the rest of the team settled into their seats.

"Why? Do you think I should be?"

"It's your big night, isn't it? I know I would be."

"You're forgetting that this is my job. I've done more presentations like this than you've done rescues." That was one thing: at least she *sounded* confident.

"Yes, but you're forgetting you've got a much tougher audience to convince here. We're not a bunch of fancy marketing suits. This is the real world. I'll just sit here quietly and wait to be impressed."

"I'd like to see that," she replied sweetly, then banged on the desk for attention as he positioned himself in the front row, one long leg crossed over the other, arms casually folded across his chest. This was his territory, and he wanted her to know it.

As her eyes swept over her audience, she was congratulating herself on the decision to keep her jacket on. It gave her a semblance of control at least. She reminded herself to take a deep breath. *You can do this*, she told herself, *and it can't be that bad, can it? Not as bad as the last product presentation you made…oh heavens, no…*

Besides, she was sure she could detect a touch of nervousness among the normally blasé crew. Maybe a tiny edge of hysteria to the laughter? A tiny trace of fear on the face of Will? Perhaps it was just wishful thinking…

She picked up the envelope and smiled brightly.

"OK. Are we ready, gentlemen? It's the moment you've all been waiting for. First of all, I want to thank you all for daring to take part. I know it's been a leap of faith for some, but I'm certain none of you will regret it. With the models concerned, I know this calendar is going to be an enormous success. Huge!"

The sniggering broke the tension and—miracles would never cease—she noticed that even Will had managed a smile.

"I'm going to hand them out one by one. First—and may I say the best, in my opinion—Bob."

Walking confidently toward him, she handed Bob his picture. She'd barely moved on to her next target when she heard his howl of laughter, followed by a shriek from Suzanne.

"Bob, darling, I may be a GP, but you don't see that every day. I congratulate you," she giggled, patting him on the back.

"That ice axe doesn't leave much to the imagination," roared a deep voice Emma recognized as one of the local hoteliers.

Thank goodness for that. The banter had started. Some of it risqué, some just plain rude, and all of it music to her ears. The exact opposite, in fact, to the nightmare scenario that had been passing through her mind all day: a horror-struck silence.

She felt her shoulders sink in relief as she carried on handing out the photographs, pausing here and there to make an encouraging remark. She knew she needn't have bothered. The calendar boys were too busy trying to outdo each other with insults.

"Bet that climbing harness chafed, Phil…"

"Jason. What the bloody hell were you doing with that helmet?"

They were all out of their seats by now, gathered in huddles, ridiculing each other's photos with good-natured howls of derision. Only one person was still in his seat. Still sitting there with one long leg resting across the other, a cool gleam of amusement in his eyes. Will was waiting patiently for her to come to him.

Emma sat down beside him on the empty chair and pulled the last print from the envelope. Without saying a word, she offered it to him and saw the tremor in her hand transfer itself to the photograph.

His fingers brushed hers as he took it, sending a shiver of excitement through her that connected with something deep inside. He made her suffer for a moment by placing it facedown across his lap.

"Aren't you going to look?" she said quietly.

"Is it compulsory to do it in public?"

"Why? Do you think you've got something to worry about?"

"You tell me…"

As Will turned the print over, Emma's deep blush gave him all the answer he needed. There he was, standing behind the cairn. In his shades and boots, backlit against the late-afternoon sun, casually holding a climbing helmet with the rescue logo on it. His body didn't look too bad, he had to admit, but it was his face that bothered him. He couldn't care less whether anyone thought he was handsome or good-looking. That was ridiculous. But he did think he looked a bit, well, world-weary. Where was the zest for life he'd once prided himself on?

His lingering look was not lost on Emma.

"What do you think, then? Very tasteful, aren't they?"

"You might have told me to smile."

"I don't recall you being too happy to be there, and anyway," she added, lowering her voice, "it's called the mean and moody look."

Her voice was so smooth and silky, had so much of the vixen about it, that it took every ounce of self-control he had to stop himself from pulling her across his lap and forcing a kiss on her. A full-blooded French kiss to jolt her out of her cool poise.

He didn't know what had come over his colleagues. She'd swept all before her with her blithe confidence and charm—even gruff Bob and Suzanne. He'd been amazed at the relish the plain-speaking doc had shown for seeing her colleagues stripped on a calendar. He'd have thought she'd have seen enough of it in her day job. A large hand appeared and swept the photo from his fingers. It was Bob Jeavons.

"What made you think you needed a pile of rocks that big, Will? A few pebbles would have done, eh, Emma?" he roared.

Emma smiled weakly, hoping against hope she didn't have to reply. Torn between scoring points and admitting she had, actually, taken a peek at the original.

"You'll not get the chance to find out, Bob," said Will evenly.

"Unlike half the female population hereabouts!" he bellowed, handing back the picture before being hauled away by Suzanne to get his opinion on Mr. October's equipment.

Will's face twisted into a grimace as Emma regarded him like something a particularly snooty Persian cat had brought in. He tried a diversion tactic. A risky one.

"You do realize we'll be the laughingstock after this?" he demanded coldly. "We're making complete fools of ourselves. Don't you know what the other teams are saying about us?"

"Will, surely it can't be that bad?" she soothed. "My charity client made a fortune out of their calendar. They got heaps of coverage—even made the regional TV news. It shows you as a modern, caring organization that's not afraid to laugh at itself."

"No one will take us seriously ever again after this."

"For a successful businessman, you're not very commercially aware, are you? And I'd have thought as an entrepreneur, especially one with his eye on the main chance, you'd have been more open-minded. It is the twenty-first century, you know. Time to stop living in the past and to move on."

His face darkened. Emma hadn't been able to resist a barb about his property plans, but it was something else that seemed to have upset him more.

"Stop living in the past?" he echoed. "Well, perhaps it is time I moved on, if that's what you recommend."

Emma didn't know why but she suddenly felt ever so slightly afraid of him. Tinged with her anxiety was a frisson of desire that made her breasts prickle. Suddenly, he got up and strode away, the print discarded on his chair. She picked it up and slotted it carefully into her folder before escaping into the tiny kitchen to make a tray of tea.

Pouring out the drinks, she asked herself, once again, why Will had to be like this. Everyone else was thrilled. The black-and-white images were beautifully shot and very tasteful. They were funny and sexy, and she knew they would be flying off the shelves by Christmas. The thought crossed her mind that perhaps it wasn't the photos that had provoked such a strong reaction—perhaps it was her.

Half an hour later, the meeting was over, and Emma was helping to stack the motley collection of chairs around the edge of the room. Out of the corner of her eye, she saw Will appear in the doorway. This time, he didn't offer to help.

"See you at the weekend then, Emma? We're off to Stickle Crag to do some rappelling. Why don't you come along?" asked Suzanne as they added the final two chairs to the stack.

"That's very kind of you but—"

"Go on," urged her friend. "It'll be far more interesting than listening to budget figures and the maintenance reports you get in the monthly meeting, and there'll be the chance to see Will dangling off a rope. You don't want to miss that, do you?"

Emma hesitated. The last thing she wanted to do was watch people launching themselves off a cliff. She was absolutely hopeless with heights. She'd once had to leave a cocktail party when Jeremy, worse for wear as usual, had started fooling around on the balcony, pretending to climb over the rail. He'd known she hated it but thought it was funny to tease her.

Suzanne's voice cut in. "You could even have the chance to do a bit of dangling yourself. Why don't you have a go?" she suggested.

"Me?" asked Emma, incredulous. Although she knew Suzanne was being friendly, the idea of actually rappelling made Emma shudder. There was no way she could do this, no matter how much she wanted to fit in. "I'd better not," she said. "It's way out of my comfort zone. Maybe in a few months."

"Out of your comfort zone?" said Will, walking over to them. "What was it you said back there—that some of us had had to take a leap of faith? Well, I think it's time for you to take one."

Emma felt her heart quicken. Everyone could hear him, and she could feel the situation rapidly getting out of hand. Will was in a provocative mood, and this time, she didn't feel in control. "I...I don't think..."

"What? Don't think you can do it? You can, Emma, if you really have faith in yourself and your friends."

"Will, don't torment her," warned Suzanne.

He was determined, it seemed, to have his revenge for being forced into doing the calendar. She felt her hands shaking as he pushed harder. Her palms were sweating too, and her pulse was racing.

"I really don't think it's me, walking backward off a cliff."

"I think it's *exactly* you, Emma…willing to step over the edge."

Step over the edge? So that was what he wanted. Something snapped inside her. Well, she'd damn well show him she wasn't afraid of anything he might care to try with her. She glared at him defiantly.

"Well, have you got the nerve?" he asked, locking eyes with her.

She smiled politely, knowing that everyone was listening. "I suppose I'm willing to try anything once."

Will raised his eyebrows in surprise, making it obvious he hadn't thought she had the guts to do it.

"Bravo." He applauded softly. "See you on Saturday then."

And he strode out the door without a glance behind, leaving Emma shell-shocked. What the hell had she gone and done?

Suzanne put a hand on her arm. "You don't have to do this. Don't let him back you into a corner."

"What choice do I have after a challenge like that?" cried Emma. "When I persuaded everyone else into doing something I would never dare do. Though why Will had to do this to me, I don't know. Surely I haven't upset him this much."

"For someone in communications, you're doing a great job of ignoring the signals," said Suzanne, shaking her head in disbelief. "He likes you, Emma. This is just his very funny way of showing it."

———

It took precisely five minutes before Will would have given his right arm to take back his challenge. Barely had the Range Rover passed the gate of the parking lot when his conscience gave him the kick in the stomach he knew he deserved.

What kind of a man was he to force a woman into a corner like that? A woman he liked and respected, even. A woman he'd like to try and persuade into his bed… *Will Tennant, you deserve a medal for stupidity.*

Emma's   reaction   to   his   challenge,   meanwhile,   was   more straightforward. She had gone home and started on a family-size block of chocolate while she tried to make sense of her latest encounter with Will.

She was completely confused. Half the time, he seemed to be giving her signals no woman could possibly misinterpret. Flirting with her outrageously, darting hungry looks at her that made her squirm with shame and desire.

Then he'd challenge her and goad her, try to humiliate her in front of friends! Why did he suddenly have to turn so prickly…so defensive… as if he had something to fear from her, when really, it was *she* who was in danger from *him*.

He could have asked her anything but this. Scuba dive with sharks, trek to the North Pole, date her dentist. She felt nauseous on the third rung of a ladder for goodness' sake. And as for walking backward off a cliff…

That night, she thought of phoning Suzanne, of getting the GP to explain that it wasn't safe for her to go rappelling. Not with her fear of heights. Well, it would be as good as a doctor's sick note. In fact, it *would* be a doctor's sick note.

So it went on for the next six nights. Should she? Shouldn't she? She damn well wouldn't. Yes, she damn well would. Then, in no time, it was Saturday morning, and Suzanne was knocking on the door of her flat, ready to take her to her fate.

"Nice day for it after all," Suzanne said as Emma sat, pale and silent, in the passenger seat of the doctor's Volvo. "I was out on call in the small hours and was quite worried. It was so windy, I really did think we'd have to call the whole thing off."

Emma mumbled something polite and wound down the window for some air. She could feel the warmth of the sun on her face and a breeze that was now no more than fresh. Although it had rained and gusted hard all night, causing her to wake at every rattle of the windowpane, the showers had conveniently cleared away just before Suzanne had arrived. Conditions had rapidly become ideal for sunbathing, picnicking, or stepping over the edge of a cliff.

She'd already spent half an hour at the base going over safety procedures with Suzanne. Her friend was so calm and matter-of-fact as she ran through the equipment and techniques, you'd have thought she was showing her how to operate the latest dishwasher.

"I'd rather do this any day than have to present those photos to our lot," Suzanne confessed as they reached the top of Stickle Crag. "Now, off you go. I'll see you later."

"What do you mean?" cried Emma. "I thought you'd be here with me."

"You'll be perfectly safe with Will and Bob. Someone needs to stay at the bottom, and I thought you'd feel happier with me there waiting for you."

"Oh," she murmured, her legs already doing a fair imitation of a jelly on a warm day. "Aren't you at least going to wish me luck?"

Suzanne laughed. "Luck doesn't come into it, Emma. We don't rely on that, you'll be pleased to know. Now get on up there, and try and enjoy yourself," she called as she set off back down the fellside.

Ahead of her, Emma could see the team practicing rescue techniques on the cliff edge. She paused for a moment to try and restore her shredded nerves. Her stomach rumbled alarmingly, and no wonder. She'd hardly had anything for breakfast and not much for supper the night before. A sudden ripple of breeze set the goose bumps prickling on her arms.

Spread out in front of her was a scene that made her catch her breath. The lake plowing its shining furrow through the steep-sided valley and in the distance, the sea all but lost in the midmorning haze.

She took a deep breath.

"Pretty impressive, huh?" said a voice beside her.

"Absolutely amazing." Emma swallowed a lump in her throat that wasn't inspired by the view. When she turned to look at Will, he was holding a harness that, she knew immediately, was meant for her.

She shivered.

"Are you OK?" he asked.

She nodded, because her throat had gone dry.

Once again, Will reflected as he regarded Emma trembling in front of him on the hillside, she was unsuitably dressed for the great outdoors. Her tight jeans and T-shirt would have been perfect for a shopping trip or a spot of gardening. But for rappelling? Come on. At least her walking boots were now respectably scuffed and muddy. It never ceased to amaze him that she could look so businesslike one minute and so casually sexy the next. He'd lain awake at night lately trying to decide which turned him on the most, but since he couldn't think of a more enjoyable cause for insomnia, he didn't worry too much about the lack of sleep.

———

Emma was terrified. Why, oh why, had she ever agreed to do this? Perhaps he might take pity on her. Perhaps he might take her aside and tell her she didn't have to go through with it…

"Emma," he was telling her softly, "you don't have to do this, you know. I shouldn't have goaded you, and I apologize."

The way out—he'd presented it to her on a plate. All she had to do was say *Thank you very much, Will. I'm very grateful to you for rescuing me. What do I owe you?* It was tempting, but Emma forced herself to shake her head. She was determined to show Will just what she was made of, no matter what it took.

"I'm fine, thanks. I've psyched myself up, and I'm going to do it. Let's just get it over with, shall we?" Then she added, "Are you going down with me?"

"Only if I absolutely have to," he replied with a wicked grin that let her know just how he'd interpreted her innocent remark.

"For goodness' sake, let's get on with it," she pleaded.

"OK, but it will help a lot if you try and relax. It really won't be that bad."

He held up the harness. For one awful moment, she had a vision of a hangman's noose, but his cheerful grin didn't look too much like that of an executioner.

"So it's you I've got to trust?" she said through clenched teeth.

"I'm afraid so. Your life is in my hands."

Her face told him it was an ill-advised joke.

"OK. If you're ready, let's get you into the gear." He bent down in front of her. "Step inside—no, not like that, like this."

Emma stepped into the loops of the webbed harness and allowed him to pull it up to her waist. Then he started doing up the straps, pulling them tight around her middle and thighs. He would have enjoyed the experience, but he could already feel her trembling. He marveled at her guts. Even though she must be terrified, she was going to go through with it. He wanted to hug her, but instead, he told himself he had to stay cool and detached.

That was how he would have treated any novice, and he reminded himself that Emma was no different.

"Is that *strictly* necessary?" She laughed nervously as he checked the straps around her thighs again. He gave the fasteners one last hard tug as he doubled them back.

"Compulsory," he said with a look so dark and sexy, her legs almost buckled. "Now put your helmet on."

As she did up the chin strap, he started to get into his own gear.

"Wh...what are you doing?" she asked through clenched teeth.

He stood up and looked at her with amusement. "Getting ready, just in case I'm forced to go down with you." After a final check on both of their harness straps, he straightened up. "Give me your hand then."

"Why?"

"So I can help you over the edge. It's a bit...greasy."

Emma forced herself to look ahead to the cliffside. Bob, standing a few feet below them, waved cheerily at her.

"What do you mean, a bit 'greasy'?" she asked.

"Just a bit damp on the ledge there after the rain. There's some lichen and moss but nothing to worry about, not with your boots on."

Emma grasped his hand and shuffled forward.

As he felt her fingers close around his, Will could feel the damage the adrenaline was doing. Her pulse was fluttering like a captive bird's, giving him an intoxicating sense of power and responsibility.

"Nothing can happen," he said gently. "You're roped on to me and that big rock over there, so don't worry."

"You'll be fine, lass," said Bob, smiling reassuringly at her. "Trust Will. He could do this with his eyes closed."

Will squeezed them shut and grinned. "What a good idea."

"Don't joke!" cried Emma.

Opening his eyes, Will smiled and led her gently forward to within a few feet of the edge.

"I can't do it," she whispered through dry lips, seeing the sheer rock face and Suzanne, doll-like, at the bottom.

"It'll be fine. Like falling off a log," said Will.

As she risked another peep over the edge, Emma could feel the trail of sweat slithering down the back of her T-shirt. Her heart was banging away like an overloaded washing machine, and her stomach felt like it was on the spin cycle too.

"How far, um…down is it?" she asked.

"Fifty, sixty feet. Not far, but don't think about that. Just keep your eyes on your feet, and let out the rope very slowly and steadily like Sue showed you."

Emma kept his hand in a viselike grip. "What if I slip or get stuck?"

"We'll have control of the rope up here. We can stop you instantly."

"P-Promise?"

"Absolutely. Now, can you turn round?"

Like an arthritic crab, she managed to shuffle her feet until her back was to the ledge. Knowing that a chasm was inches from her heels was almost overwhelming. Will still had her hand held tightly, and she focused on his face. At this moment, she didn't care what he had done or to whom. Only that she trusted him.

"Are you fit?" he asked.

"I—I don't think I can do this…"

"Yes, you can," he said firmly. "You've had the safety lecture, you know what to do, and most of all, we're here for you. Now, gently lean backward into the harness."

"But that rope—it won't take my weight."

"Yes, it will. It could take a bus and still not break."

"I'm not a bus."

"And you won't fall. Now relax back…that's it…"

Emma was absolutely on the edge now. Her thighs were shaking with the tension as she crouched down in the harness and sank back into it. Beneath her feet, the rock was still wet from the rain. It was awkward, and the ledge was tilted slightly. As she leaned back even further, her feet slipped on the lichen, and suddenly she lurched sideways.

"Will!"

A moment later, her feet were scrabbling on the ledge again as Will hauled her back onto the cliff top. She grabbed a tissue from the pocket of her jeans and wiped her eyes, heart thudding.

"It's OK," he soothed.

"I told you I couldn't do it," she wailed.

"You just overbalanced, that's all," he said, keeping her hand in his. "I told you it was bit greasy up here. Just take a bit of time to get your balance, and we'll have another go. You've already done the worst bit, believe me. Emma, look at me. We're going to do this."

A few minutes later, she was ready again. Aware of the slippery piece of rock, she leaned back into the harness again, trying to focus on Will and not the thin air behind her. Slowly, inch by inch, Will let the rope out and gently sent her over the edge.

"Focus on feeding the rope through," he called as she shuffled her feet down the rock face.

Emma could hardly hear him. Her brain felt scrambled. It was difficult to describe the feeling. Her breathing seemed heavy, and every movement she made was very deliberate. The wind had started to gust a little. The slate loomed in front of her, dark and glistening from the rain. It was green with lichen in places. Green and slimy.

The wind whipped a strand of hair from her helmet into her eyes. She heard a bird cry as it wheeled around the crag.

Momentarily, she looked down. She was vaguely aware of Suzanne, but she seemed a long, long way away. Suddenly, a rush of nausea threatened to overwhelm her, just like when Jeremy had been leaning over the balcony at that party.

Her fingers locked on to the rope, and she froze.

Waiting above, Will felt the rope stop moving through the figure of eight. He paused, surprised to feel his heart beating faster. Something was wrong. Emma had been doing so well, so why had she stopped? What was the matter? Usually, when someone had found the courage, as she had done, to step over the edge, they had no trouble tackling the rest. But he had seen it happen before when he'd been instructing. Occasionally, people did get stuck halfway down and, he thought with a stab of guilt, she *had* been terrified. To do what she'd done with so much fear—most people would have scrapped it.

"Emma, are you all right?" he called, seeing her halfway down the rockface, unmoving.

There was no answer.

He tried again. "Emma, can you get going again?"

Usually, when novices got the jitters, he'd have waited a short time before taking any action, let them sort it out themselves and regain their confidence. But this wasn't anyone.

"I'm going to get her," he told Bob.

"Wait, lad. Give her more time."

Will hesitated. Bob was right and yet…it was his fault she was in this situation, and he wasn't going to let her suffer a moment longer.

He peered down again. "She's not going anywhere, Bob. That's long enough."

"Try and talk her down," urged Bob.

"No. I'm going down there myself." He called to Emma, "Just stay where you are. I'm coming."

In a few bounds, Will had rappelled down the crag and was alongside her. He found her with her eyes screwed tightly shut, her knuckles white, gripping the rope at her side as if her life depended on it. At that moment, he hated himself for having put her in this situation.

"Emma, it's Will. Open your eyes."

She shook her head, then opened her eyes.

"Are you all right?"

Another shake.

"Not feeling faint? Dizzy? Sick?"

"A bit sick and…terrified."

"Can you move?"

"No."

"Yes, you can. Let out the rope a tiny bit."

"I'll fall."

"You can't—it's impossible. I promise you. I'm here, and I'm going to help you down. Cross my heart...you'll be fine."

"I can't. I just daren't let go."

"You can do it. I know you can. I have faith in you—you can do it, sweetheart."

It was the endearment that did it. The simple, silly word that fathers and mothers, relatives and friends—and even strangers in shops—used every day. A casual sweet nothing that meant so much to her.

Slowly, her fingers allowed the rope to slip an inch.

"Good girl," he whispered, coaxing her, gently encouraging her.

Another six inches.

"You're doing fine, Emma, sweetheart...fantastic...not far to go..."

Another few feet.

Now she could see the fellside beneath her and Suzanne at the bottom. Only a few feet to go now, no higher than a bedroom window. The relief was intoxicating, and she let out some more rope, eager to be home.

"Whoa!" he cried. "Not too fast!"

In a few seconds, her boots made contact with the hillside, the sweet and solid, wonderful ground. She wanted to kneel down and kiss it. Will was beside her, his hands trying to unfasten the harness as she jigged up and down in delight, high as a kite on the endorphins pulsing through her body.

"Well done!" cried Suzanne, patting her on the back. "You did really well!"

"Well...I did freeze a bit..."

"You were fine! Happens to all of us at one time. I was stuck for twenty minutes on my first go," said Suzanne, but Emma wasn't fooled. "She was amazing, wasn't she, Will?"

"Yes, she did very well," he said, searching for just the right mix of measured praise and studied nonchalance. Because if he didn't, he'd be throwing his arms around her, telling her how proud he was that she'd even gone through with it in the first place, let alone managed to get going again.

"Now I know you're both being far too kind," breathed Emma.

Suzanne shook her head in exasperation. "Stop putting yourself down, Emma—it takes real guts to do what you just did. Now I really must go back up top and help Bob with the equipment. I'll see you back here in"—she looked at her watch—"about half an hour, if that's OK?"

"Suits me fine!" said Emma, still riding high on adrenaline. "Thank you so much."

"It was a pleasure, wasn't it, Will?" said Suzanne.

"Oh, *absolutely*."

Suzanne rolled her eyes at him and started back up the slope as Emma stood watching him, unsure of what to do next.

"Will," she said, coming nearer to him.

He carried on packing the harnesses into his rucksack.

"Thanks for rescuing me."

"Just my job," he said matter-of-factly, fastening the buckles.

"Well, you were very good at it. I would have been up there all day without you."

He gave a wry smile as he straightened up. "I'm sure someone would have come and coaxed you down by sunset."

"But *you* did…and I'm so glad it was you."

Suddenly, he was right in front of her, looking at her so intently that her heart started thudding faster than on the cliffside. She saw something in his eyes. A new light she'd never seen before. She was sure of it, and now here he was, a breath away from her, a foot above her, his head dipping inexorably toward hers.

Before she even had time to stop and breathe, let alone to think, he was reaching for her with both arms and gently pulling her toward him. As she stood on tiptoe and brought her upturned face to meet his, she felt the lightest touch on her lips.

It was a soft, velvet kiss.

The moist warmth of his mouth stunned her with sweetness, even as his stubble rasped against her tender skin. And his hands. They were holding her around the waist, his fingers slipping in the sheen of sweat on her back. And unmistakably, pressed against her, she felt his body, hard and unyielding. She twisted the soft cotton of his T-shirt in her fingers and darted her tongue into his mouth, seeking out more.

There was no more.

Will had opened his eyes and looked into hers, seeing them gleaming and hopeful, waiting for something. Something he wasn't ready to give...

"Emma," he said softly, dragging his hands from her waist and taking a step back. He felt his heart pounding and his stomach churning at the mistake he'd so nearly made. Because in that moment, when he'd seen her flushed cheeks, her touching gratitude for doing something he had done a dozen times before, he just hadn't been able to stop himself. Hadn't been able to deny it: that powerful need to protect her, to wrap her in his arms and shelter her.

And he had wanted something else. Something more basic and earthy, and he'd wanted it right then and there. He'd wanted to pull her against him and force her to feel how hard she was making him. How hard to the touch and how soft inside. For that moment, he'd felt he had to have her, and if that meant going down on his knees and begging her to come to the cottage, he was ready to do it.

But now?

He had to get away from her. Away from the overwhelming feeling of lust and something far more dangerous that had threatened to make him say something very silly indeed. So he'd dropped his arms from her waist and let her down.

Gently but very, very firmly.

"Emma, we really have to be going now," he said.

Turning away, he shrugged the rucksack onto his back.

———

Emma's lips were searing from his kiss. She could still feel his firm grip on her waist, his touch on her skin, the force of his erection pressing against her, but he was already on his way, striding down the hillside, putting more and more distance between them by the second.

The adrenaline ebbed away as fast as a mountain stream. Her legs didn't want to support her anymore, and she sat down heavily on the fellside. When Suzanne came to collect her, she had no idea how long she'd spent sitting on the grass, staring sightlessly out over the landscape. All she knew was that Will had ignited a fire that had threatened to consume her at any moment. A fire that he'd put out before it had even had a chance to flicker properly into life. Now he'd left her, cold and empty, as he walked off down the hillside.

Chapter 5

WELL, THAT HAD KNOCKED HIM FOR SIX, THOUGHT WILL AS HE strode across the parking lot back to the Land Rover. That kiss—that flick of a small moist tongue darting into his mouth, her small, determined hands on his back, grasping his T-shirt, holding on tight. And his fingertips on her bare skin, pressing against the fine muscles of her back, gripping her flesh, hot and sweat sheened. Her beautiful breasts had been pressing against his chest, and he couldn't believe how turned on he'd been. He'd wanted to grind his pelvis against hers, lift her legs, and hold her to him as she wrapped herself around him.

But he hadn't. He hadn't because that would have been crazy—he was crazy. This was what happened when someone got too close and was in danger of making you care about her. Really care…

The gears on the Land Rover crunched alarmingly as Will pulled away from Stickle Crag parking lot. He winced. Even his driving was going downhill.

What had he thought he was doing anyway? To kiss her like that, take her in his arms, touch her… Well, he didn't do close, and he didn't do caring. He did casual, fleeting relationships. A drink, dinner, no-strings sex, and then end things before the slightest hint of anything emotional.

Then again…maybe he'd misread the signals. Maybe that was all she'd wanted too. Perhaps these days, he was getting paranoid, and all Emma wanted was his body. He sure wanted hers, naked, spread-eagled across his great big bed.

As he squeezed the vehicle into a too-small space outside the base, bells were going off in his head, deafening alarms that told him she was dangerous. Beautiful, sexy, and the biggest threat he'd encountered for a very long time.

Hauling the rucksacks into the equipment room, he dumped them on an old table.

A threat? he repeated to himself. *How could Emma be a threat? Come on, Will. Don't be such a wimp. She's gorgeous, she's available, and she's got the hots for you. Since when did you let an opportunity like that pass you by?*

Thrusting the ropes and harnesses roughly onto the shelves, he felt his stomach clench. He didn't look too closely to see if it was regret, desire, or something else, but even he couldn't deny it. Emma alone had brought on that kick and that fierce ache.

"Will, mate. Everything all right?"

He turned to find one of the other volunteer rescuers grinning at the door.

"Fine." He forced a smile to his face. "Fancy a pint later?"

"OK, why not?" the other man said. "I think the missus will let me out, if I'm very good. She wants me to put up a few shelves this afternoon."

"The joys of DIY," laughed Will, trying not to think of taking a naked and panting Emma over a flat-pack table.

"See you in the Dog around eight-ish, then?"

Will turned back to the equipment, still feeling shaky with lust. "Yeah, sure," he grunted.

The man had gone, and Will found himself preoccupied with Emma again. He'd missed an opportunity back there, he told himself. If he got the chance again, he wouldn't pass it up. He was a grown man, and he knew how to control his emotions. They'd been kept under lock and key for two years now, and he definitely wasn't going to let Emma change that.

———

Emma leaned against the kitchen worktop and waited for the reassuring whistle of the kettle. Shifting against the counter, she felt her aching back protest. Her thighs objected too, and as she reached for a mug, she saw the grazes across her knuckles. She must have knocked them when she slipped against the rock at the top of the cliff.

She sloshed the boiling water on a tea bag in the bottom of the mug because she couldn't be bothered to get the teapot out. Not for one person. She couldn't face waiting for it to brew either, so she squashed the tea bag against the mug with a spoon before tossing it at the trash can. It missed, spattering brown liquid against the cupboard.

Who cared about cleaning anyway? Who cared about anything? It had only been a kiss, so why were her eyes stinging as she felt his mouth on hers again and again?

Later, the mug of tea cradled in her hands almost cold, she tucked her legs underneath her on the sofa and gazed through the window of the flat. Once again, she was back on the fell, with Will's arms around her, molding her like putty, making her soft enough to agree to anything he might have offered. Back then, for the brief moment she'd felt his mouth hot against hers and the unmistakable hardness of him against her stomach, she'd felt that one night would have been enough. Even if he'd asked her to make love with him there and then on the hillside, she knew she'd have said yes.

But now she knew she wanted something more...something more *extraordinary* than that. More than just sex. Something Will Tennant didn't have to give—or didn't want to. She bit her lip and thumped the mug on the table in disgust.

What else could you expect from a serial commitment-phobe? A guy who had led a woman almost to the altar before beating a retreat and who now relished playing with Emma's feelings as much as the challenge of getting her into bed.

From now on, she vowed, it was strictly business between her and Mr. December—and he was going to know about it.

———

"You've got a visitor, Em."

Emma glanced up from the computer screen in the tourist center to find Jan Edwards beaming down at her. Her post-kiss resolve to become a workaholic had lasted, well, considerably less time than it ought to have. But how she'd longed for a bit of peace and quiet at first. And she had to admit, life had been satisfyingly dull these past ten days or so.

"There's someone to see you in the boardroom," repeated Jan.

The boardroom? Someone to see her? Emma felt a small knot starting to form in her stomach before a jolt of common sense unraveled it. She told herself it was impossible. She smiled back at Jan, realizing it must be the calendar designer or the printer.

"Is it Lakeland Graphics?" she asked, refocusing on the keyboard.

"No-oo."

"Westmorland Print, then?"

"Wrong again, Em."

She clicked on the Print icon so she could send her cottage holiday article to the printer.

"A strippergram?"

"You're getting very warm."

Emma lifted her hand from the mouse and sat back slowly in her chair.

"OK. Hit me with it."

"It's Mr. December."

"Right."

"'Right'? Is that all you're going to say, babe? Not 'oh my God' or 'where's my mascara' or—"

"Will Tennant is the last person I expect or want to see right now." She saw her friend open her mouth to protest, but she put up a hand. "And I'd ask you to leave it there. Please, Jan."

Jan's eyes widened, and she nodded. "Enough said. That's me told off. But he *is* waiting, and he did ask for you."

"Couldn't you tell him I'm out of the office?"

"Nice try, but no can do. He's parked right next to your Mini."

"Say I'm in a meeting with the boss."

"Sorry again. It was James Marshall who told him you were here. I'm only the messenger."

"Oh dear."

Emma knew Will had her backed into a corner again, but what on earth could he want this time? It had been almost OK while he was physically out of her sight, but having him here and now…that was different. At least he was on her territory, she reasoned; that made a lot of difference, surely.

She risked a glance at the goldfish-bowl, glass office where her boss was talking on the phone. Just at that moment, he caught her eye and raised his *Warning: New Daddy* mug to her cheerfully.

"That man would be dangerous if he had a brain," muttered Emma.

"Who? Will?" asked Jan.

"No—oh, it doesn't matter." She grabbed the mouse again and grinned. "Let him wait a bit longer."

"OK, but it's your funeral." She heard Jan tutting as she walked back to her desk, and she carried on clicking at the mouse, totally oblivious to what was on the screen, panic rising. What was Will playing at, coming to the office like this? Maybe he'd come to apologize—but for what? He hadn't acted like he'd done anything wrong. He'd just rejected her. Just pulled back a bit. And it had hurt. So it wouldn't do him any harm to wait.

Sighing, Emma sank back in her chair, trying to think how she was going to deal with their meeting. He'd be expecting her to be annoyed with him, maybe even hostile, so she'd be cool, calm, and collected as if nothing had happened. Nothing, absolutely nothing, would give him the slightest hint that he'd upset her.

"Emma."

The *New Daddy* mug had appeared on the desk by her elbow. She turned to see her boss, smiling benignly as usual. She resisted the urge to tell him he had baby sick on his tie. "Yes, James?"

"Sorry to hassle you, but you do know that that Tennant guy is waiting in the boardroom for you, don't you?"

"I was just finishing off this press—"

"Only I wouldn't like to think an influential local businessman had been kept waiting deliberately by one of my staff. Would I?"

Emma nearly exploded. *Influential businessman, my backside!* she wanted to cry. Instead, she smiled, sweetly and in a nonthreatening kind of a way. "No, James."

Her boss might come across like a genial Labrador, but inside lurked the soul of a Rottweiler.

James narrowed his eyes at her. "Be nice to him, Emma. You're good at being nice to people. That's why I gave you the PR officer's job, remember?"

"Yes, James."

Ten minutes later, she found herself with a palm around the handle of the boardroom door. Five minutes previously, she had been in the ladies', reapplying her favorite cherry lip gloss, washing her hands, and trying to breathe.

None of which had helped.

And now?

She wished she'd put on a longer skirt that morning. A baggy sweater and maybe a Victorian high-necked blouse. Maybe even a chastity belt. How could she face him after what had happened? Realization dawned on her. He hadn't pulled back—she'd practically forced herself on him. Oh, the humiliation of letting him kiss her like that—of her responding so…so physically. God, she'd actually pushed her tongue into his mouth. Worse, she'd looked…well, far too needy, judging by the way he'd rejected her.

How could she have had so little self-respect—after what had happened with Jeremy too. Over and over again, for the past ten days, she'd told herself that Will had done nothing. He hadn't slept with her, promised her the earth, dumped her for her boss, and stood by while she'd been sacked.

He had done nothing.

Then why had it hurt so much?

She didn't want to answer that, especially right now when she had to face him again. Well, there was nothing for it. This was business, and she was going to show him just how businesslike she could be.

———

Twenty minutes! Will repeated to himself. Over a quarter of an hour she'd kept him waiting in this damned boardroom. There wasn't even a window, and it was time, he reminded himself, he could ill afford to spare in the middle of the workday. Hey, he'd even canceled a meeting with his chief buyer to come here. Maybe he shouldn't have bothered…

He took a slow, deep breath, the way he did before he tackled the last, difficult section of a particularly tricky climb. It would be worth it, he told himself, when she saw how professionally he could behave, how magnanimous his proposal was, and that there were no hard feelings over the calendar. For whatever else he was, Will told himself, he was a consummate professional in every sense of the word. OK. Maybe strike out the "consummate" bit. That probably wasn't a good word to use in reference to Emma, but "professional" he liked. In his business, in his role as rescue team leader, in everything as far as work was concerned, he would show her he could be dispassionate and objective and fair.

If only she would bloody well deign to come down and speak to him.

He knew she was here. James Marshall had told him as soon as he'd entered the foyer. Besides, her trendy little car was outside—the one with the nodding dog in the back window. He supposed it was meant to be ironic. The kind of thing that was considered trendily tacky in London but that folk up here just thought was daft.

He smiled to himself, then noticed the clock on the wall… This was getting ridiculous. How much longer was she going to make him suffer? Right, he decided, she had five more minutes before he had her paged by reception. Five more minutes before he had her cute derrière hauled down here.

———

Emma sucked in a last breath, straightened her back, turned the handle on the door…and felt her legs melting.

Will was standing at the head of the table. Six feet three inches of clean-shaven, suited, and booted danger. Every inch the successful managing director, he looked just as at home in a boardroom as he did on a mountain in combats and shades. As she walked toward him, her hand outstretched, she felt a momentary wobble. He clearly wasn't in the mood to take any prisoners, and neither was she. Her nose twitched. What was that fabulous smell? She almost had to stop herself from sniffing the air. She even recognized the brand of aftershave he was wearing—had almost bought a bottle from Harvey Nichols for Jeremy until she'd seen the price.

Where had he gotten it from up here? Damn the man!

His eyes narrowed as she approached. *Backbone*, Emma told herself, like her old hockey mistress at school. Not that she'd ever been any good at hockey.

"Mr. Tennant. So sorry to have kept you waiting. I had a call from the national press to deal with. Unavoidable, I'm afraid. You know how it is with journalists."

———

Will knew things weren't going well when he felt his dick jump to attention as soon as the door opened. It seemed as though Emma only had to step into a room now, and he was losing it. No bloody wonder, though… she had that suit on for a start. The black one she'd worn at the mountain rescue base the first time he'd met her. The fitted jacket was buttoned up and stretched tight across her breasts, and he could just see a scrap of lace peeping out from the V at the top. Around her throat, she was wearing a necklace with a simple drop design that pointed the way tantalizingly to her cleavage.

And the skirt—it was, as ever, just long enough to be businesslike but easily short enough to inspire disreputable thoughts. But worse than all this were her shoes: black high heels and, if he wasn't mistaken, sheer black thigh highs. They had to be. There was no way, he thought, that Emma Tremayne would wear tights, not in a building this overheated…

He forced himself to concentrate on her face, giving what he hoped was a confident and conciliatory smile, but she looked unimpressed.

"Do take a seat, Mr. Tennant," she said coolly.

"No need to be formal," he snapped, instantly regretting rising to the bait. To his surprise, she backed down and smiled back at him.

"I'm sorry. Do take a seat, Will, and tell me how the tourist board can help you."

Why was she acting like this—so calmly, so reasonably, so…plain bloody weird? And why wasn't she being sarcastic? It was scary.

In fact, he didn't quite know how to handle her in this mood. He'd breezed in here, totally in control, ready to take charge and make an offer that he knew would floor her and she'd find impossible to refuse. But somehow, without a single word, she'd put herself in the driving seat the moment she'd opened the door. He watched, fascinated, as she perched on the chair on the other side of the desk and placed her suede folder on the wooden surface. Unzipping it with slender fingers, she opened the writing pad inside at a virgin sheet of paper.

She clicked the top of an elegant silver pen and waited for him. He didn't know what to say. He'd expected anger or hostility, but she just looked blank. As she leaned forward, writing something on the pad, he noticed the teardrop on her necklace, hanging pendulum-like above the promising cleft between her breasts.

He swallowed. His silence must have been unnerving her, for she had started doodling on the paper. Then she looked up at him and asked again, "Will, can you tell me what you want with me, please?"

There was a slight tremor in her voice. Now, she looked something beyond numb, something else that he didn't want to recognize. She looked weary. A small voice nagged at him and wouldn't be silenced, whispering that he had…oh God, he'd hurt her back there after the rappel. His pulling back had been that fraction too late for both of them.

He told himself he was being ridiculous, that he was sure he'd done nothing wrong. And that if they had started a relationship then, if he had taken her back to the cottage or her flat and had sex with her, if it had lasted more than a night, even a week, the pain of letting her down, as he inevitably would have had to, would have been far more acute.

"Will, I don't want to be rude, but I really am very busy, so if we could just get down to business, I'd be grateful," said Emma, her pen poised over the paper, waiting for him.

He found his carefully prepared speech, his generous offer, to be delivered oh so casually, was somehow stuck in the back of his dry throat. He didn't want to cough to clear it and give his nerves away.

"Sorry?" she asked, completing a fascinating spiral on the notepad. "I didn't catch that."

"How do you stand it in here? It's so damn stuffy."

"It is rather warm. Shall I open the door to let a bit of fresh air in?"

"No." He knew he was making a right mess of this. "Look, I'll get straight to the point."

"That would be good."

He resisted the urge to respond, to lean over the desk and wind his fingers in her hair, taste her lips, shimmering temptingly with a shiny gloss. He could have sworn he could smell cherries, ripe and inviting. As he swung his laptop case from beside his seat and onto the desk, Emma sat up straight and placed her pen beside the suede folder.

The act of opening his laptop made him feel in control again, and he withdrew a spiral-bound sheaf of papers and placed them on the table. *No beating about the bush*, he thought. *Give it to her straight, mate.*

"We've been giving the mountain rescue calendar careful consideration and I'd like—that is, my company, Outside Edge, has decided that we would be prepared to act as main sponsors for the project. With our backing, you'll make far more money than on sales alone." He pushed the presentation folder toward her. "I think you'll find it's a generous package. Here are our proposals, and if you need anything else, our marketing department is ready to give you all the help you need."

Emma paused before placing a hand on the folder and drawing it toward her. "That's very generous of you—of Outside Edge, Will."

He grinned broadly, thinking how great this was. She was grateful and impressed—just what he'd hoped for.

"But I have to say I'm a little confused. I thought you were totally against the idea."

"I'm only thinking of how we can benefit the rescue team. The calendar's clearly going ahead, so we might as well make it a success." Will hoped she wouldn't suspect the real reason, that he would have more influence over the project as the sponsor. And though he didn't like admitting it, not even to himself, more control over her. "Besides, what was it you told me at the photo meeting? Something about being more commercially aware and open-minded? I decided to follow your advice."

"Well, I assure you we'll give your offer careful consideration."

Nice one, he congratulated himself.

"However, I ought to tell you that we already have an excellent sponsorship deal in progress with a major manufacturer of walking equipment—"

"Like who?" he cut in, far more abruptly than was polite.

"I'm afraid I'm not at liberty to tell you that at the moment."

Will stared hard at her, trying to see whether or not she was taking the piss out of him or even seeking revenge for the rappelling—not that he'd done anything wrong—but he detected nothing. In fact, she sounded almost mechanical, and the spark in her eyes, the one he found so sexy and fiery, wasn't there. What the hell was the matter with her?

"Right…well, I suppose I should have offered sooner. I suppose I shouldn't be surprised that you had already thought of getting a sponsor."

"It was part of the plan. I did mention it at the original meeting at the rescue base. You were late, if I recall rightly."

To his alarm, she had already started to shut her notebook and zip up the folder. Will started to panic a little, telling himself she surely couldn't just dismiss his offer—dismiss him—like this. He had to provoke her into some sort of reaction.

"There's something else," he said, getting desperate. "And I won't beat around the bush."

Emma laid her folder back down on the table and stared at him. Will noted with satisfaction that the spark was there again. "That would be good," she said.

"You've seen all the press speculation that my company is involved in a new project at Lakeshore House. I'd like to do some joint PR on the project with the tourist office. In fact, I want you to help us draft some launch material."

"Can you give me some background? Like what you plan to do with the hotel, for instance?" said Emma. "You have secured the property, I take it?"

"I'm not at liberty to tell you that yet."

"Then I'm not at liberty to write anything. And anyway, we can't help you publicize a commercial project, if that's what you have in mind."

Will knew he'd shot himself in the foot. Asking her to help had been a last-ditch attempt to keep her in the same room as him, and it hadn't worked.

"I can't tell you the details yet," he said defensively.

Emma finished zipping up her folder without making a note and snatched up the proposals. "When you do feel able to reveal all, let us know. If it's appropriate for us to get involved, then I'll get one of the PR assistants to put some drafts together."

"I thought you would be doing it personally," he said, disappointed.

"Don't worry. It will all be done efficiently. If it's something we can get involved with, that is."

She got to her feet, so Will did too.

"Emma, wait a moment."

She smiled apologetically. "If that's all, I have to be getting back to the office. I've a date with a printer."

Will felt he couldn't stand this…this cold politeness. It was so not Emma…

"Look, I hope I haven't upset you," he blurted out. "I mean with the rappelling. I shouldn't have asked you to do something you didn't want to."

"You can stop feeling guilty. You didn't make me do anything I didn't want to do. In fact, it was my decision entirely. And I've faced the consequences."

The consequences? What did she mean by that? he asked himself. This was excruciating. He couldn't let it go at that, even though Emma obviously wanted to.

"I really must get back to the office. *Please.*"

She went to put her hand on the door, but he moved swiftly between it and her. She clutched the folders to her tightly, but his hand had flown to her arm before he knew it.

"What do you mean, 'the consequences'?" he asked.

"Sore legs and hands. Bruises and aches in parts of me I didn't know I had."

"Purely physical damage, then?"

"Why? Should there be any other kind?"

"Trauma," he cut in. "It was quite an experience to go through, your first rappel. Tricky too. Some people—in that situation, I mean—find it hits them later."

She gave him a cool smile. "Really? No, I can't say anything hit me later. A cup of tea, a bit of medicinal chocolate, and I was fine."

"You're sure?"

"Absolutely. Now, are you going to let me out?"

There was no way, decided Will, that he was going to let her escape before he found out what was the matter with her.

"No, Emma, you can't go just yet. We can't carry on like this—not behaving civilly to each other. If you're going to carry on doing business—if you're going to carry on working for the rescue team, I can't let that happen. It's just not healthy—could be dangerous, even."

"Don't be silly. There is nothing uncivil between us."

"Really? Convince me, then."

In a moment, Will had pulled the folder from her hands and placed it on the table. The lack of resistance was the first thing that surprised him. Then he cradled her face in his hands, and the madness took over. His lips touched hers, and he felt the gloss sliding against his open mouth, the ripe-cherry scent of her making him almost dizzy. For a moment, a long, awful moment, there was no response—nothing.

So he pushed her harder, increasing the pressure on her mouth, and suddenly, she gave in to him. She opened her lips and let him slide his tongue deeper into her mouth, wondering how she tasted so much sweeter than cherries.

He carried on with the kiss, bringing one hand to play with the buttons of her jacket and unfastening them roughly. He didn't give a thought to her expensive, provocative suit; he only wanted to close a hand around her breast and feel its weight, its full beauty. Impatiently, he flicked open the last button, tugged the lapels apart, and looked down at her beautiful breasts, stretched taut under a silk camisole.

Emma was breathless. He could see her chest heaving, hear her ragged breathing. She clung to his body as he pulled her against him.

"See? See what you do to me, Emma?"

He slid his hand under her top, rolled her nipple between his fingers, and felt her shiver as the nub hardened. He couldn't believe what he was doing, but nothing mattered now. All Will knew was that he wanted to explore every inch of her luscious body and be allowed to bury himself inside her.

"I need you, Emma. Right here and now."

"No...no, we can't—"

Will was already bearing her back against the wall of the office. "Why not?" he murmured roughly. "Surely, you're not afraid, Emma?"

He dropped a hand to her thighs and pulled up her skirt. He splayed his hand across the silky nylon of her stockings to the warm flesh above, then higher still to her panties. His finger swept across the front of the lace to find it damp—beautifully moist. Easing a hand between her legs, he cupped her and felt the warm wet rush of desire against his palm.

"Will, oh..." she murmured in indignant pleasure as he tugged her panties down her thighs and her bottom made contact with the cold wall. She squirmed as Will's fingers slid between her legs. They were so warm inside her, and she was so wet, she could feel desire pooling between her legs. As his fingers slipped deeper, she could feel his breath, hot against her cleavage.

Lust frayed his voice. "Sweetheart, that is so beautiful..."

She hated it even while she whimpered in pleasure and arched her back to draw him in further. Hated him for pleasuring her and herself for loving his touch. He moved his hands to her backside, gripping her soft cheeks as he pulled her against him, making her feel how much he wanted her through the rough cloth of his suit. As he kissed her, the rough rasp of stubble against her mouth made her whole body tingle.

Somewhere, next door, upstairs, who knew where, a telephone rang out, and the sound of laughter drifted through a wall. Dimly, she heard the chatter of a photocopier, the noises of a busy office in the middle of the day, and the realization hit her. Here she was, half-naked, backed against a wall, by a man she barely knew. Worse, she wanted him. Wanted to have wild, dirty sex with him against the wall and over the desk and on the cold tile floor of that overheated, airless, steamy room. Even as he pushed his tongue into her mouth, she knew that it was cheap and tawdry, that the tenderness, the warmth, she craved from him was missing.

She forced herself to remember: Will cared nothing for her.

He just wanted to make her another notch on his bedpost. He'd had the chance for tenderness back there on the mountain, and when she'd dared to reach out to him, he had rejected her and left her alone in a world that wasn't hers. She couldn't forget the look in his eyes. She had opened herself to him then, in that heady moment when she thought he really felt something for her, and he had shut her out.

The buzz of the phones called her back to reality. This was her hard-fought, hard-won new job here, the new life she was battling for. Free of arrogant men who picked her up, used her, wrote their own story on her, then crumpled her up and discarded her.

Gripping his biceps, she squeezed through his suit jacket, harder and harder. "Stop it." Her voice was quavery, not like it usually was. "Stop, please."

Will felt her fingers grasping his arms but carried on kissing her.

She dug her nails in.

He opened his eyes and snatched his head back, still tasting cherries on his lips. He saw the smudge of lipstick around her mouth and felt the smoothness of her bare flesh in his hands.

"Will, stop this right now," she said firmly.

"Emma—I thought…"

"This is not what I want. It's a disaster waiting to happen. Embarrassment for both of us. I have work to get back to." Her voice was tight and prim. "I have a life to get back to. Leave me alone—*please.*"

She tugged her skirt back down her thighs, and he dragged himself off her and watched as she refastened her jacket with shaky fingers. Lead settled in the pit of his stomach, and he felt he'd made one huge error of judgment.

"I'm—I'm sorry. That was…" *Stupid, mad, humiliating?* Having come to his senses, he couldn't give what he'd just done a name. "It was totally unprofessional of me. I misunderstood, misread the signals."

Emma couldn't look at him. "I have to go. I need to go."

"Not yet. Not like this."

"What did you think we were going to do, Will?" she snapped. "Rip our clothes off in the middle of the office? Have a quickie up against the wall? Take me over the desk? This is my workplace!"

"Emma, I'm not an animal. I—I misunderstood. You seemed to be enjoying it too. For God's sake, I'd never make you do anything. I'm not that—"

"Kind of guy? Maybe, maybe not. I don't know, but I'll tell you this. It was crazy of me to let it go that far, and frankly, I feel sorry for you."

Will let her move to the door. When she turned back to him, he saw a new Emma: buttoned up again, the bolts firmly locked against him. Her voice sounded as icy as any mountain ridge in winter, and one never likely to thaw again.

"I'll pass your offer about the calendar on to James," she was saying primly. "But I have to tell you, the sponsorship package is being finalized now, and I doubt if we can change it. You were just that bit too late."

Then she was gone, leaving three words burning into him.

Sorry for him? Those words branded him with the pain of loss and humiliation. What on earth had Emma got to feel sorry for him for? Unless… *No*, he told himself, *it was impossible*. Whatever Emma might have heard about him on the village grapevine—almost certainly had heard—she couldn't know everything.

That he'd jilted Kate, that he was a bastard, a lady-killer—all these she probably knew and he probably deserved. But not *that*. He shook his head and looked around, suddenly aware of voices outside the door, of just where he was and what he'd tried to do there.

He was back to square one with Emma—no, make that square minus one.

Chapter 6

THE TOWEL DISPENSER NEARLY CAME OFF THE WALL AS EMMA stood in the ladies'.

"Why won't you work?" she cried in frustration as dozens of paper sheets flew out onto the tiles. Rescuing one, she wiped the smudged lip gloss she'd been trying to apply from her face, dreading one of her colleagues coming in. She thrust the gloss into her jacket pocket and gripped the edge of the washbasin. She thought she'd been so clever, so cool and calm back there—the mirror showed otherwise.

Why did he have to be on top all the time? she asked herself. Mr. Lord of the bloody manor, Mr. High-and-Mighty Will. She hated him and hated herself more, because when he'd tried to kiss her again, blast it if her legs hadn't wobbled. She'd wobbled all over, in fact, and when he touched her…there. When she'd felt his hands on her breasts and his finger skimming between her legs, she'd been desperate to have him inside her there and then, against the wall. And part of her was whispering that he must like her. He certainly wanted her, so it must go deeper than that, surely…

She tried again to redo her lips, telling herself that. Will Tennant just wanted to have control. He obviously expected every woman to be at his whim. To swoon in his arms and be there—or not—as he pleased. How dare he behave in that arrogant, macho way? It was ridiculous, not to mention wholly inappropriate. In fact, if he'd been her boss, she could have had him prosecuted for sexual harassment. It was worse than that, however. He was, effectively, a client.

She groaned aloud. So why did he have to look so gorgeous? Wearing that expensive suit and silk tie. Looking so serious and businesslike—it

was unfair. Why couldn't she have stayed calm and unruffled and professional? Why did she have to respond?

One thing was for sure, today had proved that Will only wanted
power over her in every way. Well, Emma Tremayne wasn't going to do
control freaks or bastards ever again, so that was tough for him.

She tried out a smile in the mirror and winced.

Pathetic.

But she had to go back upstairs very soon, or Jan would send out
a search party, maybe even with a Labrador. Oh heavens, James—what
could she tell him? He'd be delighted to get a sponsor like Outside Edge
for the calendar and would be furious to find she'd turned down the offer.

Glancing at her watch, she decided she had to make some attempt to
rescue the situation. Maybe if she was lucky, she could phone Echo GPS
while James was at lunch and try all her powers of persuasion to get them
to agree to the deal she'd been trying to set up. It was only at the early
stages at the moment, certainly not the almost-done deal she'd led Will
to believe. Accepting another favor from Will was out of the question.
She could handle this part of life herself, and she certainly didn't need a
handout from him.

—————

As he drove out of the parking lot, Will knew he was lucky not to scrape
the wall of the narrow entrance to the tourist center. As it was, he was so
intent on berating himself that he nearly clipped Emma's Mini.

You stupid, stupid idiot, he thought furiously. *What on earth made you
think you could impress Emma—control her like that—hey, even jump her?*

It seemed that every move he made with Emma was wrong. From
the first time he'd seen her on the mountain, he was pushing the self-
destruct button. He should have known she wouldn't be impressed by
an offer so obviously calculated to patronize her. As for virtually pinning
her against the wall of a meeting room, just thinking about it made Will
groan in embarrassment.

OK, he told himself as he squeezed the Range Rover into the flow
of traffic, she hadn't thrust him away, not at first. He'd seen and felt her

physical response to him, but he'd certainly pushed her way too hard. Briefly, she'd responded, but in the process, he'd confirmed every one of her prejudices about him; that he was an arrogant, sex-crazed, macho man. Well, maybe there were worse things to be.

Like a coward.

———

Twenty minutes later, Will was striding through the offices at Outside Edge, snapping at his PA to hold his calls. He could see by the look on her face that he'd upset her but told himself that was tough. He shut the door of his office firmly on her protests, knowing it would cost him a bunch of flowers tomorrow and a hell of a lot of groveling.

For the rest of the afternoon, what had happened in the meeting room with Emma nagged at him. He knew he wanted her in his bed just as much as ever, but he also realized he wanted her to respect him. He'd behaved like a schoolboy these past few weeks, sneering at her ideas, goading her into doing something she didn't want to do. And when she did do it, taking all the guts she could muster and thanking him—actually thanking him for helping her when it was his damn fault in the first place—he'd come on to her and then pulled back.

He sat back in his chair and threw his pen on the desk. So not only had he humiliated her, he told himself, he'd made a clumsy move on her in her own office as well! Was it any wonder she'd rejected him, that she was confused and bruised and angry and scared? Bloody hell, he'd never have spoken to him again if he were her.

And yet…if she didn't like him, if she'd finally washed her hands of him, why had she felt so warm to his touch? So unmistakably turned on in every way? It was driving him crazy.

He glanced at his watch. Four thirty. He needed to take his mind off Emma or his business would go down the tubes. Snatching up his cell phone, he punched Max Coleridge's number. He needed to focus on something cold and dry and boring, and he had just the thing. The legal issues with the new outdoor center he was trying to push through. Yes, they'd do nicely as a substitute for a cold shower.

———

Later that evening, Will hadn't even gotten past the main course at the Coleridge farmhouse before he found out that if he wanted to cure his addiction to Emma, he was looking in the wrong place. Cozy domesticity on a plate. Love and sex—personified by Max's wife, Francine, and her swollen stomach, which tonight, he found strangely beautiful. In fact, he found himself longing to stretch out his hand and lay it on the taut skin of her abdomen. Hell, what was the matter with him? Surely, he wasn't feeling broody? *Guys don't have biological clocks*, he told himself. Still, as he saw Max resting his hand proudly on his wife's bump, Will felt a pang of longing he had no desire to acknowledge.

He tried to focus on the wineglass in his hand, a blush zinfandel that glistened on the sides of the glass as shiny as Emma's lip gloss, or her eyes as she'd gazed up at him on the mountain…

"Penny for them?"

He looked up from his glass. His ears registered that someone had been speaking to him, but he had no idea what they'd said. Emma had taken over his thoughts once again.

"What's up, Will? You've been staring at that glass as if it had poison in it. Are you still worried about getting the outdoor center idea past the planners?"

"No, Max. Not really. Though it's going to be tricky. We've got some opposition, and there's a chance it might go to developers if we're really unlucky."

Francine laid her knife and fork across her plate. "It's not this calendar, is it? Max has told me all about it, you know." She turned a dazzling smile and a pair of dark French eyes on him. "I hear we are going to see a lot more of you when it is finished."

Will shook his head and laughed. "Why on earth would I be bothered about that?"

Max was in a provocative mood. "You're going to be on the top shelf of all the newsagents in the Lakes in a few months' time, mate. Probably the local papers too. I'm not sure I'd want my white bits lusted after by all and sundry."

"In your dreams, Max."

"Ah. So it's a pride thing? You really don't mind being pinned up on the wall of someone's tea shop? Or at the local WI Hall?"

"I shall buy at least ten copies, and I shall put them up in the prenatal clinic as warning," said Francine.

An indulgent smile curved his lips. He couldn't be annoyed with Francine even if she was pushing her luck.

"You buy as many as you want, Francine. Buy the whole lot, if you can, and burn them for me," he said lightly. "But don't put them up on any walls—not unless you want to put your friends off men for good." Reaching for the wine bottle, he found it was nearly empty. "Max, get this clear. I couldn't care less about being seen with my kit off. I just happen to think it's totally the wrong image for the squad. We're trying to appear professional, not a bunch of attention-seeking jokers. There's no need for it, as you well know—I did offer to fund the center."

Max shook his head. "You can't go round solving people's problems single-handedly, mate. Give them a chance to help themselves."

"But whose idea was the calendar? Bob's or Dr. Suzanne's?" asked Francine.

"I know," cut in Max. "Emma Tremayne's."

Francine shifted in her chair, and Will saw her abdomen ripple as the baby thrust out a foot or a fist or some tiny part of its body. He got a funny feeling in his mouth, a kind of tingling. Weird...

"Who is this Emma?" inquired Francine. "I didn't know she was on the team."

"She isn't," he declared.

"Emma is their new PR lady," explained Max. "And what a PR lady..." He sighed. "Long, dark hair, curves in all the right places, lovely voice. Hasn't she, Will?"

"Max..."

His eyes glittered in triumph. "I've got eyes, mate. I saw what you were like at the Wordsworth Center—like a stag in the rutting season."

"Thanks, mate. Attractive image." Yet he had to admit, Max was right. That was exactly what he did feel like when Emma was within fifty feet.

"Is this Emma on your hit list?" said Francine, making Will conclude she wasn't as blameless as she looked.

"Definitely not. She's just been drafted into helping us with the fundraising. It's only Max that seems to think I've got a crush on her. He's wrong. I haven't," he said, draining the last of his wine from his glass.

"Really?" said Max, sounding unconvinced. "A gorgeous woman asks you to get your kit off for her, and you object? You must be losing your grip, Will. Until a few months ago, I thought you never refused a request like that from a single woman."

"Max, you make me sound a complete bastard. Sorry, Francine," he apologized.

"To be fair, you do have quite a track record with the ladies," went on Max easily. "What about that blond nurse or the girl with the mile-long legs and her own four-by-four dealership? And that posh one? An Honourable, wasn't she? At least she was until she met you." He laughed at his own joke, leaving Will fuming inwardly behind a mask of good humor.

Will turned to Francine, planting a kiss on her cheek. "There's only one woman I'm interested in right now—the one who's going to have my goddaughter or godson very soon. How long now, sweetheart?"

"Five weeks," she groaned. "But I do hope he or she will put in an appearance sooner than that. Would you like some more wine?" she said, indicating the empty bottle.

"Love to. But sit down. I'll get it. I know Max's wine cellar better than he does by now. Red or white?"

"There's already a bottle of Meursault in the fridge. The corkscrew's in the kitchen drawer. Nothing for me, thanks."

He was halfway out the door before he heard Max call after him, "There was no mistaking your reaction to her at the Wordsworth Center. What other woman could get you soaking wet without needing rescuing? Mind you, she didn't look too thrilled to see you. You looked like you'd already had a lover's tiff to me."

"Things aren't always what they appear, Max. You should know that by now."

In the safety of the kitchen, Will pulled the cork from the wine bottle, his mind working overtime on how to distract his hosts from any jibes about Emma, the calendar, or his love life.

Condensation oozed down the side of the bottle as the straw-colored liquid swished into the glass with a satisfying glug.

His fingers closed around the stem.

If only he were about to share this nice glass of chilled wine with Emma on the sofa at his cottage. She'd arrive, fresh from work, in *that* suit, and he'd show her into the drawing room. Imagine, he thought, her slim little fingers caressing the bowl of the glass. Her full lips sipping the wine as she tucked an unruly strand of mahogany hair behind her ear. Her fiery green eyes regarding him, not with contempt but with desire as she made it clear she wanted him every bit as much as he wanted her.

He would take the glass from her hand and place it slowly and deliberately on the coffee table. Then, just as slowly and deliberately, she would slip her jacket off her shoulders, unzip her skirt, and ease it over her hips. Naturally, in his fantasy, she wouldn't have a blouse on—just a black half-cup bra, which she would unhook before releasing her full breasts. Or maybe even that camisole.

Black thigh highs too, of course. Oh yes—sheer, sexy stockings and her most impractical heels. He felt himself grow hard at the thought of her removing that lot.

As for the rest, there would be…not a lot. Nothing at all when he'd finished with her. A silky thong perhaps or a pair of lacy mini-shorts stretched tight across the peachy curve of her bottom. Whatever, he would take them off and toss them carelessly aside, just to let her know she wouldn't be needing them for the rest of the evening.

She'd be naked then, and the tiny down on her honey-colored skin would rise under his fingertips as he traced a path with his tongue around her taut nipples, over her gently curving belly, and between her thighs.

He wondered if, for their first time, they'd make love on the rug in front of the hearth or with her pressed over the slippery chintz of the chaise longue in the drawing room. He would definitely have to have her in his four-poster at least once. That went without saying.

Damn!

Cold wine was running down his fingers and pooling around the base of the wineglass. Grabbing a cloth from the sink, he tried to mop the counter as the puddle expanded and began dripping over the edge of the granite worktop. He'd just poured a good part of a bottle of Max's best Meursault onto the kitchen floor!

Hastily, he wiped the tiles with a paper towel and filled another glass. Shoving the nearly empty bottle into the fridge, he hoped his friend would soon be too mellow to notice.

Right, that was it. He was going back into the dining room to enjoy the rest of his dinner and to forget all about Emma Tremayne, but even as he crossed the hall, the realization dealt him a body blow.

Forget Emma? Just who the hell was he trying to fool? He had to bring back the focus to his life: concentrate on his business, push through his plans for the outdoor center, maybe even fit in some climbing. All the things that should demand his attention, that he'd once enjoyed—correction, still enjoyed—doing.

Chapter 7

"Oh come on, Emma. It'll do you good. You've had a face like a wet weekend for ages now."

"It's kind of you, Jan, but—"

"Kind?" Jan almost snorted with derision as she plonked herself down on Emma's desk. Emma looked down at her notepad. She'd doodled endless mountains and ridges all over the page. She wondered if it was Freudian.

A hand, tipped with long red nails, was slapped down over the page.

"Don't be so daft," scolded Jan. "I don't ask people out for an evening out of sympathy. I ask them because I like them. It'll do you good to get a few glasses of red down you. I won't take no for an answer."

Two weeks had gone by since the encounter at the office. Two weeks in which she'd tried hard to wipe Will out of her mind and forget what she'd let him do to her. Emma thought she'd been doing well. She didn't think of him more than a few times a day now and certainly didn't get his photograph out more than once a night. She didn't try and recall the feel of the touch of his lips on hers more than a few times. Not at all today...

She smiled at Jan. "OK then, sounds like I don't have much choice."

With the proofs approved and the calendar moving on to the printers' stage, she'd had absolutely no reason to visit the rescue base. The marketing team at Echo GPS was putting her sponsorship proposals to the board, and things were looking promising.

Although she'd tried hard, she couldn't think of a single excuse for staying in on a Saturday night—and Jan really wouldn't take no for an answer.

———

Emma and Jan were sitting with their drinks in the Black Dog, a traditional Lakeland pub with a hole-in-the-wall hearth, flagged floor, and ceilings to bash your head on—especially if you were six feet three inches. Emma heard Will Tennant's expletive from her seat in the tiny, packed bar before she saw him.

She groaned inwardly and felt her stomach give an annoying little flip. Now, wasn't that just typical? In London, you could go a lifetime without ever seeing a stranger twice, but in her few short months up here, she'd learned you were lucky if you got as far as the mailbox without saying hello to at least three people you knew by sight and half a dozen you'd never met before in your life.

Being sociable to complete strangers, she had to admit, was one of Bannerdale's strong points.

Not tonight.

Tonight—Emma thought as she heard a grunt from the pub door—living in a village with a smaller population than the Rogue PR building was a pain in the bottom.

"Sorry," exclaimed Will to no one in particular as he rubbed his head ruefully after banging it on the low beam inside the porch of the Black Dog. He straightened up as he walked into the bar, followed by some of the other rescue team members. Emma caught Suzanne's eye and waved at her. Jason, the red-haired builder, blushed.

Will didn't seem to have noticed her, and he certainly didn't look as if he'd lost any sleep over her. In fact, he looked dangerously attractive as ever in his battered jeans and long-sleeved T-shirt. There he was now, tall and confident, and already ordering a round of drinks. And he was not alone—oh no. Even above the hubbub of the crowded pub, Emma couldn't fail to hear the shriek.

"Will! Darling!"

"Oh. Hello again, Tara."

She saw a young woman, barely more than a girl really, in the tightest crop top and trousers she had ever seen, launch herself on him like an overexcited puppy. Will brushed his lips across her cheek, and the teenager wound her arms around his neck like a lovesick boa constrictor.

Emma met his eyes over the girl's shoulder. All her resolve to stay cool and indifferent evaporated. *You pig*, she thought, *a girl old enough to be*—well, not quite Will's daughter, but almost. But even she had to admit he didn't look too thrilled with the situation himself. Good grief though, the girl had her talons in his backside now. She could see him trying to pull them away, but the remorseless Tara only grabbed him again. *Serves him damn well right*, thought Emma with disgust.

"Who's that girl?" she hissed.

Jan put her wineglass down long enough to take in the tightly clad figure shrink-wrapped around Will's powerful frame.

"Oh…that's the youngest McKinnon sister. Mummy and Daddy own a couple of swanky hotels on the lake. It looks like young Tara's got her claws into your friend Will—literally. I'd have thought she was a bit of a baby, even for him. But maybe that won't bother Casanova." She held up her glass. "Anyway, it's your round, Emma, and I'll have dry white and soda this time."

Moving to the bar, Emma was still cursing the village's shortage of salubrious pubs. *Why tonight?* she asked herself. *Why did he have to walk in here?* Still, she told herself, just because he was in the same bar didn't mean she had to speak to him.

However, she also knew that ignoring Will wasn't going to prove that simple. Her only strategy was to join the queue at the bar, keeping as much distance as she could between herself and Will and Tara. She was still close enough to hear them, though.

"Will, aren't you going to buy me a drink, darling?" squealed Tara, swaying on her vertiginous heels.

"I'll get you an orange juice. *If* you take your hands away from my backside."

"But it's such a lovely one," she slurred, squeezing harder. "And I don't want orange juice. I want a proper drink with vodka in it."

"I really think you've had enough already, pet."

"Don't be so boring," she replied petulantly. But Emma saw Tara swap her grip for a stranglehold around his neck.

Saw his grimace too, as he replied, "Boring or not, that's all you're getting from me, Tara.

"Two orange juices please, Dave," Will called to the barman. "And whatever the lady at the end of the bar is having."

"Which lady would that be, sir?"

"The cracking one with long, dark hair trying not to look in my direction right now."

"Ah, that one, sir." The barman came over to her and inquired, "What'll it be, madam? The gentleman is paying."

The cracking one with long, dark hair. Hmm. Very smooth. Too late, she realized she should have answered sooner, because Will was now doing it for her.

"She'd probably like champagne…but as this is Lakeland, a pint of Bluebird."

"No! I don't drink pints!"

"White wine spritzer, then, madam?"

"Yes please…I mean no!"

Dave had already turned his back and started pouring the wine. Tara snatched her arms from Will's neck in disgust and stormed off to the ladies'.

Emma was mortified at falling into Will's trap. His arrogance infuriated her. He obviously thought it was funny to act like he owned the place…and her—and she'd fallen for it, hook, line, and sinker. She glanced across at him angrily.

He wasn't smiling now. He looked serious and handed her the drink.

Emma took the wineglass as if it were a poisoned chalice, ordered Jan's wine and soda, and went back to her seat without thanking Will. She saw him shrug his shoulders and return to his friends in the corner of the bar, watching her from a safe distance. When she reached their table, Jan wasn't there. She spotted her through the old arch into the pub lounge, chatting away at breakneck speed with Pete Harrison, the photographer from the photo shoot.

So it had come to this, reflected Emma. Here she was at last: drinking chardonnay alone in a bar with Will Tennant a few feet away, throwing a too-casual glance in her direction every few minutes in a way that made her feel like a suspect under surveillance.

She decided that as soon as she'd finished her poisoned chalice, she was going to call a taxi and leave. She'd barely taken a sip when the space next to her was filled by a friendly face.

"Hi, Emma."

Emma felt relieved and smiled. "Hi, Suzanne."

"Haven't seen you for a bit," said Suzanne, putting her glass of Coke on the table. "What have you been up to?"

"Oh, you know, just busy. You know how it is. I've been busy tying up a sponsorship deal for the calendar."

"That sounds promising."

Nodding vigorously, Emma crossed her fingers. "I hope so. If it comes off, it should swell the funds a lot."

"We've missed you at the base."

"I don't have any real reason to visit now…the calendar's at the printers."

"You don't need a reason to come down to see us. You're almost an honorary member now," said Suzanne, grinning. "Especially after your adventures at the rappelling."

Emma pulled a face.

"It's not because of Will, is it?"

She tried to hide her discomfort with a smile. "What has Will got to do with anything?"

"He's not the reason you've stayed away, is he?"

"Of course not. Why on earth would he be?"

"He did give you a hard time over the calendar…and if you don't mind me saying, it looked like the two of you had words after the rappelling…"

Emma wished Suzanne wouldn't sound like she was trying to coax "the real trouble" out of a reluctant patient.

"We just don't see eye to eye, you know that."

"You could have fooled me!" laughed Suzanne. "But why don't you get on? What's he done to upset you?"

"He hates the calendar."

"Come on. That's not all. Is it?"

She risked a glance at Will, joking with his friends, then looked down at her hands as they gripped the glass.

"He's got a bit of a reputation."

"Who with? You can't mean Tara McKinnon?"

"Not just her."

"Well, you needn't worry about Tara," said Suzanne patiently. "She's much too young, much too in your face, and far too brainless for Will. For heaven's sake, he's pretty well-off and, though I hate to say it, a very attractive guy. He's bound to have his fair share of admirers."

"He doesn't have to act on all his offers though."

"Emma! Don't be so naive. He's not a monk, but he's not Casanova either."

"There's something else…Kate Danvers."

Suzanne looked taken aback but picked up her wineglass. "What about Kate?"

Emma almost wished she hadn't mentioned Kate, but it was too late now. "Well. There's no nice way of saying this, but I know what happened on their wedding day. He jilted her, didn't he?"

With the glass midway to her mouth, Suzanne paused. "Who told you that?"

"I just heard…on the grapevine. It is true, isn't it?"

Sue placed her glass carefully on the table. "I'm afraid you'll have to ask Will himself. Though you'll be a braver woman than me if you do."

"But you're not denying it, are you?"

"It's not for me to discuss his private life. Talk to him if you want to know the intimate details, and don't rely on what others tell you." She squeezed Emma's arm gently. "I'm afraid I've got to get an early night. I've got morning surgery tomorrow, and I can see that Tom's desperate to get off home. Let's hope we see you at the base soon, and please, remember what I said about getting your information firsthand."

As she nodded goodbye to Suzanne and her husband, Emma was left alone to think over the GP's words. That was it—she'd decided. She was simply not going to sit on her own in a pub any longer. She finished up her wine at an unhealthy speed and reached into her bag for her cell phone to call her own rescue service: Bannerdale Taxis.

As she keyed through the contacts list on her phone, Emma was suddenly aware of a pungent combination of beer and tikka masala. The smell overwhelmed her before she even heard the rasping invitation.

"On your own, love?"

Oh fantastic, she thought. Here was another jack-the-lad trying to buy her a drink she didn't want. Only this one had definitely not been on orange juice and seemed to have consumed the entire menu of the local takeout. She could hardly fail to notice as he was now leaning over her head, leering down her top, and about to occupy the remaining space on the bench seat before she could move to fill it.

"No, I'm with a friend…"

It was pathetic, but it was the only safe reply she could think of in a moment of panic. Drunk the guy might be, but he was still a lot bigger than she was. She was in no real danger, but getting out of this situation without making a scene wasn't going to be straightforward or pleasant.

"Well, whoever he is, he doesn't seem to be looking after you very well." Masala man leered, his inviting grin looking anything but.

Emma caught another whiff of curry and couldn't help but hold her breath.

"If you don't mind my saying, love," he rasped, "what kind of a bloke leaves a lovely thing like you sitting on her own in a pub?"

"This kind."

Inwardly, Emma sighed with relief as she saw Will standing about six inches behind the drunk. The mask of politeness on his face barely concealed the hostility underneath, and he had a deceptively smooth edge to his voice. Suddenly, she was very glad she wasn't in masala man's doubtless smelly shoes.

"This 'lovely thing,' as you so accurately describe her," said Will, "is with me, and she doesn't need a drink or your company. So if you'll just leave us to get on with our date, I'd be greatly obliged."

Emma saw panic register on the drunk's face as he stood up and found he reached to the top of Will's shoulders. He was met with a smile about as warm as the glaciers that had carved out Bannerdale.

"Sorry, mate, I—I didn't realize you and the lady were together…"

"Well, now you do, *mate*. Goodbye, and have a nice evening."

The man was already beating a hasty retreat to the bar when Will turned back to Emma. His smile now, she had to admit warm enough to melt a glacier in ten seconds flat, was already defrosting her resolve and threatening to move her on to a slow cook.

"What's this? A rescue-o-gram?" she joked, trying to laugh off the incident that had left her more disturbed than she cared to admit.

"I only step in when I think I'm needed. You seem to need it more often than most." He placed two glasses of Coke on the table. "Well, are you going to let me sit down? Or am I going to get the brush-off like our charming friend there?"

"There really isn't room for you here…"

"Oh, I think there is. If you don't mind getting up close and personal. Now squash up," he said as he nudged his way onto the bench. "I can only get half my bottom on this seat at the moment."

Emma knew there really wasn't room, not for someone that big—not in that small a space. Before she knew it, his thighs were pressed right up against hers. His arm was resting along the back of the bench, and his fingertips couldn't help but keep brushing her far shoulder every time they made brief but frequent contact with her silky top. She could smell him: clean skin mingled with a subtle, spicy aftershave.

Although she knew it was impossible, she thought he might actually hear her heart beating. Worse, she knew very well he was now in the perfect spot to see down the front of her top, to her cleavage. She had to get a grip. Be cool, calm, and collected, she told herself. Resist all his attempts to…to do whatever he had planned this time.

———

Will knew he was pushing his luck. He shouldn't really be crowding her like this. He should be taking his time, taking things one step at a time, coaxing her, gently but firmly, the way he had on the cliff when she'd frozen. Not rushing in on her like he had at the office, like a bull at a gate. But hell, she looked so mouthwateringly gorgeous, he couldn't resist it. And now, squashed up this close on the pub bench, she was driving him crazy. He was trying desperately—and mostly failing—to be a gentleman. But that silky top, the buttons open enough for temptation, was proving a hell of a distraction.

She had such lovely breasts. Firm and generous. He'd made a study of them and was currently in a debate over which particular bit of her was more luscious. Maybe it was the whole gorgeous package wrapped up in an irresistible, feisty sweetness. A blend of softness and spirit that he'd tried to resist for a whole week. Finally, when he'd seen her there in the pub, by far the most gorgeous woman in the place, he'd given in to temptation.

After she'd given him the brush-off at the bar, he'd resolved to take the hint and leave it. Better for them both if he kept his distance as he'd been struggling so hard to do. But stand by and see her propositioned by a drunken lout in a bar? No man with an ounce of self-esteem could let that happen to any woman. It was his duty to step in.

Except he wasn't any man, Emma wasn't any woman, and if he'd really wanted to do his duty, he wouldn't be sitting here now, squashed up so close to her you couldn't have slotted a beer coaster between the two of them. If he really wanted to do his duty, he'd already be giving her a lift home or, better still, have called her a taxi and walked away from all temptation.

———

Emma felt fire touch her face—and other places she was ashamed to admit to. It had been just about OK while she wasn't physically in his presence. In the safety of the flat or at work, she could almost convince herself she had forgotten him, that he meant nothing to her. At a range of zero inches, she had absolutely no defenses. No protection from his physical presence and, worst of all, from the brisk tenderness that was threatening, once again, to strip her bare, body and soul.

"Where's your groupie?" she asked. She'd meant it to sound witty and flippant. Too bad it came out as petty and jealous.

Will didn't seem to take offense. "If you mean Tara, she's gone home to her mummy," said Will. "A friend called her brother to come and rescue her." He grinned and tapped the cell phone in his pocket, making it clear who the friend was.

"So she's not one of your conquests?" Emma persisted.

"My *what*?"

"Your conquests." *How incredibly silly that sounded*, she thought suddenly.

"I'm not sure exactly what you're getting at, but if it's what I think, then—no. Tara McKinnon is definitely not one of my 'conquests,' as you so delicately put it."

She hadn't thought it was possible for him to get any closer to her, but she was wrong. She could now feel the muscles in his thigh tauten with the tension, and she realized she had, after all, touched a raw nerve.

"Is that why you keep avoiding me?" he said evenly. "Because you think I'm on a quest to have my wicked way with all the women of Bannerdale?"

"The thought had never crossed my mind."

"Never?"

She shook her head firmly.

"That surprises me, considering what happened in your office."

"I'd prefer it if we didn't discuss *that*."

"No hard feelings, then? On your part, I mean."

"I won't dignify that remark with an answer."

"You just did."

"You really are impossible, Will. You know that, don't you?"

"I do try."

She could have sworn he shuffled up a little closer to her. Then, smiling, he added, "So despite all the evidence, you're not afraid that I might try to add you to my roll of dishonor? Just like all those other women?"

Emma shook her head. He really was outrageous, she thought. Sexist, despicable, and totally outrageous. So why, a small voice whispered in her head, was her heart trying to escape from her chest?

Her next words, meant to seem cool and smooth, came out squeakily. "Let me make this clear. I am not afraid of anything you might have in mind for me. I should have thought that much was obvious by now."

"Good. Because in that case, you'll have no objection to coming out to dinner with me."

"Yes. I mean, no."

"You seem a little confused…"

"On the contrary. I'm quite clear—and the answer is no. We are, in effect, colleagues. And I don't believe in mixing business with pleasure. You of all people should know that by now."

If she'd wanted to remind him of their meeting in the office, she had a nasty suspicion it hadn't worked. Because of all her remarks to him, she suddenly realized this was probably the most unwise of all. He smiled at her and remarked, slowly and deliberately, "So going out with me would be considered a pleasure?"

"I didn't mean it like that. You know I didn't."

"Strictly business, then?"

Yes—an incredibly dangerous business, she might have replied. "I don't think it's a good idea," she said, snapping her mouth shut.

"Oh."

He looked so downcast, like a little boy who'd been denied a special treat, that Emma's heart almost melted. Her insides had already started dissolving sometime earlier.

"Not even to give me a chance to prove myself? Show you I'm not as wicked as you seem to think I am? You know I mean well. I even offered to sponsor the calendar, not that you accepted my generous proposal. What about accepting this one? Dinner, on me."

She shook her head resolutely and moved to pick up her wineglass. "I'm not allowed to accept business gifts."

Will's hand closed around her fingers on the stem. His eyes were intent, not teasing now. Suddenly, he looked different. Serious and, she had to admit, sincere—which was more of a turn-on than anything he'd ever done before. Her womb clenched in response. No. It couldn't be possible. Will didn't do sincere; he did one-night stands, disappointment, and rejection.

But how hard it was to refuse him! His voice was deep and steady, its calm resolve reminding her of when she'd been stuck, terrified, on the cliff face. Why did he make her feel she had no choice but to do whatever he wanted?

"I know you don't trust me," he said. "Or is it that you don't trust yourself?"

She was crumbling as she felt the heat of his strong fingers around hers, looking into his dark eyes. She was opening her mouth to reply when the words were snatched away by a loud beeping coming from the direction of his trousers. She couldn't possibly have thought of a more appropriate warning alarm.

"What's that noise?"

"My pager." He frowned and glanced briefly at the electronic screen clipped to his belt. "We've got a call-out. I'm afraid I'll have to go."

"Right now?"

He was already getting to his feet as he answered, "Yes, right now." But as he grabbed his car keys, he leaned down and added softly, "Think about what I said, Emma. That's all I ask—and keep an open mind."

Then he was gone, leaving her lost in a whirl of confusion.

What did he mean "keep an open mind"? Suzanne's cryptic remarks hadn't helped either. She hadn't denied he'd jilted Kate, but she had made her feel rather silly on the subject of Will's love life. The GP was right. Will was the most eligible man for miles. He was entitled to sleep with whom he wanted, as often as he wanted. But that wasn't good enough for her. She finally acknowledged what she had known since she had sat, bruised and sore, in his car. She felt the kick at the core of her body as a physical pain.

She wanted Will for herself—exclusively, and for a lot longer than one night.

From what she'd seen and heard so far, he didn't believe in exclusive, and he certainly didn't believe in long term, yet he had asked her to give him a chance. *A chance for what?* she asked herself. Was it to show her that she meant more to him than a one-night, one-week, maybe one-month stand? The problem was that when she'd put her trust in someone before, it had ended with the loss of a man she thought she loved and of a job she *knew* she'd loved, as well as total humiliation. But this was Will, and somewhere deep inside, the desire to give him a chance, against all her rational instincts, was growing...

"Sorry to disappear like this, Emma, but I got talking to Pete here. Remember him? From work?"

Jan was back with Pete in tow. *The poor guy looks shell-shocked*, thought Emma.

"I feel so guilty, leaving you on your lonesome like this all evening. Though you don't seem to have been that lonely. Wasn't that the lovely Will I saw you with just now? Anyway, Pete's invited me back for coffee, so if you don't mind..."

Emma shook herself into awareness. "Of course not." She smiled, realizing how desperate she was to have space to think in peace and quiet. "I fancy a walk in the fresh air."

"Oh no, you don't. We're not letting you walk home on your own, are we, Pete? You can share a taxi with us," said Jan.

"It's not far," she replied firmly. No way was she going to play third wheel to her friend and Pete.

"I know that, you daft thing, but hadn't you noticed?" said Jan, pointing to the tiny pub windows. "It's pouring down!"

It was true. The raindrops were streaming down the leaded panes, but Emma wouldn't be persuaded. She grinned at Jan. "I'll get a taxi. I promise."

"Well...if you're sure you'll be OK."

"Absolutely fine." She smiled. "Now, get off home, and don't do anything I wouldn't do."

When the magical taxi finally appeared, the barman was waiting to lock the door behind her, and the driver wasn't too happy at having a fare that took him all of a mile up the road. Even less impressed when, half-way there, Emma changed her mind and asked him to pull up outside the mountain rescue base, now blazing with lights from the vehicle bay and all the windows. She paid him the full fare and a generous tip and stepped out into a downpour.

Even though it was the close of May, an unseasonably cold wind was driving the raindrops almost horizontally off the dark fells, against her face. The mist was already down almost to the rooftops, and the blackness hiding the mountains was total. Even the few yards from taxi to base left her brushing the water from her jacket. She headed straight for the control room, where Bob Jeavons was coordinating the call-out. She saw his look of surprise at her flushed face.

"What on earth are you doing here, pet?" he asked.

"I was in the Black Dog and heard you had a call-out. I came to see if there was anything I could do to help."

"That's very good of you, but I'm not sure what there is *to* do."

"Is Will with the team?"

"Of course, love." His eyes narrowed, and Emma could see he was puzzled by her question. "Nearly everyone's out on the search—the dogs too. Two teenagers are missing on Black Fell. It's going to be a very long night."

Bob was right. It was going to be a long, wet night for everyone out on the mountain, for both searchers and the youngsters who were lost. She shivered as she thought of the grit it took to drop everything and head off on a night like this to help a stranger. The compassion needed to care for someone in distress who was helpless and relying on you. Risking yourself too—for nothing other than the satisfaction of helping people who couldn't help themselves.

She thought she'd seen something special for her from Will—when he'd dressed her hands, on the crag side in his brief kiss, tonight when he'd asked her to give him a chance.

"Can I do anything? Make you a cup of tea?" she offered desperately.

"That'd be good," said Bob. As she left the control room, he added, "Then get yourself home. Will won't be back for hours."

Emma knew he was right. She shouldn't really be here. Hey, she didn't know why she was here, or maybe she did—and that scared her. She decided to make herself useful while she tried to figure it out. She crossed the corridor into the poky kitchen under the stairs and put the kettle on. She found a couple of mugs and unearthed some tea bags. The kitchen must have been a store cupboard once, she thought. There was barely space for the essentials, let alone for any comforts.

When the tea was brewed, she put the mugs, plus a bag of sugar, out for Bob on a battered old tray. Then she set off for the control room. As she did so, an idea had already formed in her mind—not about the calendar but about Will. It was nearly midnight by now, and ignoring Bob's advice, she dragged an old chair—a relic from a school staff room by the looks of it—into the kitchen. She tucked her feet under her and sat down to wait throughout the long night.

———

"Emma!"

In her dream, she was outside in the wind and rain; she could feel the gale buffeting her and the droplets of water running down her face. She opened her eyes and blinked in the glare of the strip light in the little kitchen.

"Wake up. What are you doing here at this hour?"

It was Will, shaking her gently. His hair was stuck to his head, and he was completely soaked through. Water was dripping off his coat onto her face and arms. And he had never looked so meltingly, heart-stoppingly gorgeous.

She uncurled painfully from the chair and winced as the feeling started to return to her limbs. "What time is it?" Her voice sounded sleepy and strange in the tiny room.

"Nearly 4:00 a.m., Emma. What on earth are you doing here?"

"Waiting for you…for you lot," she ventured.

Even in her befuddled state, she couldn't mistake the look of pleasure, however fleeting, on his wet face. His dark brown eyes were gleaming, like sunlight on the surface of a lake.

"Did you find the runaways?"

He grimaced. "Eventually. They were halfway up Black Fell. No proper gear and no food and drink apart from a couple of bottles of vodka. They set off after tea from a campsite 'for a walk.' Then the mist came down, and they got lost."

"Are they OK, though?"

"Cold, wet, and terrified. I don't think they'll do it again. They'll be fine." He smiled. "But they've been packed off to the hospital for a checkup anyway."

She noticed that her top was wet from the rivulets of water that had run off his wet coat onto her, soaking into the fabric.

"Sorry!" he laughed. "I'll go and get out of this stuff... Will you still be here when I get back?"

"I'll make you all a hot drink."

"Great."

Emma felt her stomach flip. She might have offered him the earth, not tea, for the pleasure she saw in his eyes. Then he went off to change while she took a deep breath in preparation for what she was about to do. She made the drinks and handed them around to those team members who had returned to base to stow the equipment and vehicles. Then she walked back to the kitchen, stood by the sink, and waited.

So what happened now? The decision she'd come to before she'd fallen asleep had taken her over. Was it a leap into the unknown? An irrevocable step toward...who knew what? Her own mug was cooling in her hand when he came back, rubbing his glistening hair with a towel. He closed the door softly, leaving them alone in the tiny enclosed space. As it shut with a click, she could feel her pulse begin to quicken and her stomach flutter.

"Well, Emma?"

"Well what?" she said, stalling.

"Have you thought about my offer?"

"What offer's that?" she said, suddenly feeling reticent.

"To take you out to dinner. Purely platonic, cross my heart."

Emma thought she'd seen that gesture somewhere before and hadn't been convinced. "The last time you made that promise was when you were cleaning my hands. You said it wouldn't hurt, but it did."

"I didn't say it wouldn't hurt. I said I'd be as careful as I could... *there's a difference.*"

A big, big difference between saying he wouldn't hurt her and saying he'd try not to. But was being careful good enough for her?

He checked his watch. "Look, it's half past four in the morning, and I'm shattered. Is there any chance of a reply this side of Christmas? Will you come to dinner with me or not?"

"I have replied—and the answer's no."

He threw the towel down on the chair, making her jump. His eyes were dark again. "Don't play with me, Emma!"

His vehemence, the sudden change in tone, shocked her. This wasn't the manner of a man who simply wanted a conquest, just to get her into bed. It was something more than that—as if her reply really meant something to him, unless he was just worn out from the night's work. Maybe she was worn out too...

"I won't come to dinner," she murmured, "but I will spend the day with you."

Will nearly had to hold on to the door to steady himself.

A whole day and an evening. But that meant she might... The effect was instantaneous, and in this confined space, there was no way of hiding it.

"Purely on a platonic basis of course."

"Of course," he echoed, but he was smiling broadly. "I'll play the perfect gentleman. Cross my—"

"Heart and hope to die? I think we've already agreed that one's worn out its welcome."

"But you will come?"

"I said yes, didn't I? Or has your hearing been affected by the rain?"

"I just couldn't believe my own ears. OK then. We'll start with lunch—what could be safer than that?"

Oh a lot of things, she thought. Stepping into a cage of tigers, playing Russian roulette, thinking she could spend an evening with this man without wanting to be touched by those long, strong fingers, taste the sweet heat of that mouth again. She suppressed a shiver.

"Lunch certainly *sounds* very innocent, Will."

"And afterward, if I behave, you'll let me take you out for dinner?"

"Now that doesn't sound so harmless…"

"What could be more straightforward than a man taking a woman out for a meal? You can go halves, if you like," he offered, his eyes glinting mischievously.

"I fully intend to."

"Just like student days—paying your own way, eh?"

"I don't want to owe you for anything else after recent events."

"That's settled then. I'll pick you up on Saturday morning," he said, grabbing the towel from the chair. "And now, I'm going home to my bed, if that's all right with you, Emma." And he was gone, leaving her astonished at her own daring.

———

She'd waited for him. All night.

He'd gotten his wish. Emma had agreed to spend a day with him, and a small voice inside his head was whispering that he didn't deserve it. No matter how hard he tried to tell himself that lunch meant a sandwich and dinner meant…well, dinner, he couldn't help thinking of all the other delicacies that might, if his wildest fantasies came true, be on the menu.

Despite being up for nearly twenty-four hours, six of them hauling equipment two thousand feet up and down a pitch-black fellside, sleep wouldn't overtake him. He opened his eyes and threw back the duvet in frustration, stretching out his arms until he touched the outer edges of the bed. Oh God…his bed. He couldn't help picturing her on the white covers, spread out like an exotic flower, ready and waiting for him.

He groaned and pulled the covers back over his aching body.

Finally, he was willing to admit that much. He cared about her. Her determination, her spirit, the vulnerability that made him want to protect her from the world. He smiled at the archaic thought. She'd have killed him for that one.

And he was going to be a very good boy. He'd prove to her he could keep his hands to himself. That he wasn't the crass, sex-mad wolf she obviously thought he was. Correction: he wouldn't *behave* like a sex-mad wolf. Obviously, he was desperate to take her to bed. Just the thought of it was driving him mad, but he would wait, no matter what it took. Until she was ready for him. *All in good time*, he thought, *but please don't let it be long.*

A watery sun broke through the clouds, and a refreshing breeze rattled the windowpanes of Ghyllside Cottage. Will reached for his watch from the bedside table and saw it was already almost 6:00 a.m. Despite the fact that he'd already had one drenching that morning, he decided that a cold shower would be a very good idea and headed for the bathroom.

Chapter 8

THE KNOCK ON EMMA'S DOOR THAT BRIGHT SATURDAY MORNING was as she'd expected: overconfident and very loud. Not a good start to her date—no, she corrected herself—trial by combat with Will.

She'd had some restless nights over the past week, waking at odd hours, her stomach fluttering, wondering if she'd been right to take a chance on him and give him the benefit of the doubt. Stepping into the wolf's lair was a risky move but the only way to find out what she needed to know. Could a man who seemed to have behaved so ruthlessly be ready to give more to her? She'd be safe, wouldn't she? After all, he'd promised faithfully it would be strictly hands off. She had to hope that, on this occasion, Will Tennant was a man of his word and, more important, that she could keep her part of the bargain.

Taking a deep breath, she opened the door to find him standing there, a gift-wrapped parcel under one arm.

"Hi there," he said casually, bending down to brush her cheek with his lips. The resultant fizz went all the way down to her toes and straight back up through the middle. Not good—it was barely 11:00 a.m.

She saw him take in her floaty skirt and camisole top with a critical look.

"Well? Will I do? I assume we are going for lunch?" she said, and then she noticed the combat trousers, T-shirt, and inevitable boots. "Or maybe not…"

"We are going to lunch—and personally, it would suit me fine if you stayed just as you are. But I'm afraid you're going to have to lose the skirt for now. The top can stay, though…as long as you bring something warm to put on over it."

"You had better not be planning what I think you are," she warned.

"If you mean climbing, then no, not today. But you will need these," he added, offering her the package.

Taking it cautiously from his hands, she took in the sophisticated handmade paper and soft-wired ribbon. They made her think of only one thing: provocative underwear. Surely, it was beyond the realms of possibility he would have even dared…

"I hope this isn't…"

"Call it a peace offering."

She pulled apart the paper with trembling fingers and pulled out a pair of combat trousers. Trendy in a high-tech sort of way but undeniably practical. She didn't know whether to laugh or cry. Will, on the other hand, looked perfectly relaxed, stretched out on her chocolate leather sofa, a gleam of amusement playing in his eyes.

"Of course, you'll need a rucksack too, and maps, maybe a survival bag…"

"Tell me you're joking!"

"Nope. Deadly serious. You can come into one of the shops, and I'll fix you up with everything you need"—he started ticking items off on his fingers—"compass, flashlight, whistle—"

"A whistle!"

"Oh yes. Essential, and what's more, I'm going to make sure you know how to use them properly." He grinned broadly at her. "So what do you think?" he asked, indicating the trousers dangling from her fingertips. She was holding them like a poisonous snake that might strike at any moment.

"Very nice."

"*Nice*… Is that *it*? Is that all you're going to say? If you're out on the fells and get soaked through in those tight jeans you insist on wearing, you'll regret it," he explained patiently. "These are far more suitable, although I nearly didn't hand them over when I saw that skirt…"

"In that case, I'll go and change right now."

As she wriggled into the trousers in front of her bedroom mirror, Emma could tell straightaway they were a little bit too small. She peered at the label in the waistband—she must have put on a bit of weight in the past few months. Not that it mattered too much. She'd lost a good few pounds in her final months in London, all of which and more had now found their way back onto her hips and tummy. Getting dumped and fired on the same day had done wonders for her figure, she thought ruefully.

And as for the trousers…well, he was only being thoughtful; he really did care what happened to her on the fells. It was such an…unexpected gift. So practical…so unlike anything Jeremy would ever have bought for her. She pulled a face in the mirror. He would have howled in derision at the thought of her in walking trousers. La Perla, Agent Provocateur, he would have approved of, expected even—but North Face or Columbia? Never in a million years.

Her stomach flipped. This gift, so mundane, so not her, had touched her because she had to acknowledge that Will wasn't just having a joke at her expense. He wanted her to be safe, to fit in with this new world… his world.

No, don't go there, she told herself. *You'll only crash and burn.* As she went back into the living room, any thoughts of asking him to change them for a bigger size had been set aside.

"Perfect," he exclaimed as she stood in the middle of the room, red-faced under his gaze.

"And you're sure they fit?"

"Like I said—you look perfect," and he jumped to his feet, indicating there was to be no debate on the matter. "Get your boots on. We're going."

———

A few minutes later, as they took the twisting Lakeland roads at alarming speed, she risked a glance at Will. He was wearing his wraparound sunglasses and driving along with one hand, the other resting casually on his thigh. If he hadn't been wearing walking gear, he'd have looked every inch the clichéd seducer.

Emma wondered if he would really stick to his promise to keep things platonic. Surely, she said to herself, at some point today—or more likely tonight—he'd make a move on her. He had to. She didn't know what she was going to do when he did, and worse, she wasn't sure whether she wanted him to or not. Even the thought made her shift restlessly in her seat. She wanted his body, there was no denying that, but she also wanted to see if he could keep his word.

She fiddled with a button she hoped would open the electric windows.

"Comfortable?" asked Will, rapidly changing down the gears to negotiate a sharp hairpin bend. "I can turn up the air-conditioning if you want."

Shaking her head, Emma tried to show a keener interest in the scenery. She flinched as they rattled over cattle grids and skimmed alarmingly close to dry stone walls. Finally, he stopped the Range Rover in a tiny pull off at the side of a track. For a moment, she half expected him to press a button, recline her seat, and jump her. Instead, he got out, hoisted the inevitable rucksack out of the boot, and pointed to a steep path up the hillside.

"Go on," he said, seeing her hesitate. "It's not far."

It was a warm, still day as she trudged up the hillside beside him. This time, he hadn't lied. It really wasn't far, and suddenly, ascending a cleft between two crags, he halted, pausing while she caught up with him. Spread out on a small plateau below them was a miniature lake, still and inky blue, the perfect mirror image of the mountains upended in its glassy surface.

"Will this do for our picnic?" he asked.

The view took her breath away. "It's beautiful." *Dark and beautiful, like you*, she thought. Heaven knew what lay beneath the surface either.

Unpacking the rucksack, he brought out two plates and some cutlery, a bottle of champagne, and two fluted glasses. After spreading out a picnic rug on the grassy hillside, he proceeded to take out some smoked salmon, strawberries, and cream. A mayfly buzzed past her lips, and Emma realized her mouth must be hanging open in astonishment. She rapidly shut it.

"So this is essential equipment for a mountain rescue leader, is it?" she asked, smiling.

"Of course. On his day off, anyway. What can I tempt you with?" he asked mischievously. "Foie gras? Gravlax? Champagne?"

"All three," she replied, watching him uncork the champagne with quiet efficiency. It took her back, over half a year now, to London and Jeremy. He always made a great show of opening any bottle. Half of it had usually ended up on her dress or the floor, but Will had managed not to spill a single drop. She shouldn't have been surprised really, so why had her heart flipped as the cork had whispered out of the bottle?

She held the glass he handed her up to the light and indicated the bottle.

"Will, did you know this was Krug Champagne?"

He whistled. "No! You don't say? Well, I thought it was a bit pricey for a bottle of plonk." He was laughing at her, and she had to admit, she deserved it. "We may be a bit rough and ready up here, but we're not complete heathens. I can read a label." He took a sip from the glass. "And I like having the best. Nothing sinful about that, is there?"

Seeing the expense he'd gone to, Emma was reminded that he was, after all, a wealthy guy. She wondered again about his business and his plans for the hotel. She really knew very little about him, despite the fact that they'd shared some very intimate moments.

"Depends on who you use to get the best," she replied.

"I think this conversation is heading in the wrong direction," said Will evenly. "Now eat up. I'm not carrying this lot down with me. Strawberry?" he asked, offering her a basket.

Emma took the fruit from him, feeling his fingers against hers as she did so. She pulled out the green stalk, resolving to use this day as the chance to find out more about the real Will, if there was such a thing. Then she popped a berry into her mouth and bit into it, the blend of tart sweetness almost stinging her mouth. A trail of juice escaped her mouth, and feeling it slithering down her chin, she wiped it away with her finger and licked it clean.

When she looked up, she saw he was watching her.

"Another?"

"Better not."

"Whatever you say." He smiled, placing the basket back down on the ground.

She wondered if this was the moment he'd make his move and glanced at him as discreetly as she could. But he just sat there innocently, eating the rest of the strawberries, not even trying to tempt her again. When they'd finished the picnic and he'd demolished the strawberries, she leaned back against the grass and gazed out over the tarn, placing her hands behind her to steady herself.

Big mistake.

Her little finger made contact with his. Just a tiny brush, but it was enough to make her sit up again and hug her knees with her arms. The temptation to slip her hand under his was almost overwhelming. She knew it would be warm and strong and rough. Her breasts prickled, and she felt she simply couldn't stand the tension between them any longer. Scrambling to her feet, she dusted the strands of grass from her new walking trousers.

"Can we go down to the tarn?" she asked, her throat dry and scratchy.

"If you'd like to," he replied, stretching out his limbs before getting to his feet with casual ease.

"Does it have a name?"

"Not this one." He smiled. "It's too small. Come on. I'll show you something."

She followed him down the slope to the ragged oval of water nestling in the bowl of the hills. Her gaze took in the reeds growing at the edge and the white water lilies, clustered near the fringes, waxy and lush.

"Look at those," he said, pointing to the lilies.

"Oh! I've never seen those growing wild, only in the park," cried Emma, surprised at her own delight in something so simple. A sudden impulse struck her, and she picked up a pebble from the handkerchief-sized beach.

"We used to do this at the seaside, Steve and me," she laughed, flinging it across the water. It skidded once and then sank silently below the surface.

"Who's Steve?" asked Will casually.

"My brother. He's three years older than me."

"Ah. He lives in London, does he?"

"New Zealand, actually. I miss him. A webcam's all very well but no substitute for the real thing."

"Lucky Steve. North or South Island?"

"Wellington. Do you know it, then? Have you been?"

She watched him rake a hand through his thick, unruly hair.

"A few times. I spent six weeks there on business a couple of years ago," he added wryly. "Well, it was part pleasure too. We organize adventure holidays for the business, and I went to develop some contacts. And yes, before you ask, I did go climbing—and rafting and bungee jumping."

"Bungee jumping! Now I know you're completely mad. You will never ever get me doing that."

"You'd be surprised what you could do if you really set your mind to it."

She caught her breath, desperately hoping he wouldn't mention the rappelling. She was too ashamed to be reminded of that day, of needing to be rescued—of needing Will and of being humiliated. She risked a sideways glance at him, holding her breath for a moment.

"What does Steve do out there? Is he married?"

Emma's shoulders sank in relief.

"Oh yes, and he's got two children. He's an accountant—very exciting. You know, when we were young, we used to go almost every year to Cornwall with Mum and Dad. Drove them mad, we did, scrapping like cat and dog." She knew she was babbling now. Babbling and hunting on the shore of the tarn for another flat pebble. "Still, he did know how to skim a stone." She sighed, watching another attempt sink into the tarn.

A sharp pang of something that felt like regret struck her without warning. "Looks like I've forgotten how." She paused for a moment, watching the ripples on the surface. "Have you got any brothers or sisters, Will?"

"No. I'm one of a kind, you'll doubtless be pleased to hear."

"Did you mind? Being on your own, I mean?"

"Sometimes," he replied and then added as his eyes rested on the distant mountains, "I wouldn't like to have just one myself... What about you?"

She was crouching down now, examining stones for their skimmability. The midafternoon air was thick and still. Miles up in the sky, a distant airplane droned softly. She hoped he couldn't hear her heart beating.

"I hadn't really thought about it. I don't know...definitely one. Maybe two..." She straightened up with a clutch of suitable stones cradled in her hands. "Maybe. One day."

As she said it, something kicked inside. Two children? One day? Where had that come from? Being an auntie, even at a distance, was cool, but being a mum? Whew, that was scary. She was only twenty-eight, and there was no earthly reason why she should even be thinking about a family. Maybe, thought Emma, pretending to scour the shingle for stones, it was only Will asking so explicitly that had forced her to think whether she *actually* wanted kids at all.

She took a few paces to where the water was lapping at the pebbles and launched her stone. It didn't even bounce once.

"Oh dear." This wasn't going very well. She tried another, which managed one and a half before disappearing, then dropped the pebbles onto the beach in disappointment.

"Try this one." He was right beside her, taking her hand and placing a flat, glistening stone in her palm.

She gazed at it as if she'd never seen a piece of rock before.

"If you don't mind me saying, you'd do better if you stand like this..."

He was right behind her now, one hand on her arm. The pebble was moist and smooth in her hand, a contrast with the heat of his touch.

"You hold it like this," he said, curving her fingers around the stone. "And then you let go..."

He pulled back his wrist suddenly, sending the flat rock scudding out over the water. It skidded and bounced six times before disappearing beneath the surface.

"Wow, six!" she cried in delight.

"It's just having the right technique." Will smiled. "And the right stone." She turned around to find him gazing down at her. "Isn't it, Emma?"

His hands were holding her waist gently, and it would have been easy—so very easy—to stand on tiptoe and seek his mouth again, just as she had before. Yet he had pulled away from her then, left her empty and cold, and she wasn't going to make the same mistake twice.

As she stepped back and he let his arms fall, she felt the disappointment physically as a tight knot in her stomach. She'd wanted so much to feel his arms around her. Wanted to taste him, let him lower her onto the grass and make love to her. To hear him say she wasn't just another conquest, that she was special, that she really meant something to him...

Instead, he asked her a simple question—one she'd been dreading ever since he'd knocked on her door that morning.

"Emma, why are you here in Bannerdale?"

Relief flooded through her. She had her answer already prepared.

"I got offered a fantastic new opportunity."

"Ah." He nodded his head. "Of course. The job with the high-powered Lakeland tourist board. I can see how a top-ten London consultancy couldn't compete with that." Then he added, very softly, "I think I've just had the press release version. What about the truth?"

She should have been annoyed, insulted even, but she wasn't. There had been no trace of sarcasm in his words. Just a feeling that he was getting far too close for comfort.

"I...I...made a mistake."

"A mistake? What kind of mistake would drive an intelligent, successful woman all the way up here from London?"

She wiped the palms of her hands on her trousers. "I was...in a relationship with a man..."

A slight breeze had started rippling the surface of the tarn and distorting the perfect image of the mountains. She shivered.

"In a relationship with a man. That happens quite often, I believe, even in London..." He was smiling gently. "But it doesn't necessarily have to be a mistake."

"It is when he's your biggest client and…" She hesitated. She had never discussed the gory details with anyone, not even with her friends, certainly not with her parents, though they knew what had happened. And here she was with a…she was going to say a stranger, but that would have been wrong. Completely wrong.

"And…" he encouraged.

"He's also sleeping with your boss."

"I can see how that would be awkward," he acknowledged. "But it wasn't your problem. It was hers—I assume it's a her—and his. Anyway, who are these charmers?"

"She's called Phaedra, and he was—is—Jeremy. He's the marketing director for Viper. They make GPS systems for hikers. I expect you've got their stuff in your shops."

"I have indeed…but maybe not for much longer." He caught her expression of surprise and moved briskly on. "So your boss stole your boyfriend and then sacked you. Nice one. Sounds like rough justice to me. Come on, Emma. Let's hear it all. You've started now."

"I—I shouldn't be telling you this…"

"Why not?"

"I feel silly. I expect I was a wimp and it served me right," she ventured, not wanting to look at him.

"Somehow, I think not."

"When Phaedra found out—about Jeremy and me moving in together, I got the slow torture treatment. Not one big thing, just a constant stream of snipes and nitpicking, but it wore me down. She found fault with everything I did, pushed me on to all the minor accounts, and took me off Jeremy's business altogether. I thought she was just a bit jealous or maybe worried I'd tell him more than I should about how she was overcharging his company. But I never gave her any cause, and I really thought she'd get over it."

It sounded pathetic. But the pain afterward hadn't felt trivial. The loss of her job and the betrayal of the man she thought had cared for her had felt like the end of the world.

"But surely you told this Jeremy what your boss was up to?" demanded Will. "He must have supported you."

Emma rested her eyes on the ground and shook her head. "I said I thought she was a bit jealous, but he said I was imagining it, that I was getting paranoid. And"—she lifted her eyes to Will's face—"you know what? He was sleeping with her the whole time. Everything I told him was getting back to her and making things worse and worse. I lasted six months before I finally realized..." She took a deep breath.

"Why didn't you take her to a tribunal, for God's sake?" he cut in. "No one should have to suffer that. Why on earth did you let them do that to you?"

She flinched. Will sounded angry now, angry with someone, but she wasn't sure who exactly. At the people who had caused her so much pain, or with her for being weak enough to let them do it?

"Because I loved him—it felt like I did anyway. And I was hurt and weak. Oh, I suppose I could have sued her for breach of contract. But who wants their love life argued over by strangers and splashed all over the papers? That's not good for a PR exec, is it? You see, we were presenting a proposal for Jeremy's new brand. Phaedra was humiliating me in front of him for not having the campaign finalized. Then..." Emma cursed herself as she felt her eyes stinging again. She absolutely did not want to cry in front of Will. "I—I thought he'd try to stand up for me, but he looked...just like a rabbit caught in the headlights, and that's when I knew. I just knew. He was stuck between a rock and a hard place, wasn't he? He had the two of us there, both waiting for him to take her side, and he did nothing. He was a—a..."

"Wanker?" asked Will innocently, making Emma want to hug him.

"I'm afraid 'wanker' is too good a word for him. He'd been getting off with me and Phaedra. I shouldn't think he had much time for anything else. 'Coward' is more accurate, actually. When he didn't defend me or even try and smooth things over, it all clicked in one moment just like that..."

Her voice trailed off. The tarn, the blue sky, the sound of birds and a distant plane, all that faded as Emma found herself back again in the boardroom at Rogue. She still remembered, suddenly, staring first at Jeremy, then at her boss. He had looked irritated and embarrassed.

Phaedra had concern on her face and triumph in her eyes. She had laid her hand on Emma's arm and mouthed, *I'm so sorry*, as if she'd had to break the news that someone had died.

Emma felt she had—inside.

"You see, when it came down to it, Jeremy was a complete coward. He knew on which side his bread was buttered, and he chose Phaedra."

"God knows why," muttered Will.

"I'm sorry?" Emma shook her head, only half listening. In her mind, she was still back in London, and suddenly an image popped into her head, bringing a half smile to her lips. She shook her head at the recollection. "At least I went out in style."

His voice softened. "That doesn't sound like you." He reached up his hand as if to touch her cheek and then dropped it again and took a step back, letting her continue. "What did you do, sweetheart?"

Emma heard him clearly now. His voice was calm as he encouraged her, just like on the fellside.

Gulp.

Emma hesitated for a moment.

"Come on, out with it."

"I was very calm, really, considering. It was a hot day. Phaedra had ordered in smoothies, so I picked up mine, called her a lying bitch and him a two-timing snake, and threw it over them both."

"Cold, were they?"

Emma raised her eyebrows inquiringly.

"The drinks?"

"Oh yes. Very cold and very messy."

She saw him look at her with great earnestness. "What flavor?" he asked.

"Sorry?"

"What flavor smoothie was it?"

"Mango."

He raised his eyebrows now. "Good choice. I hate mango."

"I would have thrown a kiwi one too, but I couldn't reach it."

She saw his face break into a huge grin as bright as the sun dancing off the surface of the tarn. It reached all the way to his eyes, crinkling the corners. How could he be a man to hide anything? To do what he'd done—to her and to Kate? How?

Then Emma started laughing too. Here in the quiet of the mountains, a million miles from the pain and upset, with Will next to her, she could finally see the humor in the situation.

She would never fathom him out—this man who seemed to care so much for people yet seemed to have treated Kate and other women with such casual cruelty. Perhaps he didn't know what he'd done to her on that fellside, when he'd built up her hopes and then rejected her. Or come on to her so…so calculatingly in her office.

Perhaps it had meant nothing to him. Not after what he'd done to his fiancée and the other women he'd used for nights of casual sex. They must have gotten hurt too, if they'd wanted more from him than he would give.

She didn't believe it. Today had given her a glimpse of what he could be, of what he might be underneath the professional rescuer, the serial seducer. She was sure there was a gentler, more vulnerable man trying to reach out. Someone with secrets that went beyond village gossip. Someone who cared about her beyond scoring points off her or getting her into his four-poster. There had to be more layers to Will than there had seemed at first, if only she knew how to uncover them.

———

Behind his laughter, Will was vowing that, come Monday morning, he was going to end his contract with Viper GPS, and if he ever got his hands on the wonderful Jeremy, he'd have him dangling off the end of a rope from a cliff, and he might even let go.

The urge to protect and care for Emma was scaring him silly.

So far, he'd behaved like a perfect gentleman. It hadn't been easy. The moment he'd walked into the flat and seen her in that skirt, when he'd thought of unzipping it and shimmying her out of it, wriggling her tight little bottom into the trousers he knew were a little too small. That image had ensured his drive to the picnic tarn had been pretty uncomfortable at times.

When she'd tasted the strawberries and the juice had trickled out of her cute mouth and when her fingers had brushed his and she'd snatched them away...that had raised his temperature too. Maybe she was feeling the sexual tension between them as much as he was; maybe she was scared he'd make a move. If she'd left her hand there a moment longer, she'd have felt the tremor in his own fingers. It wasn't just lust but something that went deeper...when she'd told him what had happened to her, how she'd been betrayed and cast aside, he'd felt moved. He sensed a new bond between them—he understood her humiliation and shame and the desire to hide it all and run away.

Then, when he'd touched her, helped her with the stones, her hand in his, the intimacy had felt like a balm. What he was feeling now, standing here with Emma, was new and yet familiar—the echoes of past embraces and shared understanding. They resonated almost painfully in his heart.

As she'd looked up at him, her eyes unnaturally bright as she'd told him how she'd been betrayed and hurt, he'd ached to take her in his arms and comfort her. And to lower her to the fellside and make love to her slowly, tenderly, deeply, as she deserved.

No, he reminded himself, she must come to him willingly.

Will felt the hairs on his arms stand on end, and the afternoon breeze freshened. Looking down at his watch, he made a decision. "Time to pack up and go."

Emma's face fell. "But it's only three o'clock."

"I've got to call into the base before I go home," he said, avoiding her gaze. "And you need to get ready for tonight. I expect that could take some time."

Seeing her fire up in indignation, he set off quickly toward the picnic site.

"By the way, you'll be pleased to know you can dress up as much as you like," he called over his shoulder. "In fact, it's compulsory."

He drove her home steadily, carefully, knowing she was worryingly quiet. He mustn't hurt her, he realized. She deserved more than that. No matter how tempting it was to kiss her, to have her soft golden curves pressed against his body, to know her, inside and out, he knew she deserved so much more than that. He'd messed up so badly in the past, and he wasn't sure he could be trusted tonight. In fact, he knew damn well he couldn't be trusted. He hoped that this time, no one would have to have their hopes and dreams shattered into a thousand pieces. Because if he got it wrong again, he didn't think he could live with himself.

––––––

Sitting next to him, Emma was already regretting their conversation by the tarn and the way she'd bared her soul and told Will everything about herself.

She risked a tiny glance at him while he was concentrating on a hairpin bend. Their journey home was virtually silent. Will kept his eyes on the road and both hands on the wheel. They had almost reached the flat now without a single comment escaping his lips. Emma tried to relax and enjoy the passing mountains and lakes, set off to impossible perfection by a ludicrously blue sky, but it was a hopeless cause.

She felt no further on with him than she had that morning, but then again, her mind kept returning to his question about having children. She wasn't sure which was more disturbing: him asking her or her response. She told herself she was being ridiculous. It had just been a casual remark that she'd answered on the spur of the moment. She also resolved that things were going to change that evening. She was going to get some answers out of him if it was the last thing she did.

As they drew up outside the flat, he didn't offer to get out of the car.

"Pick you up at six," he called, leaning across the passenger seat.

"Six?" she protested as he started the engine. "That's a bit early for dinner."

Will just grinned and pulled away, leaving her standing at the bottom of the steps to her apartment.

Chapter 9

STEPPING INTO THE HALL, EMMA GLANCED AT THE CLOCK ON THE wall. Four o'clock. That left two hours to get ready. Even for an occasion that required "compulsory dressing up," there was plenty of time. Throwing her house keys on the hall table, she went straight into the bathroom for a shower, switched it to power setting, and let the jets of water pummel her skin.

As she stood under the stream of water, she wondered what she should wear. She'd planned on jeans and a top after her previous experiences, and she certainly didn't want to look as if she'd tried too hard. So nothing too short, low cut, or flamboyant. But now—well, it would have to be something smart.

Later, as she dried her hair, a horrible thought struck her. What if he was being ironic! She wouldn't put it past him. What if they were going to the pub or a barbecue at a friend's house?

No. Even he wouldn't do that to her. He'd said dinner, so it must be a restaurant or a hotel. There were several very good and expensive ones on the lakeside and a couple with Michelin stars up in the hills. One had even boasted a famous footballer and his wife and an infamous Hollywood couple—now divorced, she reflected ruefully—as guests.

If it was one of these, she would wear something really nice. The black silk dress, maybe…the one she'd bought to wear for a PR awards ceremony, but then she'd been fired before it had even been out of the shopping bag.

She took it out of the wardrobe and slipped it on. It was a tiny bit tighter around her breasts and hips than when she'd bought it—she had definitely put on a bit of weight. She sighed. It would have to do, and the boned bodice did show off her cleavage—not too much, she hoped; she didn't want to look like she was encouraging him in any way. Although it only had tiny spaghetti straps, the skirt hung halfway down her calves. She had a final glance in the mirror and congratulated herself. All very simple and modest. Absolutely nothing to worry about.

––––––

Sometime later, Emma found herself studying the clock again. It was ten to six. She felt a bit fluttery, and it occurred to her that this was so much like a first date, it was ridiculous. Heavens, she wasn't some nervous teenager; this was only Will. Infuriating, annoying, gorgeous Will.

She had to do something to take her mind off her nerves. Maybe she needed to touch up her lip gloss—a bit more wouldn't do any harm.

In the corner of her bedroom, the laptop was still on from the day before. Emma looked at the bedside clock and saw that she still had a few minutes before Will would arrive, so she clicked the mouse, hoping for an email from Steve and Gina in New Zealand.

The message she found waiting was not from that far away. It was from London. From Echo GPS, in fact, sent quite late on Friday evening, and when she'd read it, she forgot all about her lip gloss and sat back in the chair.

The irony of it brought a bitter smile to her lips.

Hi, Emma,

Good news. I finally got the board to say yes to your Bannerdale Mountain Rescue calendar proposal. They have agreed that Echo GPS systems will be the main sponsor in return for meeting all the production costs. Your PR strategy really impressed the directors, and we look forward to discussing it in detail next week.

Yours

Rachel Brockhouse
Marketing Director, Echo GPS Systems

P.S. Our MD has asked me to let you know we have a vacancy for communications director coming up at our London head office. I strongly advise you to apply. You did a fantastic job with Viper GPS before you left. Your work for them cost us a 5 percent market share! I look forward to announcing the calendar deal to my old adversary Jeremy Forbes. Do you see much of him these days?

Leaning back in the chair, Emma sighed. Well, that was a surprise for the books. Persuading her ex's main competitor to sponsor the calendar was a major coup. She'd done a good job—so good that Echo GPS wanted her to work for them. After only six months up here, she had the chance to go back to London again. A job with Echo would mean more money, a higher profile again, parties, events. Everything she'd left behind and once prized so highly.

When the one thing she wanted was here.

He is here.

In fact, he was late, and by the time she'd managed to get up from the chair and find her lip gloss, it was twenty past six. Perhaps he wasn't coming. Perhaps she should reply to the email right now. Except she didn't know what to reply.

It was the most fantastic offer, and six months ago, she'd have jumped at the chance, but now? Emma didn't want to think about what it all meant, her lack of excitement, her utter confusion in fact. For it meant admitting how very deep she was in up here, with the people, her friends, the place, and worse, with Will.

Even though she had no reason to believe he felt anything—anything other than lust for her—she hoped… No, that wasn't fair, she admitted to herself. This afternoon, he had shown her respect, affection even, that he cared about her. But nothing to compare with what she knew was growing in her heart for him—what had been growing since that day on the mountain, even though he'd laughed at her, goaded her, and challenged her. She was still here, waiting for him, with no certainty of getting anything from him.

As she began to wonder whether or not he would turn up, she heard the metal staircase protesting as someone heavy took the steps—two at a time. Then there was a knock on the door, as loud and insistent as she would have expected. She smiled to herself. At least some things about Will were predictable.

"Hi there, Emma."

She opened the door to find him standing there, to her astonishment, in a dinner suit and white shirt. The only thing missing was the bow tie.

"Well, I did say dress up," he added, obviously reading the surprise in her eyes. "Sorry I'm a bit late. I had to help Bob with a comms problem in the control room, and I had a real rush in the end." He rubbed the top of his head. "Hair still a bit damp, I'm afraid. I've only just come out of the shower, and I didn't have time to tie this properly before the taxi arrived," he said, pulling a black silk tie out of his pocket.

"I suppose I'll have to let you off this once." She relented, holding open the door. Still, she was puzzled. Not even the swankiest hotel on the lake shore demanded black tie. They must be going to one of those open-air concerts or even a business dinner. She hoped not. She'd have to share him with hundreds of other people. On the other hand, it would be so much safer, and perhaps that was the idea. She wasn't sure whether he wanted things to get cozy or not...

She showed him into the living room, and he stood rather awkwardly for a moment before looking at his watch. "Emma, I'm sorry, but we need to go. I know it's my fault that we're late, but..."

"It's a bit early for a dinner, isn't it?"

"I thought we'd have a drink first, and the table's booked for a quarter to seven—they couldn't fit us in any later. They're doing me a favor as it is." His voice tailed off as he met her eyes. "By the way, you look gorgeous."

Totally gorgeous and totally beddable, he thought. Her dress was sensational, especially the way the silk clung like a second skin to her hips. And the way her cleavage almost spilled over the top of the...he didn't know what it was called, but it looked like an eighteenth-century corset to him. Whew. The fact that the dress was long only tantalized him more, and he longed to explore what lay underneath.

"Thanks," muttered Emma. "I must get my handbag." Her face was turning pink as she darted out of the room, leaving him standing by the fireplace.

This was going to be so awkward...it was turning into a date. But if he hadn't complimented her, she would have been so disappointed. When she got back, he was struggling to tie the bow tie in the mirror above the mantelpiece.

"Blasted thing. Really awkward...always takes me ages...OK?" he asked, turning around to face her as he gave the silk one last tweak.

"Absolutely fine." She smiled, wondering if his self-deprecation was just a tactic to put her at her ease. So far, he was doing a good job of the gentleman act, though how long he could keep it up remained to be seen. Oh God, she was obsessed—good job she hadn't voiced *that* one out loud.

"Have you got one of those shawl things or something?" he asked as he followed her to the front door. "I mean, you look great, but it might be a bit cold out."

No danger of that if you keep looking at me like that, thought Emma. *Or if you keep looking like that, full stop.* The suit enhanced the breadth of his shoulders and his height. He must have been nearly a foot taller than her, even in her killer heels. He was good enough to eat. She grabbed a pashmina off the bedroom chair and wrapped it around her before following him out the door.

"Is this enough to protect me from the elements?"

He smiled. "I should think so. Now, are you ready to set off?"

"Set off?"

"Yes." He checked his watch again. "We need to get going—now."

"Where's the taxi?"

"There isn't one."

"But you said you'd got here in one..."

"I did, but we're walking to the restaurant."

"Walking? In these shoes? In this dress? Will, even you must know this is not an outfit for doing anything other than stepping out of a car and into a building. I can't possibly get more than a few hundred yards in these."

"That's all we need" was the enigmatic reply. By now, he had her totally confused. There were a few tea shops close to her flat—and the Mereside Inn, a modest hotel-cum-pub. But nothing, absolutely nowhere, that merited a little black dress and a dinner suit.

As he followed her down the driveway, Will debated whether to give her his arm. It was steep, and those amazing shoes really did have very high heels. He tried to think of them in purely practical terms, but seeing the thin straps circling her slender ankles, he was struggling.

In the end, he decided not to touch her. Once he laid hands on her, he was afraid he wouldn't be able to let go, that his hands would travel from her arm to her waist and maybe his fingers might accidentally brush that pert rear. He was glad too, if he was really honest with himself, that she'd hidden that delicious honey-colored skin underneath a demure shawl. Otherwise, he didn't think he could get through the evening.

"OK. Now where?" she demanded at the foot of the drive, hugging the shawl tighter around her as if she could read his mind. The early evening breeze was refreshing, tugging at her carefully swept-up hair.

"Over there." He nodded his head toward the lake.

There was only the Mereside Inn opposite. "But that's a pub. My local…not that I go in there all that often."

"Trust me," he replied, knowing she wouldn't. He decided to throw caution to the wind after all and risked a hand on the small of her back, guiding her in the direction of the pub beer garden. She moved briskly forward. Even through the fine wool of her shawl, the warmth of his touch was only just bearable.

"Carry on," he said, steering her through the tables and chairs toward the lakeshore, ignoring the amused glances from drinkers enjoying the early evening sun.

At the edge of the garden, stretching out over the water, was an old wooden jetty. Emma caught her breath as she got her first view of the restaurant.

All thirty-four feet of her.

A yacht was riding tranquilly at the pier, her slender mast pointing at the few pale pink clouds barring the otherwise perfect sky. A smile touched her lips as she saw the name on the hull.

Artemis.

Greek goddess of the hunt. She glanced at Will to see if he'd spotted the irony, planned it even, but she saw only a look of pleasure in his eyes. Later on, she might have to enlighten him.

She turned to see him, watching her silently, waiting for her reaction.

"If you wanted me to be impressed, you've done it," she admitted. "Mission accomplished on that score."

"Not what you were expecting?"

"Two minutes ago, I was expecting a pub meal in the beer garden, so yes, I'd say this has definitely come as a surprise."

"I thought you'd have had your fill of three-star restaurants down in London. This," he said, looking out over the shimmering lake, "you can only experience right here."

Her eyes took in the jagged mountains across the lake, now turning indigo against the setting sun. She continued to look at them because she did not dare risk a glance at him, her heart was so full.

"For once, I'll agree with you. We could only do this in Bannerdale."

"Hi there, Will. You're a bit late...as usual!" The shout came from on board the yacht. A trim, gray-haired woman dressed in a sweatshirt and jeans beamed at them as she uncoiled a rope with brisk efficiency.

"Sorry, Jane!" he called back. "I had business at the rescue base."

"I've heard that one from you before. What's with the fancy suit? A special occasion?" teased Jane Stanton, the yacht's owner, as she climbed deftly onto the jetty.

"Emma here thinks I live and sleep in hiking gear. I wanted to show her we can be civilized in Bannerdale. Where's Charles?"

"Just preparing to get us underway. Aren't you going to introduce me, then?" she asked, kissing him on the cheek.

One thing was obvious, thought Emma as Jane greeted Will like an old friend: he'd done this many times before. His easy familiarity with the Stantons told her that much. She should have known she wasn't the first to get this kind of treatment, but just for a moment, she'd let herself believe this was laid on especially for her. Suddenly, her pashmina didn't seem warm enough.

"Ready to climb on board?" asked Will, unaware the warm reception he'd received had provoked a frosty one from Emma.

"I'm terribly sorry, but you'll have to take those off," apologized Jane, pointing to her shoes.

"Sorry?"

"It's the stiletto heels, I'm afraid—they don't do our deck any favors. Do you mind?"

"Er...no, not at all. I wouldn't want to cause any damage, naturally," she replied.

"Thanks for being so understanding. Jump on as soon as you're ready," said Jane cheerfully, climbing back over the rail.

Fine, Emma thought. Now she'd be barefoot for the whole evening. Will must have known she wouldn't be able to keep them on. She bent down to take off her shoes, but someone got there first.

Will was actually kneeling down on the jetty in front of her. "Let me help you. I know I should have warned you, but you could hardly walk down here in boots with that outfit."

She pursed her lips. "I suppose I'll have to forgive you then, but I'm quite capable of taking my own shoes off."

They were the most ridiculously impractical and mouthwateringly sexy pair of shoes he had ever seen. As he loosened the buckle, he couldn't help encircling her ankle with his thumb and finger. He swept his hand down the smooth blade of her skin as he slipped off the shoe, expecting her to snatch her foot away at any moment.

She didn't.

She let him hold it for way longer than he deserved, and when he finally placed her bare foot down on the wooden jetty, she wriggled delicate toes painted in a shimmering pastel shade. And then actually held on to his shoulders for balance as he unbuckled the other shoe. He felt like a servant granted a special favor by his mistress, and funnily enough, he didn't mind.

"Will, we must get underway." Charles Stanton was leaning over the rail and beckoning them to get on board.

That was one mercy, concluded Emma as she felt the cold jetty under her feet: she could climb on board more easily without shoes. Taking them from Will, she popped them onto the deck and let Charles hand her over the rail before Will could get the chance.

Once on deck, she stopped to catch her breath. She'd been on a floating gin palace in Cannes once with Jeremy—a corporate bash to celebrate the launch of their latest GPS system. This bore no comparison. Jeremy had been drunk on the free champagne by nine o'clock, and she'd spent the rest of the evening boosting the egos of braying executives.

This was not as glamorous but somehow more real and far more beautiful. As they glided away from the shore, the light breeze on land was translated into a stiff wind, setting the sails flapping and the halyards clattering against the mast. On the deck, a small table was laid out for dinner between the bench seats.

Charles handed her a glass of Pimm's as the yacht tilted alarmingly first to port and then to starboard. As they sailed across the lake, she clutched her drink in one hand and the rail in the other. One moment, the water was inches from her back; the next, she was soaring through the air, the waves skipping by six feet below. Will, lounging on the cushions on the other side of the boat, looked like he'd seen it all before.

"You've chosen a nice night for it," commented Charles. "For once, it's dry and we've got plenty of wind. Otherwise, it would have been the iron sail for us, and that's hardly romantic, is it?"

Hardly romantic? Even if they had had to resort to the engine, Emma couldn't think of anything more romantic. If she'd been trying to get herself into bed, she'd have chosen this method too. It was obviously Will's certain seduction technique. The sinking feeling in her stomach was impossible to ignore. She glared at him as he admired the scenery, his hair tousled by the wind.

———

He knew she was eyeing him, and he knew it wasn't a friendly look. He sighed as he gazed out over the lake.

He'd really thought he was getting somewhere on the quayside. She'd

allowed him to guide her toward the jetty and—he couldn't believe it—
take off her shoes. It had certainly been no hardship, kneeling down in
front of her, having no choice but to touch her skin.

He watched her as she pretended to take an interest in a passing
yacht, his eyes drawn again to those slender ankles and calves and higher,
to where her thighs were pressed tightly together. She wriggled her toes
against the deck, and even that slight gesture turned him on.

He noticed the shawl was still bound protectively around her. He
should be wrapped around her instead. He should be huddled up close
to her, keeping her warm with his body...

Emma swung around and darted a wary glance at him, opening her
mouth as if she was about to say something.

"Sorry to disturb you, but would one of you like to choose some
wine?" Jane Stanton had popped her head out of the saloon gangway.
The aromas of cooking wafted out from the door, and Emma wished she
could summon up an appetite.

"Thanks, Jane," said Will, then turned to Emma. "Do you want to
choose?" he asked.

"It's OK," she muttered to him. "You do it."

Emma realized she needed a few moments away from his far-too
direct appraisal. As he ducked his head beneath the cabin door, she took
a sip of her Pimm's and tried to imagine that she was in the South of
France on a sultry August night. She wasn't alone for long.

Charles Stanton appeared, bearing a tray of canapés. "Lovely evening," he said, offering the tray. "Will's been lucky—it poured down the
last time we saw him."

She decided to ask a question she already knew the answer to. "Does
he do this often, then, hire *Artemis*, that is?"

"Oh yes! He's been on here...let me see...it must be four times since
last summer."

"Oh." So it *was* his favorite seduction method, and what woman
could resist it?

"He's one of our best customers," continued Charles. "He's always
bringing clients on our corporate sailing days, but"—he lowered his

voice—"I probably shouldn't say this, but this is the first time he's ever brought a young lady on board."

Her stomach flipped as the wind tore another strand from her hairdo. Her mind focused on those three words: the first time. She knew her delight at hearing them was way out of proportion to what it should have been. It didn't mean he hadn't taken a woman out to dinner before. But not here—like this. For one night, at least, she was special.

"I'll leave you to it," Charles said as Will emerged from the cabin.

The hesitant smile that greeted him was such a contrast to her previous scowl that he had to swallow hard.

"So. What have you chosen for us?" he heard her asking.

Us. The breath caught in his throat. He waited for the lurch of panic that would tell him to run away from the intimacy of the word, but it didn't arrive. All he felt was a sense of warmth, pleasure, and togetherness, which was all much more scary.

"White, I think…yeah. Something French anyway. To tell you the truth, it's just slipped my mind. I hope it's OK."

She shuffled along the seat, leaving a space next to her. "I'm sure it will be fine. Look, why don't you join me here? It's silly shouting at each other across the boat like this, don't you think?"

"Oh absolutely," he replied, treating her to a glance so sexy she almost melted. He sat down tentatively, keeping a discreet distance from her. She knew he was trying to give her space. If only he knew she wanted the opposite from him: closeness, warmth, affection.

The ensuing silence was punctuated by the cries of gulls and the rush of the water as they made for a small bay on the opposite shore. "Do you know about the name of the yacht?" she ventured. "*Artemis*—interesting choice."

He looked at her quizzically, but his tone was amused. "Why do I feel I'm about to be taught a lesson?"

"Artemis—virgin goddess of the wilderness," she declared. *And fertility*, she could have added, but she decided to keep that one to herself. "She hunted down a man called Actaeon who watched her bathing naked—"

"Bathing naked?" he echoed.

"Oh yes. She turned him into a stag and set his own hounds on him."

He cleared his throat. "Sounds like a real charmer. Still, that's something else I didn't know about you. You're an expert on mythology."

"Classics MA." She nodded sagely.

"Wow. I'm impressed."

Teasing him was fun and sexy, but she couldn't keep up the pretense any longer. "Actually, I read it in one of my niece's Horrible History books. I did English at university."

Will was too warm. He wanted to undo his bow tie and the top button of his shirt. And to take his jacket off. But it would have looked odd when a fresh breeze was whipping up whitecaps on the lake and pricking Emma's flesh with goose bumps.

"Where are we going?" she asked.

"Over into that little bay," he replied, glad of a subject that didn't involve wet and naked goddesses. "We'll have dinner there, where the water's calm."

Ten minutes later, the yacht was almost motionless, riding gently at anchor in the bay. Dinner was served on the deck, the food giving them both a relatively safe topic of conversation. Emma didn't know how she managed her starter and main course; the butterflies in her stomach left no room for anything else. A gentle fluttering stirred every time Will looked directly at her or refilled her wineglass…or just breathed in and out.

Lust must affect men and women in different ways, Emma concluded, seeing him devour his own meal and half of hers. All that walking and climbing, she thought, and he was so terribly big. Tall, that is, tall and strong… Oh, for goodness' sake, she had to try and calm down. Dessert arrived, and with it the chance for Will to point out the fell tops they could see silhouetted against the setting sun.

The evocative names—Harrison Stickle, Pike o' Blisco, Crinkle Crag—rolled off his tongue and set off the butterflies as she heard a tiny, incredibly sexy trace of his Cumbrian accent. She saw the pride in his eyes as he told her about the climbs he'd enjoyed, the rescues he'd helped with—some ending happily, humorously even. Many not.

She found herself warming to his unashamed passion for the place he lived in, the people and landscape. There was no cynicism now, no glib remarks or sarcastic comments. It seemed natural to take her chance. "Will," she ventured as he slotted the bottle in the ice bucket, "this afternoon, you asked me why I was here in Bannerdale. I told you the truth. Now it's your turn—why are *you* here?"

"Always have been—apart from university," he answered, placing his glass on the little table.

"Where did you go?"

"Scotland."

"Why?"

He grinned. "Big mountains."

"Ah, silly me. Should have known." There was silence. "You're not helping me out here..."

He smiled and put down his napkin on the table. "I studied geography. I was all set to be the archetypal bearded teacher in tweeds and brogues."

The image brought a giggle to her lips. "Somehow I can't quite imagine that...but then again, you do have the makings of a beard sometimes...all that designer stubble..."

Laughing, he rubbed his chin. "Life's too short for male grooming, but I do make an effort for special occasions." The look he gave her was so knowing that she felt her stomach clench with desire.

"And?" The word came out as a squeak. "Let's have your life history. You can't get away from me here, on this boat."

"If you really insist, but I warn you, it's very boring. Born and brought up here. Bannerdale Primary School, local comp, university, and a postgraduate certificate of education. Then the geography teacher bit. That lasted six months. Told you I was boring."

She wagged a finger at him. "You're not getting away with that. I want to know more. Much more."

"Ask away then."

"Anything?"

"You can ask anything you want." He smiled. She was well aware he hadn't *actually* promised to answer.

"Don't worry, I will—but don't forget it was your idea." She made a show of considering her first question. "OK then. Number one, what made you start your own business?"

"I was a useless teacher." His eyes were twinkling. "Seriously, I really like kids, but it wasn't for me, the day-to-day and all the admin. I'd always wanted to start my own business, stay as close as I could to the great outdoors. I suppose I would have launched Outside Edge one day, but Dad dying made it happen sooner than I'd expected."

"Oh. I'm so sorry…" Her voice trailed off as her enthusiasm for the game drained away.

"It's all right, Emma. You haven't upset me," he said, reassuring her. "It was a long time ago. I don't mind talking about it now. He had a heart attack while he was out walking the fells on his day off." He gave a bitter laugh. "He never smoked or drank much, always kept in shape—I suppose that's just the way it goes."

"When was this?" she murmured. "You couldn't have been that old."

"I was twenty-four, and Dad was barely fifty. The rescue squad went to help. Bob Jeavons was there, in fact, but there was nothing they could do. That's that, I'm afraid."

"Life's so unfair," she said limply. "I mean he was young, your dad, far too young. It must have been a terrible shock for you and your mum. I've been lucky." As he let her closer to him, her heart started to beat a little faster.

"He made sure he looked after us, though. He'd worked so hard, saved all his life, so there was a decent amount of money and some insurance. Not loads, but Mum insisted on me having every spare penny. It got me started in the business, and things just grew from there."

He got up from the table on the deck and motioned to her to sit back on the bench with him. Still, he didn't crowd her or offer to put his arm around her, but she could feel the heat from his body and smell his sharp citrusy aftershave.

She knew he was being deliberately vague about his success. He must have worked incredibly hard to go from one store to a big network in ten years…and he was harboring ambitions in property too, if the hotel was anything to go by. It was on the tip of her tongue to ask him about it, but it seemed trivial after what he'd just told her. Trivial and churlish. He had a right to do whatever he wanted with his money. It wasn't as if he'd inherited a fortune or a stately home or anything. Still, it would be nice to see him doing something positive rather than just expanding his empire even further.

"Where does your mum live?" she asked tentatively.

"A cottage in Bannerdale. She moved out of our family home when Dad died and made me have the profits to start the business. The cottage is what the tourists call 'quaint,' which means no double glazing, steep stairs, and an open fire. Mum refuses to move even though I've offered to buy her something more practical. She just won't have it."

"I'm sure she likes her independence," commented Emma, smiling inwardly at his well-meaning interference. Didn't she try and do the same herself with her own parents?

She paused, held her breath for a tiny moment, then dared some more. "Is that why you joined the rescue team? Because they tried to help your dad that day?"

She saw the tiny smile curve his lips. "I was grateful to them…when I'd stopped being angry they didn't reach him in time. Of course, it wasn't their fault, but for a while, I needed to blame somebody. I was on my probationary year with the squad at the time. Everyone has to do it, to prove they can cut it with the team. I joined because—well, I just wanted to use my skills to help other people. Corny but true. I'd been climbing since I was a lad, and I know these hills like the back of my hand."

He took a sip from his glass and then set it down, leaving her waiting for more. He looked her full in the face. "Believe it or not, I like helping people, Emma."

He paused, leaving Emma unsure if he was referring to his reluctance to support the calendar or his behavior in her office—or neither. She tried not to react and took a sip of wine.

Will carried on. "You see, sometimes people get hurt, even when you don't mean them to—when it's ultimately for their own good. It's like on the hillside when someone's in pain and we have to move them or treat them. Sometimes we know it's going to hurt before we can make things better for them. It's the part I hate, but I'm afraid that's the way it is."

Emma was puzzled and a little disturbed by his words. She was wondering what he meant. Was he trying to justify the way he'd behaved toward her? No, she reasoned, she was reading way too much into things. She knew that the team often had to make some difficult decisions when they were on rescues, and it must be upsetting, no matter how much of a brave face they tried to put on it.

As if reading her mind, Will reached for the bottle. "Now. This isn't a very nice subject," he said, smiling. "Let's talk about something else. Do you want some more wine?"

She put her hand over her half-full glass.

"No thanks. And, Will, even if it hurts, I—I'd rather know the absolute truth."

"The absolute truth?" he echoed. "I'm not sure anyone wants to hear the absolute truth. An approximation maybe, a sanitized version…"

"I always want to know everything. However unpalatable." She was amazed at her daring.

"What makes you think you don't know everything? What else is there to know?" He paused, waiting for his nose to grow or to be struck down by a thunderbolt. Nothing worse happened than a gust of wind flapping the sails. He looked up at the darkening sky. "So go ahead. Ask me another one. I think I can guess your specialist subject by now."

Not really, she thought. *Not if I asked what I really want to. Why did you jilt your fiancée on your wedding day? Why don't you want a real relationship? And what do you want from me other than a night in bed?*

"I'm waiting," he teased.

"The calendar," she blurted out, then caught his exasperated look. "I know you don't agree with it—even though you did offer to sponsor it, though I'm not convinced that was entirely altruistic…"

He suddenly seemed to be studying a bar of clouds over the darkening mountains.

"It's not because you're worried about people seeing you naked, is it?"

He threw back his head and laughed at that. "We've already been through all the reasons why I didn't—still don't—agree with it...but I'll tell you this much. Being seen in the nude is definitely not one of them. On the other hand," he added, moving a little closer to her in the gathering twilight, "are you?"

"Am I what?"

"Bothered about me being seen naked by the women of Bannerdale?"

Her laugh of derision sounded hollow even to her own ears. Oh God, she hadn't thought of that. He was right; she couldn't bear the thought of it.

"Or do you think most of them have seen me already? That's what you think, isn't it?"

"Don't be ridiculous!" she exclaimed, her cheeks flaming. "As if I care whether they have or haven't."

"How would you like it, then?" he persisted, ignoring her fierce blush.

"Like what?"

"Like to have all the men in Bannerdale admiring your breasts?"

Her mouth dropped open. "That's different."

"I don't see how."

"Because a woman...she'd be viewed as a sex object. With you, it's more...well, a bit of a joke."

"Thanks. You sure know how to boost a man's confidence."

"I didn't mean it like that. I didn't mean you personally..."

"So you *would* view me as a sex object, huh?"

"Stop it!" she cried, but she was trying to stifle her laughter. "Stop trying to twist everything I say. I know you hate—hated—the idea, and I'm...um...very grateful to you for taking part against your better judgment. It *is* going to be a success, and it *is* going to raise a lot of money for the base. Even you can't argue with that."

"You're right, and I don't want to argue with you. You don't honestly think I want you to fail, do you? Because if you do, we may as well go home right now." He took her hands in his and rubbed his thumbs gently over the palms, caressing the skin where she'd grazed it after her fall. "I only wish good things for you. I would never want you to be hurt." He lifted his eyes to hers and looked into them unflinchingly. "I would never want to do that, Emma. No matter what else you think about me, you must know that."

Her stomach somersaulted. The sky was indigo now, lights twinkling on both sides of the lake as she heard the rattle of the anchor being raised. The splash of the water against the bow told her they were moving again. He still had her hands in his; his mouth was inches away from hers. She wanted him so much, and it was no use now, trying to deny the absolute truth: she was falling in love with him.

Chapter 10

WILL'S MOUTH HAD BARELY REACHED HERS WHEN EMMA HEARD the noise behind them. A figure emerged from the gloom and coughed softly. "Sorry to disturb you both, but we need to know. Where are we going, Will? Back to Bannerdale or over to Ghyllside?"

It was Charles Stanton, hovering by the door to the cabin. Will was still holding her hands in his. "Thanks, Charles. We haven't decided yet, have we, Emma? Can you give us a few more minutes?"

The older man nodded. "Right you are, then. Let me know as soon as you can."

As soon as they were alone again, she dared to ask him, "How can we get to Ghyllside from here?"

"You'll find out," he answered softly, smiling and squeezing her fingers. "If you really want to, that is."

Her legs felt like cotton batting, and she was glad, so glad, she was sitting down.

"It's your choice," he murmured. "I won't try and make you do anything you don't want to."

She could feel her heart racing as she contemplated the step she was about to take. She couldn't see his face properly in the twilight, but she knew what he was saying clearly enough.

He was asking her to let him make love to her. To undress her and explore her body with those rough and tender hands…and no matter how gently, how carefully he phrased it, he wanted to take her.

And she wanted to be taken. She wanted to spend the night with him so much, she was aching all the way from her heart to her womb. But not just one night—she wanted every night. Now and forever.

But this might be the only night she'd ever have.

She felt dizzy with desire and longing, the reply catching in her dry throat.

"Emma, it's time. I need to know, sweetheart. Is it back to where we started, or are you coming home with me?"

She gave his hand the lightest of squeezes and whispered, "Home with you."

As soon as the words left her lips, Will dropped her hand and left her alone on the deck. Shivering in the damp night air, she pulled her shawl tighter. Her heart thudded. She couldn't say he'd put any pressure on her. He had asked, and she had said, clearly, yes. She wouldn't be able to complain if, in the morning, she woke up to an awkward silence and a hasty departure.

Or if she got hurt.

The yacht pressed onward toward the opposite side of the lake, where the dark shadows of trees were looming in the dim twilight. Splotches of light from a house glimmered between the branches. In the darkness, she heard him return to her side and felt his arm circle firmly around her shoulders. "Where are we going?" she murmured, already knowing the answer but wanting to hear him say it out loud.

"To bed."

Never had two such little words had the power to turn her body molten from the core.

"I'm taking you home to bed, sweetheart."

He got to his feet, pulling her up with him and pressing her hard against his body. Then he began to satisfy the hunger she'd endured ever since he had left her so empty on the hillside. His mouth was on hers, and this time...this time...he flicked his tongue gently inside her mouth, giving her a taste of the long, sweet night that was surely to come.

As his soft kiss deepened, became harder and more urgent, she dared to explore his mouth the way she'd longed to do, knowing that this time, he was going to finish what he'd started. She felt his thumb skim her nipples, and instantly, they hardened to his touch.

"Cold?" he whispered.

She shook her head defiantly.

"Good. Then you won't need this." He pulled the shawl from her shoulders and let it fall onto the deck. He bent his head and trailed his tongue along the top of her cleavage. She arched her back, pressing her pelvis against his body, and felt the hard length of him pressing against her stomach through the flimsy silk of her dress.

"Still not cold?"

"No," she murmured, pushing her hands inside his jacket, tracing his spine and the taut muscles of his back through his shirt. As she stood on tiptoe to reach his mouth again, a soft bump made her look up as *Artemis* nudged a black jetty jutting out into the lake. Now there really was no going back.

She had no problem now with letting him help her over the rail and onto the jetty in front of a large house. Light from the windows revealed the wooden slats leading from the lake onto a gravel drive. She gazed up at the house where the soft light was spilling out from some of the downstairs rooms and one of the upper ones. She didn't need to ask him. This was his home—Ghyllside Cottage.

The yacht's engine faded into the darkness as she heard Will calling goodbye to the crew. The wooden boards were damp and cool under the soles of her feet. Her bare feet.

"Wait!" she cried, dashing to the end of the jetty and grabbing his arm. "My shoes. They're still on board, quick!"

"It's too late, Emma. It's gone."

"No!" she wailed. "What am I going to do without them?"

"Stay in bed all day?" he offered. "Look, I'll drive you home via the marina tomorrow, and we'll get them. In the meantime, I'll carry you to the house."

"No," she protested, suddenly shy. "I...I can't have that."

"Fine by me. As long as you don't mind walking along the jetty, but I warn you, there are splinters in it as well as the odd slug or snail..."

"Carry me," she squealed, putting her arms around his neck.

"Good decision."

"But don't drop me!"

"Emma, what do you think I spend half my life doing?"

Being carried off to bed by him should have felt like a cliché. It didn't. It felt more sexy and exciting than she could ever have imagined. She could still feel the tension in his arms as he carried her along the jetty to the lawn in front of the house.

She wasn't a waif, and just thinking of how strong he was to carry her all that way turned her on even more. His shoes crunched on the gravel drive as they neared the house. Even in the darkness, she could see it was massive. A white rendered house with leaded windows. "This isn't a cottage," she said as he set her down in the canopied porch, and she felt the sudden chill of the tiles under her feet.

"That's what it was called when I bought it. The Edwardians must have liked picturesque names." He took a key out of his pocket and unlocked the oak door. "In you go," he said, urging her into the hall, his fingers lingering unashamedly on her silk-clad bottom.

"That's outrageous…"

"Couldn't resist it," he replied, patting her backside unrepentantly. Ignoring her shriek of indignation, Will just smiled. "Now get inside," he ordered. She was ready to combust with fury and, she had to admit, lust.

Stepping onto the polished floor of the hall, her eyes were drawn to an oak-paneled staircase rising to the second floor. Her skin tingled as his fingers brushed her bare shoulders, pulling off her shawl and dropping it on a chair.

"Do you want coffee?" he asked, dropping a kiss on the back of her neck that made the downy hairs rise in anticipation. "Or can I take you straight up to bed?"

"I don't want coffee."

"Good, because I'm not making any. Now—up to bed," he said, picking her up again without asking permission. "It doesn't have to be mine, you know," he told her as he carried her up the stairs, his eyes sparkling. At the top of the landing, he paused. "I've got a spare room if you want…"

Her eyes took in the doors leading off the landing, resting on the one at the end, soft light escaping through the half-open door.

"Were you expecting me?"

"No."

It sounded very unconvincing.

"What if I took you at your word about the spare room?" she asked.

"I hope you don't, because you know what? I might have to ignore you," he answered, carrying her to the end of the landing and nudging open his bedroom door. "Because every day and every night since I saw you on that hillside, I have wanted to take you to bed. But since I promised this could be a no-strings day, if you still want it to stay that way, just say the word."

"Will," she murmured as he put her gently down on her feet in his bedroom, "don't be so..." He stopped her mid-phrase with a kiss. While he deepened it with his tongue, she slipped the jacket off his shoulders, letting it fall to the floor. The bow tie followed, a rustle of silk against the collar. Her fingers were fumbling at the buttons of his shirt in her haste to get at his body. She hauled out his shirt, then dragged the sleeves down his arms, almost ripping off the cuffs. She wanted him—wanted him so badly she didn't care what happened tomorrow.

Then her hands moved lower, flicking open the button of his trousers, the zip slithering halfway down. Slipping her hand inside his boxer shorts, she echoed his gasp of pleasure with a moan of delight, unable to believe how hard he was.

"That's outrageous," he groaned as she wrapped her fingers around him. His hands closed on hers, gently but firmly. "No. Not yet."

"No?"

"Very, very soon, I promise. First, there's something that I've wanted to do for so long. That I've got to do," he murmured. As he held her in his arms, her legs seemed to have lost their bones and turned to unsupported flesh.

She wanted to melt like butter and let him slice through her.

He turned her around to face an antique, full-length mirror, and then she saw herself. She was leaning back against him, her cheeks flushed with desire, her nipples straining against her dress. She could feel him against the small of her back, and what he said made her legs feel very wobbly indeed.

"It's my turn to undress you. Your turn to feel what it's like to have nothing between you and me. No protection."

No protection? She'd never felt so safe or protected in her life, with those strong arms around her.

"Look at yourself," he ordered.

Over her shoulder, she saw him, holding one hand against her lower stomach so she was pressed firmly against him. The other hovered above the zip of her dress.

"I want this off right now."

His fingers lingered on the skin above the zip for a moment, sending a shiver of anticipation down her spine. Then she heard the sound of the zip being drawn down agonizingly slowly. The black silk parted to reveal her naked back and the waistband of the tiniest thong she owned.

"Will...oh..."

"You bad, bad girl."

"Don't tease m—"

He put a finger on her lips and kissed the top of her head. His hands were on her shoulders now, strong fingers sliding under the wispy straps and slipping them down. She couldn't believe someone so big and so powerful could be so gentle. And yet, of course, it was his job to be gentle and strong. He had been on the mountain that day. As he'd dressed her hands, as he'd hurt her while he was helping her. He had been as gentle as he could, as he knew how to be.

He was a man used to being in control, and she knew that. Accepted now, the brisk tenderness that was Will. Like now, as he freed her of the tight restraint of her bodice. As he peeled the black silk from her breasts, as he took them in his hands and held their weight and let out a breath that told her exactly how beautiful he found them.

Turning her to face him again, he pressed her aching nipples against his hair-roughened chest, then traced a molten arc along her shoulders and spine with his long, strong fingers. Power with sensitivity, that was what Will had more than any man she'd ever known. It was a mind-blowing combination that was overwhelming her mind and body.

Will truly believed the ache between his thighs couldn't possibly get any fiercer as he caressed the slender yet ripe curves he'd dreamed of for so long.

It could. Like hell it could.

He felt dizzy with desire. Almost out of control, and that scared him. He thought about taking her there and then, on the bedroom floor, but he wanted this to last for him and for her, for the gorgeous, willing, soft, and luscious girl he was holding. The one wrapped in his arms, wearing nothing but a scrap of cream lace, a contrast with the caramel of her bare skin. Her nipples were already hard, but he demanded more from her. He set to work with his mouth, circling her nipples with his tongue and oh so gently nipping them until she moaned aloud in pleasure.

He had never wanted to please a woman so much—or be so selfish. He had to explore every inch of her body, and to do that, he had to strip her naked. Totally, utterly bare. He slipped one finger inside the waistband of the tiny lacy thong and pulled it back teasingly.

"Please..." she whispered as he kept his finger poised in the flimsy material.

"Please yes, or please no?"

"Yes...oh, please yes..."

Slowly, way too slowly, he inched the lace down over the lush curve of her bottom, his thumbs gliding over her skin as he slid the wispy material over her thighs to her ankles and let it lie there, brushing her feet.

"Step out of it."

He was standing now, and those dark eyes were drinking her in, a shameless appraisal that inflamed her sensitized body even more.

"Well," she asked, "are you satisfied?"

He shook his head. "No. Not yet...your necklace..." He stood behind her, gently unfastening her gold chain and placing it on the bedside table.

"Now?" she whispered.

His voice was barely audible. "Not quite...your hair..."

A fierce tide of arousal ran through her as he loosened her hair and let it fall onto her naked shoulders. Untangling it, he spread it apart over her bare shoulders, leaving embers of fire wherever he touched her skin. "You're so beautiful," he whispered.

"This isn't fair," she whispered as he pulled her into his arms again. "When I saw you naked, you still had your boots on."

"You're forgetting something," he murmured, kissing her neck and shoulders. "You left your shoes behind on the yacht, and know what? You wiggle your toes when you're turned on."

He knelt down at her feet, his rock-roughened hands encircling her ankles and then sweeping over her calves and thighs in long strokes, sending wave after wave of pleasure through her. She gripped his shoulders as he reached the damp curls between her legs and touched her.

There.

Right there.

On the hot, sweet spot that had nagged at her, exquisitely, all evening. Increasing the buzzing intensity of desire that had her squirming every time he looked at her.

Oh… Emma knew she was dissolving as he slid one finger inside her. The hot, unstoppable rush of desire made her moan out loud.

"Will…oh please, I—"

"You are sensational."

As he knelt at her feet, his hands were holding the backs of her thighs. His head dipping until his mouth and tongue were pushing her to new levels of sensation, an exquisite tingling, building to a peak that centered in her swollen clit and oh…

"Enough…Will, I can't stand it…please…no more."

No more. No more because she had to be taken *now*, taken to his bed and driven into with all the power he had.

"I—I want you inside me."

"You're going to get me, sweetheart. And how."

He swung her into his arms and carried her over to the bed. Placed her onto the silk throw, the cool silk caressing her bare skin. She lay obediently in a pool of lamplight, wanting desperately to show him how much she wanted to be filled up but not daring to. Not yet.

She didn't know him well enough yet, not to open up that wide—to invite him, beg him. But he must have read her mind, because he was smiling down at her and urging her thighs apart with one big hand.

"Wider than that, sweetheart," he whispered, leaning over her now, his hands either side of her head. "Much more than that."

"What about—"

"I'll take care of it. You stay exactly as you are."

Will reached over to the bedside table for a condom and ripped open the packet. As he did so, trying not to make a hash of it, he knew that it was he who needed protection from her, and not the kind that came by the dozen—despite his best intentions, despite everything he'd fought against for the past three months. And he didn't care. He wanted to let go so much, to give in to his feelings for her, and damn the consequences.

Seeing her lying there, ready and demanding, her cloud of dark hair spread against the white pillow, he couldn't wait a moment longer to take her. He was fumbling hopelessly at his zipper now. He'd waited so long…

"Let me…oh, please let me." Her hands were wrenching frantically at his zipper and tugging at his trousers and shorts. He kicked them off, and finally, he gave her a close-up view of what she'd only glimpsed before. The hot, hard length of him.

"Emma…sweetheart…"

He buried himself within her with one slow, powerful thrust. It had been a while for her. He could tell that as she gasped at the pressure, and he didn't want to hurt her but knew he was massively turned on.

"*Sweetheart?*" His voice was low, barely a whisper. Asking a question, to which the answer was irrelevant. There was no going back now. He needed this like nothing he'd ever needed before.

Small, determined hands grasped his buttocks, stung him with their nails, and urged him in deeper. He thrust again with much greater force and felt the rope holding him back, keeping him on the edge, fraying. She began to convulse around him in waves of exquisite, clamping pressure. Her fingers were digging into the flesh on his back, but he barely noticed. He could barely see or hear anything, only *feel* her contracting impossibly around him. Gripping him like a dark, velvet vise.

The rope snapped, and Will let himself fall into oblivion with her.

———

It was too warm in Will's bed.

The morning sun was slanting through the windows, dappling the bed with bright patches of heat and light. Will's naked body was hot and sticky against hers, and Emma would have thrown back the cotton sheet that was covering them except she didn't want to wake him. Not yet. She wanted to stay like this for as long as possible and put off the moment when she had to leave his bed and go home. Maybe he planned to let her down gently but firmly. Somehow, she knew that was how he'd do it.

But not yet, she thought. *Please not yet.*

As she shifted slightly in his embrace, his arm tightened around her in a gesture of possession and protection that made her stomach flip. She tensed, still feeling the effects of a night of lovemaking after so many months on her own.

Will had taken her beyond everything she'd ever known. Again and again during the long, warm night, tender but insistent, devouring every last ounce of her. The last time, he'd sat braced upright against the oak backboard of his bed. He'd guided her onto him as he stretched her to the limit and brought her to a shuddering climax that left her wrecked and limp in his arms.

Now her cheek was resting on his bare chest, sensing the soft rise and fall as he slept. She knew him now. Knew all the little scars on his body from every misadventure. The big one on his knee from a bad climbing fall. And now she knew where the trail of hair that she'd spent so long admiring ended.

It cried out to be explored, right now, with her mouth. He had his eyes closed as she traced a moist path that led from his nipples, down his chest, and over his stomach. As she reached his navel, she felt his body quiver. "Are you awake?" she mumbled from under the sheet.

His reply was barely audible and very shaky. "No, sweetheart...still asleep, and I hope I don't have to wake up anytime soon."

———

Sometime later, Emma took a look at the clock on Will's bedside table. It was midmorning and the sun was slanting, hot and bright, into the room. Swinging his legs out of bed, he started to pull on a pair of jeans. Even from the pillow, she could see the red nail marks on his back and buttocks and let out a little cry of guilt and embarrassment. "I'm sorry…"

"I'm not," he replied, knowing what she meant without turning around or asking. He zipped up his jeans gingerly and sat on the bed next to her. "Wildcat."

"Don't tease me," she pleaded, covering her face with her hands.

"I consider it to be my role in life," he replied, wrapping a tendril of glossy hair around his finger.

She hoisted the sheet above her breasts, suddenly embarrassed by her nakedness. "And mine is to be another notch on your bedpost," she ventured.

"Make that four, sweetheart."

"And is that it?" she asked simply, her heart thudding in her chest. "Just notches on the bedpost?"

He looked at her strangely, and for a moment, she thought she'd shattered the intimacy between them. Then suddenly, he pulled the sheet off her. "Come on. Get up. I want to show you something."

"Where's my dress?" she asked as she climbed out of bed. "I haven't brought anything else to wear. You didn't tell me I wouldn't be going home."

He caught up his discarded shirt from the floor and draped it around her shoulders. "Put this on," he said, and she slipped her arms into the sleeves and rolled them up. She left the top buttons open to let the morning air cool her hot skin. The tails brushed the tops of her thighs.

"Perfect." Will nodded, feeling the effect as his jeans tightened around him. "You are absolutely perfect."

"What about my underwear?" she asked innocently.

He bent down and picked up the scrap of lace still lying in front of the mirror. "You mean this? I'd hardly call it an item of clothing."

"Do you disapprove?"

"Come on outside before I show you just how much I approve."

Emma took her lacy thong from his hand and put it on, trying to smooth down the shirt tails as far as she could. "What if someone sees us?"

He held out his hand. "They won't. There are eight acres of grounds around us. No nosy neighbors—unless someone has binoculars on us from a yacht."

She let him lead her down the staircase into the hall and into the kitchen, with its farmhouse table and range cooker. "I'll make us breakfast when I've shown you this," he offered, guiding her into a small boot room from where a door opened into the garden. He ushered her outside.

Chapter 11

EMMA HAD NEVER BEEN ANYWHERE QUITE LIKE IT BEFORE. IT WAS simply breathtaking. The broad stone terrace she was standing on over-looked lawns surrounded by shrubs and woodland. At the end of the lawns was the lake, sunlight dancing off the wavelets, the jetty he had carried her along pointing out into the shimmering water.

"Oh…"

"Like it?" he asked, almost hesitantly, and then he smiled as she squeezed his hand. "This way," he said, stepping down onto the lawn. "You'll be OK on the grass without shoes." The cool dew tickled her toes as she padded over the springy turf down to the lake. They halted where a small stream flowed out into the dark water. "Here," he said, ducking under the overhanging branch of a willow tree.

Reaching into his pocket, he took out a penknife and handed it to her. This easy familiarity was not what she'd expected…but so very much what she'd longed for.

Now she hoped she would be wrong about him again. That this hadn't been just another one-night stand. That she would find out why he'd treated Kate so cruelly. That he had a reason she could forgive and might be ready to let another woman into his life.

Her.

She cradled the knife in her hand, then gazed at him expectantly. "What am I supposed to do with this?" she laughed. "Learn bush craft? Build a fire?"

"Carve your notches on the tree." He smiled. "Four. And your initials."

"You can't be serious."

A smile spread over his face. "Deadly."

"I...I...don't know if I can."

"Just do it," he urged, taking the knife. "Here." He flattened his palm against the trunk of the tree. "I'll make the first notch." He flicked open the blade and scored a mark firmly in the bark before handing the knife back to her. "Go on."

It was trickier than she thought. She had to press deeply to make a mark, and it took longer than she'd expected to do all four. She stepped back and giggled, seeing the grooves and knowing what each one stood for.

"Now your initials," he ordered, "and before you say it, I know what they'll be."

"No way," she cried. "I'll put my middle name too. That won't look so silly."

She found the initials were even more difficult. They were hardly recognizable but at least she'd tried: EAT. Emma Anne Tremayne. There, she'd done it. She took a step back, satisfied. "Is that all right?"

All this time, Will waited patiently, offering the odd word of encouragement.

"Perfect, actually." He grinned, getting a smack on the arm for his nerve. "Now it's my turn," he said, retrieving the penknife and quickly scoring three letters. "There...W...M...T."

"What does the M stand for?" she asked.

"Ah. Now that I'm not telling you."

"Why not?" she teased, high on the happiness of the moment. "It can't be that bad. Is it an old family name like Montgomery?"

"No."

"Marmaduke."

"Of course not," he replied, sounding insulted while his eyes sparkled with laughter. He began to stride quickly up the grass slope back to the terrace.

"Mabel!" she called after him as he closed rapidly on the house.

"Now you're being silly."

Emma had to run to catch him, her feet sinking into the damp turf.

"Will, wait!" she cried, grabbing his arm. She was a little out of breath. "I want to ask you something."

"I won't tell you my name," he declared, catching her in his arms and kissing her. "No matter what you try."

"It's not that… It's more important than that," she said, eager to seize the moment. That pulled him up. He looked…she wasn't sure what—caught off-balance? She decided to take a chance.

"Go ahead, sweetheart. Ask me anything."

"It's Lakeshore House."

There it was in his eyes; Emma knew she hadn't been mistaken. There was a definite look of relief and a slumping of the shoulders as if he'd been expecting something else.

"Lakeshore House?" he echoed.

"Yes—big hotel by the water. You know very well what I mean."

"I can't seem to recall the place," he said, acting puzzled, rubbing his still-unshaven chin.

"Don't be so annoying. Of course you do. You were outside it in the Range Rover when you gave me a lift to the Wordsworth Center. After you'd patronized me for ten minutes, of course."

"Oh that. Now I remember. You weren't very nice to me, Emma, and you had a tight jacket on. A tight skirt too. Your bottom looked sensational in it."

"Stop it," she ordered, her face reddening. "This is serious. I need to know. You're buying it, aren't you?"

"Maybe," he conceded.

"To turn into second homes, expand your empire. You'll make a fortune."

"Maybe," he repeated. "Maybe not. *If* I get it." He paused on the terrace. "Emma, are you really interested in my empire, as you call it, or is this conversation leading somewhere else? Conversations often do with you." He sat down on a wrought-iron bench and pulled her onto his lap. "In fact, I wish you'd come right out and ask what you really want."

If I thought you would give me a straight answer, I would, she reflected. *If I knew you wouldn't run away, I'd ask you everything I want to know.*

Despite sharing his bed, understanding his body as intimately as her own, she didn't really know him at all.

Her arms encircled his neck as she carried on. "I…just wondered why you need to make even more money because…you don't really need to, do you?"

"Emma…"

She heard the warning in his voice but pressed on. No going back now.

"Because I'm no fool, Will. I know how much this house is worth. I mean, it's amazing. Beautiful. But you already own a big company…and if you're buying a hotel…"

"Where is all this going? I don't want to talk about business right now—and neither do you, sweetheart."

"It's not about business. It's about you—and me. My ideas, anyway." She kissed him gently to stifle any objection. "You don't think we need to raise any funds for the calendar, do you, Will? That's why you're so against it…why you wanted to sponsor it? Because, let's be honest here, you could have paid for a new base all by yourself. Couldn't you?" He started to protest, but she stilled his lips with a finger.

After a moment's silence, he said again, quietly, "Possibly."

"I don't believe you. In fact, I think you have already paid for some of it—maybe almost all of it. I've seen the target for the fundraising, and even I know it's not nearly enough."

She saw that he wasn't smiling anymore, but he didn't look angry. He stroked her thigh thoughtfully, so she tried again, "It's time for you to be honest with me, Will."

"What, about the base or the hotel?"

"Both, preferably."

He sucked in his breath. "OK. The hotel. If—and it's a big if—I do get it, I want to turn it into an outdoor center for inner-city kids. A place where they can have a go at climbing, canoeing, rappelling—all the kind of stuff that makes life worth living. Especially rappelling…"

She refused to be goaded by this or sidetracked. Not now he'd started. Besides, she'd never been so happy to be wrong about someone. "So not a luxury second-home development that will make you a fortune?"

"Not unless people want to share their exclusive apartment with fifty unruly kids having a great time thinking they're doing dangerous stuff." He smiled. "Safely, of course."

"Why didn't you tell me before?"

"You seemed to have made your mind up already."

Emma didn't want to have to agree with him, but for once, he was right. She recalled their earlier conversations in the car and in her office. He hadn't helped, though, by being so defensive. Now, however, he was smiling at her and gently stroking her bare leg. Those days, their first sparring matches, seemed so far away.

"Anyway, I'm telling you about my plans now," Will went on. "But don't get too excited," he cautioned, one big, warm hand half circling her thigh. "It may never happen. There are other big developers interested too. A fantastic old place like that right on the lake would indeed make some very swish apartments and make someone a very nice profit. Whatever you think, my pockets aren't that deep."

He shifted her in his lap so she fitted more perfectly against the hardness inside his jeans.

"Does that set your mind at rest? Not only am I hot as hell in bed, I'm public spirited too. Now, is there anything else you want to know about me? Childhood illnesses? Criminal convictions? Favorite position for making love to you? But hey—you already know that..."

"Not yet," she added softly, tracing a fingertip over his chest and refusing to be diverted. "I'm still not *absolutely* sure...and you still haven't told me if you paid for the base."

"Now that will have to remain my secret, I'm afraid. As for positions, I think it's high time you did some more research." He smiled. "Let's go inside. I can see you're getting cold." He checked his watch. "Then I've got to have a shower—I've got a lunch meeting shortly."

Emma's face fell. Was this the signal she'd been dreading? The hint? She forced her question to sound casual. "A meeting on a Sunday?" Her smile fell short of her eyes, but he was no fool.

"It's Max and Francine." He smiled, tucking a strand of hair behind her ear. "Architect friend of mine and his pregnant French wife. I think you might have met him that day at the Wordsworth Center."

"The one with the Porsche? Goatee and pink shirt?"

"That's Max. We went to school together. He never changes—always had to have the latest football shoes and gadgets." He shook his head, laughter lighting his dark eyes. "The two of us need to sort out some very boring legal issues before the planning meeting on Monday morning. I wouldn't have arranged it, but you see, sweetheart, I never expected you to stay over. I hoped, was desperate in fact, but I didn't assume."

Emma narrowed her eyes at him. Did she believe him? Probably not.

"However," he added in a serious tone, "before I give you a lift home, there's still time for you to join me in the shower. Do you have any experience of Edwardian plumbing?"

"No, but I really need to brush up on my history," she answered, squealing in indignation as he tried to undo the remaining buttons of her shirt.

As they walked back to the house, even Will's evasiveness couldn't stop her heart from soaring. He stopped again in the boot room and pushed her against the wall to give her a long, deep French kiss that made her reel with pleasure. Then he tugged her by the hand, giggling, through the door into the kitchen, insisting she share a shower with him. She flinched as her feet touched the cold kitchen tiles and stopped.

He seemed so relaxed, so happy, that Emma wondered if now was the time. Should she tell him about her job offer and see what he had to say? What his reaction would be? Should she ask him what she really wanted to know? About…Kate?

He leaned against the kitchen table, pulled her to him, held her between his legs. Standing here like…like they'd known each other for years, wearing his shirt, in his kitchen, Emma felt the intimacy drugging her. It was like a warm tide flowing through her, an emotional muscle relaxant that sucked away caution, leaving her boneless. She dared to do anything at this moment. To challenge him, to see what she really meant to him.

She loved him.

He must know that now. He must feel it emanating from every pore of her body. Everything felt so right, so easy, she felt that nothing could go wrong, not this time...

"Emma. What's the matter? You've gone quiet, sweetheart. That's not like you," he said.

It didn't raise a smile.

"Oh...it's...it's..."

His scrutiny was intense as he reached up and pulled a willow leaf from her hair. Emma stepped over the edge and took the biggest risk of her life.

"Will, I haven't been entirely straight with you. When I said there was something I wanted to know...there's something I have to tell you."

"This sounds ominous." Yet still, he was smiling. He didn't expect anything serious.

"It, well...it's not...it's just..."

He stroked her hair.

"Yesterday afternoon before you came, I had an email."

"Hmm..."

"From Echo GPS. You must know them."

"Of course. I've got their gear in all my shops."

"Well, they are the ones who've agreed to sponsor the calendar."

The relief on his face this time was tangible. He laughed out loud.

"And you thought I'd be angry...put out after you'd rejected my offer?" He stroked her cheek and kissed her hair. "I'm not that petty, Emma. You did well to get money out of Echo. They drive a hard bargain."

There was no going back now. It all came out, like a river in flood.

"That's not it. Not all, I mean. Will, they've offered me a job." Still standing between his thighs, she felt his body grow tense as her stomach began to churn.

"Not here, I take it."

"No. Not in Bannerdale. In London. As their director of communications. It's lots more money, a high profile, company car."

"Ah." He took his hands from her waist. "And are you taking it?"

"I—I don't know. It's a fantastic opportunity. And it means I could go back..."

"Home?"

"Yes. I suppose so. Home." The word sounded hollow.

"Then you'd better take it, sweetheart. If that's what you really want."

Emma felt her stomach was somersaulting. *Please, Will,* her mind begged, *tell me it's not what you want. Tell me you want me to stay with you. Ask me, please…*

Will didn't help her out, forcing her to fill the silence. "I've almost decided to…to go, but I feel…guilty about leaving everyone. The tourist office, the rescue squad, the friends I've made—"

"I'm sure we'll survive somehow," he replied bitterly. "I mean, we'll miss you, Emma, but no one would stand in your way, not if that's what you really want. I know what you've given up to come up here. It's hardly the land of opportunity, not for someone like you."

Emma wanted to scream. Will couldn't be saying this, she told herself. He couldn't be agreeing with her, encouraging her to go. Surely he couldn't actually *want* her to go. She tried again, a last-ditch attempt to make him say what she wanted to hear.

"No, I suppose you're right." She waited. "I suppose everyone will get by just fine without me. I can hardly expect them to bang on my door and beg me to stay, can I?"

There. It was out, and she couldn't have put it any clearer without actually getting down on her knees and asking him.

He had one last chance to ask her to stay and to tell her what she meant to him. The silence hung thick and heavy in the kitchen. And still Will said nothing. Distantly, she heard the throb of a ferryboat on the lake, while he seemed to be struggling. For a second, he seemed uncertain but—no. There was no uncertainty when he spoke.

"Emma, it's been fantastic having you here. What you've done for us, for the team, has been amazing. No one, least of all me, will be glad to see you go, but you have to live your own life. We all do. We can't force people to do something when their heart isn't in it. No matter how much we want to. You understand that, don't you?"

Emma felt as if someone had taken hold of her insides and was knotting them slowly and viciously. Suddenly, Will's shirt seemed much too short, with far too many of the buttons undone. As she tried to pull it further down her thighs, she noticed her feet were muddy.

"I understand perfectly," she said.

And though her legs had turned to jelly, though she felt sick and weak and knocked back, there was no way she would let him see her pain. Not ever. It didn't sound like her voice, the next bit, speaking to him politely and calmly as if nothing had happened. As if she didn't care at all that he had just sent her crashing to the ground with a few words.

"I ought to leave. I need a shower, and then I'd be grateful if you'd drive me home."

Freeing herself from her place between his thighs, she walked away. She'd actually reached the door to the hall before it came. His voice cut through the silence, more bitter and tired than she had ever heard before.

"So you understand perfectly, do you?"

She stopped, her hand on the doorknob.

"You bloody well don't understand, Emma. You can't possibly."

She turned to face him.

He was standing in the middle of the room, and she could see, even from here, the tension in his big, big body. "You *think* you understand. You think you know everything."

"Will—"

"You've heard the spin in the village, haven't you?"

Emma felt sick. She could hardly bear to see him like this.

"Will. The bastard. Left poor old Kate at the altar without so much as a by-your-leave," he went on.

"I—"

"On a mission to sleep with every woman for fifty miles, then chucks them out as soon as the sun rises."

He was almost shouting now.

"Will—"

"Well, isn't that what you've heard? Isn't that the word on me?"

"Stop this, please."

"No. I won't. Not until you've answered me. What do you think you know about me?"

She tried to reply, but the words were so faint.

"I can't hear you, Emma."

Finally, she managed to meet his eyes and winced at the pain and bitterness they held. "Yes."

Expecting a cry of indignation, a shout, a denial, he simply nodded. "And is it a good tale, Emma? A feasible one? Do I live up to the image?"

"Don't do this to me, Will. Don't make me answer."

"I'm waiting. I'm asking you, Emma, what do you believe?"

"I don't know," she cried. "I really don't and, Will...hate me if you want, ignore me if you want, but I don't care anymore. I don't care what you did to Kate or why you did it, because you didn't ask me to stay."

He sat down at the farmhouse table and looked dumbfounded. Emma was afraid. She felt like she'd felled an ox or hurt something wild and savage, but she was resolute. He wouldn't look at her, just sat there. Then, as she opened the door to the hall, he said, "Emma, it's not easy for me to—to show my feelings. It's—it's not what you think. Please, this is all so sudden. Try and understand. I need more time and space."

The old cliché. It wasn't even original, and the new Emma didn't settle for clichés or second best. It was all or nothing with Will.

It looked like being nothing.

Well, so be it, even if it hurt for a thousand years. She was determined she wouldn't be used by any man ever again. Wouldn't be second best or duped or conned, and if that was harsh, if he didn't understand, then so be it.

"Will, if it's time and space you need, you've got it. I'm leaving."

She made it out of the door this time and then heard him add, in a low voice, "I'll take you home."

"I need a shower first," she mumbled. And she did. She needed to wash all traces of Will away along with every shred of hope and faith and trust she'd had that he really cared about her. That he would ask her to stay with him—not for a day, a week, but forever. She reached the stairs before the absolute truth blinded her with hot tears.

Her own words echoed in her mind. She loved Will as she'd never loved anyone before. In the end, what he'd done in the past to someone else didn't matter anymore. Selfish, but true. It was what he'd done to her.

And he hadn't asked her to stay.

Chapter 12

WILL HAD BEEN IN SOME BAD SITUATIONS. HE'D HAD SOME close calls and been messed up pretty badly once or twice. He'd seen stuff people shouldn't have to see out there on the hills. People he'd been sent to search for, to rescue—whose loved ones expected to see them back, a little red-faced, maybe a bit bruised, but ultimately *safe*.

Except they hadn't been safe. Would never be.

It had cost him actual tears once or twice, privately of course, he didn't mind admitting that. When he'd had to deal with the inconsolable grief of a wife, a son, or a daughter. This was nothing compared to that, he told himself. Of course it wasn't. It was only love. It didn't deserve the pain he was feeling, the confusion. No one had died.

Yet still it was hurting. No matter how much he rationalized it or tried to tell himself that, in the grand scheme of things, being left behind by someone he cared for was nothing, it was hurting.

Because it was happening to *him*—and it wasn't the first time.

———

Emma's dignity made it intact as far as the top of Will's stairs before shattering as she reached the landing and stumbled into his room, locking the door behind her. Suddenly, she had no desire for a shower anymore; her only instinct was to run. This wasn't a dream she would wake up from to a bright and sunny truth; it was a nightmare. He'd raised all her hopes only to let them plummet to the ground.

She asked herself how she could have been so blind. Will was never going to ask her to stay because he was never going to commit to her— or to any woman. Oh, he liked her, loved her body, respected her, but that was as far as it went—not enough. Once again, someone hadn't felt enough to fight for her.

The fragile world she had begun to construct around her, the world in which she'd dared to hope he really cared about her—*loved her*—was shattering. No way was she going to be driven home by a man who'd just rejected her. She couldn't have dropped a stronger hint. And what was it he'd said?

You have to live your own life. We can't force people to do something when their heart isn't in it. No matter how much we want to.

The tears fell again. He couldn't have said it much plainer, could he? Then he'd added insult to injury with the oldest line in the book: *I need more time and space.*

"Well, Will," she murmured softly, "you've got it."

Inside his room, her chest heaving, she tore his shirt from her body, sending the buttons pinging in her haste to get it off. She could still smell the faint aroma of his aftershave as she pulled it over her head and threw it on the floor.

She hunted for her little black dress, eventually dragging it out from under the duvet they'd thrown onto the carpet while making love in the warm night. Her evening bag was lying by the mirror where he'd stripped off her clothes. Her shawl was still on the chair in the hall where Will had discarded it, and there was no way she was going down to fetch it. As for her shoes…goodness knew what she was going to do about them.

Her only thought was to get out of there as fast as possible, so she headed into the bathroom and turned on the shower, letting the water run so Will wouldn't suspect what she was about to do. Back in the bedroom, she sat down heavily on the bed, almost breaking the zip of her tiny evening bag in her haste to find her cell phone and call a taxi.

As she scrambled for the phone, the tears of disappointment and frustration were blinding her. She had to get away, but first, breathing would be good. Sitting on the edge of the mattress, she dragged in a few lungfuls of air. It was enough to allow her to pick up the phone again and remember that there had been another night when she'd been with

Will and needed a taxi. The night in the Black Dog, when Jan and Pete had gone home together.

The night she'd spent at the rescue base waiting for Will. She hoped it would still be there in the dialed numbers and scrolled frantically through the memory for the taxi firm.

There it was, she thought, sighing in relief, the last one on the list. Now all she needed was for someone in this godforsaken corner of England to be willing to come out here on a Sunday morning. She hoped the bit of cash in her bag would be enough or that the driver would take a card. If not, she'd have to get the rest from her flat. She'd pay the driver in chocolate, wine, or anything if he'd come and get her out of this mess.

The phone in the taxi office seemed to ring forever before it was picked up. She didn't know and didn't care what the controller thought of her rant about coming as soon as possible. All she cared was that the taxi firm knew Ghyllside Cottage and would be there in thirty minutes. Now she had thirty minutes to find some shoes and get out of this beautiful, awful house.

Yes, shoes would be good. Even black deck-busting heels or sneakers or fluffy slippers. Somehow she knew that any footwear in this house would be the size of boats. Will had big feet; she hadn't needed to sleep with him to know that. But one thing was certain: she couldn't go home in her bare feet. She had to negotiate the gravel drive for a start, and she didn't know how she was going to do that. Knot the sheet, perhaps, and shimmy down the ivy…

A cry of frustration escaped her lips. The situation would have been funny if it hadn't been so gut-wrenchingly humiliating. The knife twisted again. This must have been Kate's home before Will had turned her out. She must have spent weekends here at least—and if she had stayed here, what had she left behind?

Her eyes took in the chest of drawers under the window, the bedside cupboard where he kept his supply of condoms, and the huge oak wardrobe against the wall. Walking over to it, she unlatched the heavy door. Nothing doing. Just a few suits and shirts and jackets. Some smart shoes on the bottom of the wardrobe—all size twelve at least.

Emma slammed the door shut.

In the corner of the room, she noticed a door to a walk-in closet. Pulling it open, she searched for a light switch. There wasn't one, so she set to hunting in the semidarkness for walking boots, flip-flops, slippers, anything a jilted bride might have kept here and forgotten.

Emma was almost sobbing now. The taxi was due in ten minutes, and all she'd unearthed were fins and a set of crampons. All were now littering his bedroom floor in her frantic quest to find something to put on her feet. Grabbing at a pair of sneakers that looked promising in the gloom, she flung them at the wall in disgust as she realized they were his.

In desperation, she searched the top shelf of the cupboard. A shopping bag with foreign symbols on it caught her eye, and she snatched it down. There, inside, still in the polyethylene wrapper, was a pair of exquisite beaded sandals. Emma concluded they must have been a gift from one of his business trips or a forgotten souvenir from an exotic holiday.

One of them at least had great taste, and she suspected it was Will. If Kate had any real discernment, she wouldn't have been with a pig like him…

Past caring now, she ripped open the bag and put them on. They were a little too small, but she was pathetically grateful for small mercies this morning. It dawned on her that this was the ultimate humiliation; now she was literally in Kate's shoes, but anything was better than having to explain why she was barefoot to the taxi driver.

Now all she had to do was get out of his house.

Clutching her bag, her feet slipping over the heels of the stolen sandals, Emma gently turned the key in the lock and slowly inched the door open. It creaked slightly, and she held her breath, dreading the sound of heavy footsteps on the stairs, his voice asking her if she was ready to leave, embarrassed, scared…

There were no footsteps on the stairs.

She nudged the door wider and crept onto the landing, listening for him. Was he still in the kitchen or in some other part of the house? There was only silence, so taking her chance, she slipped softly down the oak staircase and into the hall.

As she crept across the tiles, she saw the kitchen door was ajar, but she still couldn't hear anyone moving about. Her pashmina was still draped on the leather chair by the front door, so she snatched it up before twisting the handle. The door opened out onto the gravel drive he'd carried her over twelve hours before, laughing and happy, up to his bed.

Outside, Will's black four-by-four stood on the drive.

Emma slipped past and crept around the side of the house, where the gravel drive curved away up a gentle slope to wrought-iron entrance gates set between two stone pillars. The dull throb of a diesel engine broke the silence as the taxi reversed between the entrance posts. Hitching up the skirt of her silk dress, she hurried toward it.

———

Will stood outside on the jetty, gulping in fresh air. He knew he couldn't stay out here any longer; he had to go to her.

Her words had rocked him.

I don't care what you did to Kate or why you did it, because you didn't ask me to stay.

She'd said she wanted him, despite what he might have done to Kate. No matter what she thought about him, what she'd heard, she still cared about him—just as he was, with all his faults. All she wanted was to know that he wanted her.

It seemed so little to ask and yet so much.

He couldn't let her go like this. Whatever happened, she deserved an explanation. Though the thought of telling her the truth, of baring his soul, went against every instinct. Will did not wash his dirty linen in public. He kept his private life private, his most intimate secrets firmly under lock and key, exactly where they should be.

But it had to happen, and deep down, he knew that sooner or later, someone would try to get close, pierce his armor. He'd kept himself safe for two years, but Emma had gotten so very, very close.

Will raked his hand through his hair and groaned. She was going. She was testing him. Not even an idiot like him could mistake that. But so soon?

And he did not ask people to stay. He did not beg women to stay. Not now. Not ever again.

He'd known all along what Emma must think. She was bound to have heard the rumors in the village. Someone they both knew, a colleague maybe, anyone, in fact, within a ten-mile radius could have told Emma what he'd done to Kate. They'd be ready and willing, he thought bitterly, to give their own version of what had happened two years before. He was surprised that they hadn't embroidered it to the extent of him leaving her at the altar.

Then again, he had only himself to blame. In Emma's eyes, he'd lived up to his reputation—and how. Seduced her, rejected her—twice—kept her dangling on the end of his personal rope. Then the worst part: he'd lulled her into a false sense of security until she had felt safe with him.

Only to let her down.

He shaded his eyes with his hand and stared across the lake toward the opposite shore and her flat. He couldn't let her go like this. He had to go up to his room and tell her the truth. Swallow his pride and find the courage to tell her about Kate and him. Make her understand what had happened, how he had felt, what it had done to him. There would be no going back, he knew that. If he went up there now and opened himself up, he would have to ask her to stay.

Will shivered. Even though the sun was still warm on the wooden jetty, a cooling breeze skittered across the lake and raised the goose bumps on his forearms. Then he heard it. Distorted, distant, but clear: a diesel engine idling. He twisted around to see a taxi parked at the top of his drive. Its driver was climbing out and opening the rear door.

And she was climbing in.

"*Emma!*"

She looked back at him as he broke into a run to catch up with her.

"Wait! Don't go—not like this!"

She was in the car now as the driver revved the engine and started to pull away. As he saw her look back through the window, he was shouting at her, running hard to catch her.

It was too late. He'd blown it again.

There had been no need to pay the taxi driver in chocolate or alcohol. When they'd reached the flat, Emma had found real money in the purse of her work bag. No need to explain to the driver what had happened. Seeing her evening clothes and red eyes, the man had obviously put two and two together. Even if he'd made five, it wouldn't have added up to the disaster that had happened this morning.

She'd fallen for it. The picnic, the yacht, the sunny Sunday morning coziness. The mind-blowing, tender sex. Will had pulled out all the stops, and without so much as a whimper of resistance, she'd fallen for it.

In fact, she'd asked for it. Actually asked him to take her home to bed and asked to be hurt. Maybe the seduction had lasted a bit longer than average for him, but he'd managed it. And now?

She was turning into a serial victim. She must be giving off *hurt me—I'm a sure thing* signals. She'd let Jeremy do it, and now she'd let Will do the same. She'd thought they were so different, but underneath it all, they were the same.

She needed to talk to someone—needed comfort. Jan maybe. Suzanne. Her mum. Anyone. She reached in her evening bag for her phone and found it missing. She sighed. *Well, there you are*, she thought. Now she needed new shoes, a new phone—and a new attitude toward men. A *get any closer, you rat bag, and I'll shoot you* attitude.

As soon as she thought it, she knew it wasn't her. It wasn't her instinct to keep people at arm's length. No, it was her way to trust people, to give them the benefit of the doubt. She liked people. That was why she'd wanted the tourist board job, why she'd volunteered to help the mountain rescue.

She was just way too soft and gullible.

———

God almighty, what had happened here?

Will stared in disbelief at the mess that was his bedroom. He needed his car keys and his pager, and he'd found chaos. Just what had she been doing? At first, he thought she'd just gone mad and trashed his room. God knew he deserved it.

Then he saw the paper bag with the writing and he knew.

She'd taken Kate's shoes. Of course, Emma needed shoes; she'd left hers behind on the yacht.

Picking up the bag, he swept the clothes off the duvet, cleared a space, and sat down, crumpling the bag up in his hands. Two years it had been, he thought in surprise, since he'd seen that bag—those sandals. He'd bought them for Kate en route to New Zealand, but in the rush of the wedding preparations, he hadn't gotten around to giving them to her. Then, of course, he hadn't gotten around to giving them to her at all.

The day was becoming more distant now. The once painfully perfect memory of it was beginning to blur at the edges. Even though he'd tried so many times to hear their conversation again, looking for a clue or a reason, that day was fading.

He knew this, though: he'd been laying out his morning suit on the bed and checking that he had the rings to give to Max when it had happened. In fact, he'd thought it *was* Max when he heard the bell ring downstairs. It had hit him as soon as he'd opened the door. It was unlucky for a groom to see his bride on their wedding day; even he, without a superstitious bone in his body, knew that.

Kate had only said four words to him before everything fell into place in one awful moment: "I'm so sorry, Will."

He remembered how he'd had to hold on to the door to steady himself as she'd tried to explain why she was leaving him. Why, at that moment of all moments, she was walking out on him when his life with her had stretched out in front of him, shining and happy and new. She'd done it then, she said, before it was too late for all of them.

"Do you still love me?" he'd asked her as she tried to tell him why she'd shattered his world.

"I'm—I'm very fond of you…"

She could have used any obscenity other than *fond*, a word he still couldn't bear to hear. Then he'd begged. Demanded. Shouted. But nothing would change her mind. Nothing he had could.

When Max and his mother arrived, they'd found the front door wide open and a note saying he'd called off the wedding. He'd found a place few people knew. A dark and inaccessible place where he'd licked his wounds. When he got home that evening, he was a different person. One who was cautious now, to the point of obsession, about ever letting anyone get close to him again—until Emma had breached his defenses.

And as he'd predicted, it was all ending in misery again.

Will drew his phone from his pocket and dialed, wondering if she would answer when his name came up on the screen. The ringing made him jump. It was coming from under a pile of his clothes.

Emma's ringtone. Emma's phone.

He tracked it down to the floor by the bedside table.

She'd left it behind in her haste to escape him. Escape him… Hell, he'd really screwed her up, hadn't he! He threw it back down on the carpet and let it lie with all the other debris of his life.

Stuff the phone anyway—he needed to see her and talk to her right now. Taking the stairs two at a time, he thudded through the hall and out to the Range Rover. He was going to Emma, and he was going to tell her everything.

———

In the corner of Emma's bedroom, the laptop was whirring softly. She flopped down into the chair and tapped the mouse, watching the screen flower into life. She needed human contact, a friendly face, even across cyberspace, to remind her someone still cared about her. Wearily, she clicked on a message received in the early hours of the morning. Steven and Gina. Both over the moon as they told her to expect another niece or nephew by Christmas.

Her answer to her brother's email was the best piece of spin she'd ever produced. She sounded happy and positive, and her delight in the baby-to-be was genuine—that hadn't needed to be faked. But the story she told him about her own weekend was a complete fabrication.

As for the job offer, well, that was surely a no-brainer now. Leaving Bannerdale had never seemed so tempting and so unutterably awful.

Hitting Reply, she started to compose her thanks to Rachel Brockhouse. This offer was too good to miss, impossible to miss, in fact. There was nothing for her here now. It was time to go back to reality and start over. She'd done it before, and she could do it again.

Then why did it have to be so very, very hard?

———

That bloody stupid pager. This bloody stupid job. For the first and only time in his life, Will found himself resenting being called out on a rescue. Not even on the wettest, coldest, most awful night had he ever felt that he wanted to ignore a cry for help and tell them to find somebody else because just this once, he needed to look after himself.

He'd actually had the keys in the ignition when the buzzing had started. The noise that meant he wouldn't be going to Emma. Couldn't go. Not yet. He'd had the whole of yesterday, the whole of last night off duty at his own request. Plenty of time to impress her, seduce her, to hurt her and reject her. But there was no time now to go to her and tell her the truth.

He looked at the screen and groaned. As always, it said only one word: *Rescue*. Sitting with the engine running, he called into the base. The phone crackled into life, Suzanne's calm voice unmistakable.

"Will?"

"Yeah. What and where?" he barked.

"Two climbers stranded on a crag on Ravenhowe Crag. A young lad and an older girl, late teens by the sound of it."

"Exact location?"

After a brief pause, Suzanne gave him the reference.

"I'm closer than you. I'm on my way now," he replied curtly.

He heard the doubt in her voice and felt angrier than ever. "We'll meet you there."

"Whatever."

"Will, is everything all right?"

"Why the hell shouldn't it be?"

There was a long silence, then Bob's voice, steady and calm, more like the one he used with casualties than team members. Bloody annoying, in fact.

"Will, it's me, mate. We'll be right behind you. Wait for us on—"

"Yeah, right." He flicked off the phone, cutting off Bob in midsentence.

Too fucking right they'd be behind him, a good twenty minutes behind him. Ghyllside Cottage was way closer to Ravenhowe Crag than the base, and it was a busy Sunday afternoon. Plus, he knew a back route he could take in the four-wheel drive, while the base was the wrong end of the village center.

As he roared up the drive, sending the gravel flying, he put through a call to Max and Francine. Getting their voicemail, he left a garbled message apologizing for ruining their lunch and blaming the climbers. My God, he thought, the day was turning into a complete disaster…

His shortcut cost him a side mirror by the time he reached the stony pull-in at the bottom of the incident site. A brush with a dry stone wall had flipped back the mirror and shattered the glass. Fuck that. He could easily get it fixed when all this was over.

And now he was here: Ravenhowe Crag. A safe enough climb for an experienced climber on a good day, but not a novice's route and definitely not in these conditions. The sun had gone in, and mist was swirling around the fells, obscuring the tops. It looked like summer was going into hiding again. Will tried to thrust his personal problems aside and focus on the young climbers.

They must be terrified. A teenage girl and lad, Suzanne had said. Stuck on the cliffside, too scared or inexperienced to find their way down as the weather had closed in. People had no idea how fast things could change up here. From bright and sunny to cold and wet, from a dream to a nightmare.

He felt no resentment now, only a sense of urgency and a need to get the job over and done with, for this was one thing he was good at. A problem that he could solve through straightforward sweat and toil and physical skill. Nowhere near as risky as trying to get Emma to trust him again.

He jumped down from the car and glanced up at the fell tops. His T-shirt was by no means warm enough, even down here. The temperature had dropped several degrees already as the clouds had come out, obscuring the sun. Several hundred feet up, it would be cold and damp and pretty unpleasant. So very different, he thought, to a few hours ago, when he'd woken with Emma's warm body next to him in bed.

The place she should wake up every morning. He knew now, how much he needed to say it to her: *Wake up with me, Emma, every day. I love you.*

He pulled his jacket from the back of the car and grabbed a rucksack, ropes, first aid, and drinks. He slung the rucksack onto his shoulder and fastened up his coat. The team was right behind.

They wouldn't be long. They knew exactly where he'd be.

———

Emma sat back in the chair in her bedroom and sucked in a long breath. Her shoulders felt stiff with tension, and her head was starting to throb. How could composing a simple email be so hard? She should be turning cartwheels at the opportunity that had dropped in her lap. Not that she hadn't earned the chance at this ticket back to London. She deserved this invitation back to civilization, with its buzzing streets, decent coffee, and a taxi on every street corner—that was where she really belonged.

Stretching her arms above her head, she read back the note she'd written. It was full of typos.

Hi, Rahcel, thanks for your emmail,

Fantastic news about the sponsorshpi deal. On behalf of Bannerdale MRT, please accept my thanks for your company's generosity. I aslo want to thank your ND for the job tipoff. Yes, I'd be very interested in teh role of communications Director.

You see, there's this guy I've met up here and he's absolutely the sexiest bloke I've ever known and hes a leader in the MRT and well, it's quite simple, relly. I've fallen in love with him and he just doesn't feel teh same way about me. He likes me and cares about me—he cares aboutEeveryone—but he just doesn't want to go that extra mile for me—per se

   Let's put it simply, Rachel. I love him but he doesn't love me and that's all there is to it.

She added the last few lines with her eyes shut.

"*Basicly,*" she typed, "*Id be madd to stay here and not accep your offer. I'm comigg hom…*"

Pressing her finger on the Backspace key, she held it there as moisture splashed onto the keyboard. She couldn't see properly anymore, and as the tears ran down her face, she turned off the laptop, stumbled to her bed, and gave in.

———

It took Will longer than he'd thought it would to reach the crag. Maybe he was tired after last night. That made him smile. Holding Emma, making love to her, had been the sweetest pleasure. Her body was beautiful, soft and curvaceous, and her response giving and open as he'd explored every inch of her.

That first time, when he'd thrust inside her and felt the power of her orgasm around him… Even here in the cold, when his mind should have been on *them*, he was aching for her. She was absolutely beautiful. Feisty and loving and courageous—not like him.

He'd been a coward, he told himself. He'd been so intent on never getting close to someone again and so careful not to allow anyone through his armor that he'd hurt Emma. He could see that now in absolute clarity, even here in the mist. He slowed for a moment, feeling the cold, damp air on his face.

It was getting pretty rough up here, thought Will, and the visibility was getting worse by the minute. As he stopped to catch his breath, a faint cry above him on the fellside made him stop and listen.

"Hey there," he called. "It's OK. I'm coming."

He could hear them now, and he knew he was close to the crag. Quickening his stride, his long legs soon covered the stony ground on the steep hill. Suddenly, the rock face loomed above him, and he saw them.

A teenager was perched on a narrow ledge, crying quietly. She was obviously terrified, but that was to be expected. It was the lad with her, propped against the rock, still and silent, who worried him more.

The girl shouted to him, "Please help us. My brother's hurt himself—"

"It's OK, sweetheart, we're coming. You're going to be just fine. What's your name?" soothed Will.

He could just hear her voice above the freshening breeze.

"Charlotte, is it? And your brother's Tom. Well, everything's going to be all right, Charlotte. Not long now."

As he took off his rucksack, he carried on talking to her. "Keep nice and still. I'm going to help you, sweetheart."

Reassuring her even as he unpacked the ropes and equipment, Will felt a sense of relief that was almost palpable. This was a situation he could deal with. He knew exactly what to do. He knew the crag, had climbed here himself many times—it wasn't even a difficult grade.

"Not long now," he called as he heard the girl sobbing in fear and relief. "Soon be with you, sweetheart." He was almost within touching distance of her when he heard the radio buzzing down on the fellside where he'd left it. He told himself the rest of the team must be close now, and so what, if just this once, he'd broken a tiny rule.

These people needed him—and so did Emma.

———

Emma finally managed to haul herself into the shower as the sky opposite the window deepened from blue to indigo. She turned the jet to full and tried to pummel herself into life under the stinging spray and scour herself clean of Will's musky scent.

Foamy water flowed down the drain, taking away the memory of his touch and the fleeting moment of tenderness he'd shown her. She could hardly bear to look at her body, knowing what he had done to her—recalling his fingers on her skin, his mouth on her breasts, his lovemaking.

Winding a towel around her hair, Emma grabbed a bath sheet from the hook on the door, drying her body, rubbing him away...vowing to start afresh on Monday. Where, she wasn't certain, but one thing was for sure: there would be no more Will. She would ask her boss, James Marshall, to take over the production of the calendar, and she'd never see Will again.

A dull thudding intruded through the bathroom door: the sound of footsteps on the metal staircase, followed by a loud and insistent banging on the door. Her heart started beating out a retreat. That knock. It could only be one person. The question was, did she want to answer it?

Her hand was on the bathroom door handle. She opened it a crack and peered around the jamb into the hall. A shadowy figure was waiting on the other side of the frosted half-glass in the front door.

"Emma!"

She reached the door in two strides and pulled it open wide.

Chapter 13

"DON'T YOU EVER ANSWER YOUR PHONE, GIRL?"

Emma tried not to look disappointed as she pulled the door open wider to find Suzanne there. "I left it at someone's house. I've only just gotten out of the shower."

"That much is obvious," said Suzanne, taking in her towel-clad figure. She knelt down as she unlaced her boots wearily at the top of the staircase. Her strawberry-blond crop was sticking up at all angles around her flushed face. She was wearing the muddiest pair of boots Emma had ever seen and an expression of total fatigue.

"Aren't you going to let me in?" she said.

"Sorry, Sue, you'll have to forgive my manners. I'm not feeling at my best right now."

"Me neither, and these damn boots don't want to come off!"

Emma winced as one did come off. It flew off, in fact, and hit the wall, leaving a muddy mark.

Suzanne sighed dramatically. "Sorry, it's been a bad day."

Emma had to smile in spite of how bad she was feeling. It wasn't often she saw Suzanne in any state other than total control. "It's fine," she said. "Decorating's the least of my worries." *Especially now I'm moving out*, she might have added. Showing Suzanne through to the living room, Emma caught sight of the rain running down the windowpanes. It was turning into a crappy day all around.

Suzanne's voice cut into her thoughts. "Is it all right if I sit down? I'll try not to make a mess of your trendy sofa."

"Oh God, yes. Oh, Sue, I'm really sorry. I've had a pretty lousy day too."

"Oh dear. Well, I'm afraid I'm not going to make it any better," muttered Suzanne, dropping her car keys onto the coffee table. "I'm here with news, Emma. Not that good either."

All at once, everything clicked into place: the late-night visit, the muddy boots, the frustration and fatigue in her friend's voice.

"What do you mean, not good news?" she murmured.

"Why don't you sit down?" said Suzanne gently.

Emma flopped down on the edge of the sofa Will had stretched out on so casually only the afternoon before.

"I'm afraid Will's had an accident. It's OK," she added quickly as Emma's hand flew to her mouth. "He's in Lancaster General Hospital, and he's going to be all right, but it was nasty, and if we hadn't been there—"

"No!" *Not like this*, she thought. *Please don't let it end like this…*

Suzanne reached forward and smiled, placing a hand on her arm. "Don't worry. It's not too serious. He'll be fine in time."

The rush of relief Emma felt was physical and overwhelming. Why did she feel like this? As if…as if…she still loved him…

"What's he done to himself?" she asked shakily.

Suzanne sighed. "Concussion, fractured fibula, bruised ribs. And some very impressive cuts. Not entirely sure about his leg until the consultant's seen him in the morning. Hardly life threatening, but painful, and it could so easily have been much worse."

"When did this happen? I was with him all morning. I—I spent the night at the cottage."

"It was this afternoon. It's taken us until evening to get him down, and he's bloody heavy, I can tell you. It's a wonder I haven't had some hernias to treat."

Emma didn't even smile.

"I see you're not in the mood for jokes. Cheer up. It's not that bad. He's going to be OK, you know. Physically, anyway."

"What do you mean?"

"Will needs your support right now, more than ever. He's hurt, but worse, he's mad as hell at himself. Having to be rescued by his own team…just think about it."

Will needed *her* support? Big, tough Will, who always, at the end of the day, held all the cards, who had power over her, absolutely and totally?

"How did it happen?" she whispered.

"We had some injured climbers stuck on a crag on Ravenhowe. None of us are really sure what he was doing, but evidently he wanted to be first in. Couldn't wait for us. When we got there, the climbers were safe, but Will was at the bottom of the crag."

"How far had he fallen?" asked Emma, although she knew the answer would mean nothing to her.

"Forty-five, maybe fifty feet. That may not sound like too far, but he still got away with murder," she paused. "We've had three serious falls from Ravenhowe in the past few years. One was fatal, so Will has been very lucky, thank goodness. Until Bob gets hold of him, that is," she added. "The pain he's in now will be nothing."

Emma was grateful for Suzanne's attempts to soften the blow and reassure her, but it just wasn't happening today.

"Far worse is his sudden tendency to whine. He's driving everyone mad and persuading him to let us carry him down was a nightmare," said Suzanne grimly.

"I'm sorry he's been hurt, and I'm grateful for you coming to tell me, but I don't think he'll want me there."

She snapped her mouth shut, but Suzanne continued, "All we've heard since we carried him down was your name. He was ranting about you every step of the way."

"My name?" She knew she must have sounded completely stupid, but Suzanne seemed not to notice.

"Yes. Yours. We're sick of hearing it. He's been driving the hospital staff mad to have his phone, but they won't allow it in there. So"—she heaved a sigh—"I said I'd fetch you."

"How long will he be in the hospital? Will he be all right?"

"Just overnight, I guess, until the specialist can see him tomorrow. I'm hoping his leg's not as bad as it looked when we got to him. He shouldn't need an operation, but he's definitely going to be out of action for quite a while. You know how much he'll like that."

Not going to like it? Emma knew he'd hate it. Stuck on the sofa or behind a desk with climbing and rescues off the agenda. The recovery would be far more painful than any injury. And it was true—he'd be absolutely furious with himself at having to be rescued, even if it was in the course of duty. So why did she care so much? Why, when he'd hurt her like this, did she care how he felt, about what happened to him? And why was he asking for her? A guilty conscience maybe, but more... No, it wasn't possible. He'd had his chance.

"Is he well enough to talk to me?"

"Oh yes, he's well enough to do that." Suzanne smiled wryly before getting up from the chair. "He was perfectly able to complain too, when we wouldn't let him have his phone. Look, Emma, I'm pretty tired to be honest, so I need to know: are you coming with me to the hospital or not?"

Emma gave a nod in reply. He could be asking for her to tell her goodbye. It could mean absolutely nothing.

"Go and get dressed then, girl. I'll wait for you downstairs." Snatching up her keys from the table, she smiled indulgently at Emma, who was still sitting there, feeling totally shell-shocked. "Come on, then. What are you waiting for? Get your clothes on, and get out that door and into your car before I drag you."

———

Wasn't it ironic, thought Will as he lay on his back on the narrow bed. He just hadn't seen it coming, his fall. It hadn't been from a great height, thank the Lord for that, but it had been enough to hurt him more than anything he'd ever felt before.

He'd thought he could sort everything else by himself. Overconfident Will, always in control. Now, one slip, one tiny moment of lost concentration, when he was tired and his mind was not quite 100 percent where it should have been, had landed him here. On his back, hooked up to God knew what, and *helpless*. Abso-fucking-lutely perfect.

He couldn't recall exactly what had happened, but maybe that was the drugs they were pumping into him. Maybe part of him didn't want to remember, but the climbers must have told Bob and the team everything by now. The boy had a concussion; the girl was just shocked and cold. At least they were safe. He'd managed that much. Never mind that he was going to be in trouble, that there might be an inquiry within the team, and doubtless, he'd be hauled over the coals. Him, a deputy leader too, though maybe not for much longer. Well, tough. He didn't care. After all, no one had been hurt but himself.

It was his other mistake that really upset him. The one that had ended up with Emma hurt and out of his life. Just like his fall, he hadn't seen her coming, though he acknowledged now she had been creeping into his life for months now. Since that first moment he'd seen her at the base, she'd been beautiful, confident, and, he realized now, reaching out to him. And when she'd seen him on the fell top, naked and vulnerable, he'd known then that she was special and unique.

He'd tried hard to resist the possibility of letting her close because he knew it would end like this, with them both hurt and in pain. One slip, one moment with his eye off the ball, and she'd floored him.

And now he wasn't sure if he'd ever get the chance to put things right.

———

The rain was coming down in torrents as Emma followed the doctor down the highway to Lancaster General. She knew Suzanne didn't have to go with her. In fact, she was worn out. Emma could see that. She also knew that her brusque manner hid a genuine affection for Will. Coming all this way to tell her went beyond the call of duty and was something only a good friend would do. She hoped their friendship would continue when she moved back to London to take the Echo job but knew it wasn't that likely. They'd only really just gotten to know each other.

Just like her and Will.

Emma fiddled with the radio, trying to find some music to distract herself, but she soon gave up. Nothing could distract her from thinking about Will. He deserved a hearing. Whatever he had to say and no matter what he'd done, she couldn't bear the thought of him being hurt. She didn't hate him that much. She didn't hate him at all, in fact, just ached for him to love her. The one thing she was sure she could never have.

Because, let's face it, she told herself as she queued at the busy highway junction, she just didn't belong up here in his world. For a brief, shining moment, she'd convinced herself that this was the place for her. That while this place never buzzed and sparkled like the city, something else, someone else, had rocked her world.

Not now. She was a metropolitan girl, pure and simple, and the time had come to go back to her roots. There was simply nothing to stay for any longer, no matter how much she loved him or hoped, deep in a corner of her heart, that he cared for her.

The windshield wipers could hardly cope with the rain sluicing down the screen. Even in midsummer, the sky was already dark, the lights on the highway blinding her.

An hour later, she was following Suzanne through the maze of corridors and departments that led to the side room where they were keeping him overnight for observation. As they approached the nurses' station, the staff greeted Suzanne warmly and nodded at her in acknowledgment. She paused to ask them about Will's progress, and Emma hazarded a look through the small window in the door of his ward. For a moment, she thought she had the wrong room. Was this the same big, strong guy who had carried her down the jetty and up the stairs into his bedroom? Who had made love to her for half a night and all morning? Was this the man who had hurt her so much? The one making her hurt so much now...

She felt a rush of love sweeping over her that only intensified the pain.

"OK, Emma?" Suzanne was beside her, her voice soft. "He broke every rule in the book to help those climbers, you know. Typical. He'll be in trouble when all this is over." Her smile told Emma he wouldn't. "Don't tell anyone, but I'd have done exactly the same thing." Emma tensed as she felt Suzanne's hand on her arm. "Shall I come in with you, or do you want to be alone?"

"Come in with me. Please, Sue." Her voice sounded like a small child's, then hardened. "I'll see how he is, and then I'm going. He's got five minutes. That's it."

"Really?" asked Suzanne quietly. "Don't you think he deserves more than that?"

Before Emma could answer and before she knew what the answer was, Suzanne had knocked on the door and pushed it open without waiting for a reply. The figure in the bed stirred and opened his eyes.

"I've brought someone to see you," declared Suzanne sternly.

Emma stared. Will was shockingly pale and something else she'd never seen before—vulnerable looking. As he propped himself up on one elbow, she could see the Steri-Strips covering the cuts on his forehead and cheek. His hospital gown was hanging off one shoulder where a large bruise was already beginning to bloom spectacularly. She could see the sprinkling of hair on his chest, the one that only this morning she'd kissed and explored.

She swallowed. Why on earth was she even here? What had she come for other than to say goodbye and be said goodbye to? Maybe she wouldn't wait for either of those things. Once she'd heard from his own lips that he was fine, she was out of here for good.

He leaned against the pillow. "Emma, thanks for coming."

"Does it hurt?" she asked.

"No. Not now," he lied.

Suzanne shook her head grimly. "We had to give him nitrous oxide and half the morphine supplies."

"You didn't have to cut my bloody trousers off!" Agitation made him grimace in pain.

"Standard procedure, Will. You know that. Quickest way to get the morphine in."

"You know damn well you didn't have to stick it in my arse. You know bloody well you could have done it IV."

Suzanne smiled broadly as she picked up the chart at the bottom of his bed and scanned it cursorily. "Just be grateful I was there. Otherwise, Bob would have had to do it, and believe me, he needs an *awful* lot of practice."

"Glad you find it funny," he croaked and sank back down onto the pillow.

"I see you're on the mend. And they've taken the IV away. Much better for you," she said, replacing the chart. "So I'm off. I want to see how one of my patients is getting on in geriatrics, and then, thank goodness, I am going home to my other half." To Emma's surprise, Suzanne squeezed Will's hand and kissed his cheek. "You've got some things to sort out, I expect. And, Will darling, when you have sorted things out, try and get some rest and stop making such a nuisance of yourself."

"I'm never going to hear the last of this, am I?"

"Probably not."

"You should work on your bedside manner, Dr. Harley!" he called as Emma hugged her friend goodbye and whispered "thanks" into her ear.

So, she thought, his sense of humor was back: he'd survive. The door closed with a quiet click. Outside, she could see Suzanne saying her farewells to the staff. Now, Will and she were alone together in the overheated, stuffy room. Emma hugged her bag to her and stood a few paces from the bed. The moment had to be put off as long as possible.

"Nice room. Lucky to get your own."

"Sit down," he ordered, no longer looking so vulnerable.

"I won't, if you don't mind. I'm not staying now that I know you'll live."

He ignored her. "I said sit down, Emma. This is going to take a while."

"Are you sure you're up to it, Will? It could be painful…"

"Who for?"

"Both of us."

"You're not going to get hurt by what I have to say. Me, that's a different matter, but I probably deserve everything I might get."

Her heart pattered lightly. This was the start of it, then, but he was wrong if he thought she wasn't going to get hurt. Too late for that—way too late. Dragging a chair closer to the bed, she sat on the edge of the vinyl seat, with her bag on the floor and her hands in her lap. She studied the floor for a moment before she could face him.

"How on earth did you let this happen?" she asked eventually.

"I was stupid."

"You seem good at that," she muttered.

"You're probably right, but I was obviously extra stupid today. I seem to have made a big mistake...again."

"Not like you to make a mistake," murmured Emma.

"I wasn't thinking straight," said Will, reaching over to take her hand.

Emma kept both hands resolutely in her lap, so Will laid his fingers resignedly back on the cover.

"My mind was on other things, Emma. You know damn well why," he said, grimacing as he tried to subdue the pain shooting through his leg.

Seeing his expression, Emma tried to resist the temptation to fling her arms around him, to kiss him and hold him tenderly. She stayed stiff and upright in the chair, determined that Will would never get close to her again.

He tried again. "There's something I need to explain...something you didn't give me a chance to tell you back at the cottage."

Though he was right next to her, his voice came from a long way away. Her stomach began to knot again. "I said I didn't care."

"I think you do. I hope you do, Emma."

"Will, I didn't come here to hear your platitudes or your excuses. I came to see you because you'd had an accident. I've done my duty, and now I'm going."

Going home and leaving Bannerdale. Back to the city where I belong.

She should be saying it out loud. Shouting it, but the words died on her lips.

He'd had enough for one day. She'd had enough. She reached down to pick up her bag from under the chair, but Will's strong fingers closed around her wrist. He was half leaning out of the bed now.

"Emma, you're not going anywhere. You're going to bloody well sit down right now and hear me out. Or so help me, I'll get out of this bed and make you stay!"

"Don't be ridiculous."

Take your hand away, she told herself. *Pull it out of his.*

But she kept it there, in the grip of the man she loved, still loved more than anything else in the world.

"Listen to me. I'd have been with you this afternoon if this stupid thing hadn't happened. As soon as you left, I had to go. You know the rest."

"Will—"

"Shut up, sweetheart. Just for a moment—please." He gritted his teeth as he struggled to get up but kept her wrist in a tight grip.

"You're hurting my hand."

He released the pressure a fraction. "I know what you must think."

"Do you, Will? Do you really? What would you think? I know this much. That you will never commit to a woman. Not to me, not to Kate, not to anyone. You asked me for time and space, and I'm giving it to you. I'm going home!"

"Are you absolutely decided on that, Emma? Absolutely sure that nothing I can say will make any difference?"

What I want, she thought, *is so beyond your capability, is so far and away a dream, something I will never have, that it must be impossible.*

"I'm going."

"Emma!"

As he shouted her name, Emma heard a noise outside the door and caught the nurse on duty staring at them in alarm through the window. The door handle rattled, and a nurse walked in briskly.

"Everything all right in here?" The nurse was at the bottom of the bed now, picking up the chart and frowning. "Are you sure you're OK, Will?"

"Fine," he snapped, letting Emma's arm drop into her lap but keeping his eyes locked on hers. "Absolutely bloody fine."

"We need to check your vitals," said the nurse, looking at them both suspiciously. "It's getting very late. I'm afraid you can't stay much longer, love, no matter what Dr. Harley says."

Emma picked up her bag. "I'm just going."

"She's not."

The nurse raised an eyebrow. "Staying or going, your girlfriend needs to wait outside for a minute. If you both don't mind, that is."

Emma got to her feet. "It's no bother."

She'd reached the door when she heard Will speak.

"Wait for me."

Whether it was plea or a command, she didn't know, but she walked away anyway. Quickening her step, she hurried down the maze of corridors, past the coffee machine in the reception area, to the entrance. The doors opened automatically as she approached. Walking briskly through them, she felt the cool night air on her skin and gulped in a breath. The rain had slowed to a drizzle, and the pavement was black and gleaming in the orange glow of the city lights.

She stood outside, feeling the fine rain on her cheeks, hearing it drip from the trees and shrubs onto the tarmac.

Don't you think he deserves more than that?

That was what Suzanne had said.

Emma's eyes were stinging again, blurring the light spilling out from the hospital entrance. Didn't they both deserve more than this? More than her running away again instead of staying to hear the truth, however painful?

When the door to the side ward opened again, the staff nurse found her slumped on a chair in the corridor, a half-empty cup of coffee clutched in her hand.

"I know it's none of my business, love, but I'd say you made the right decision," she said kindly.

Emma got to her feet and threw the cup in a nearby bin. "I hope so. I really do. Are you sure he's going to be all right?"

"He'll be fine, but try to be gentle with him," the nurse warned, her eyes twinkling.

Be gentle with *him*? Emma almost laughed in derision but settled for an ironic smile. As she hovered in the doorway to his room, he was sitting upright.

Had he expected her to wait? She wasn't sure.

"Come over here, sweetheart," he said gently.

Part of her hated herself for turning around and giving in, for doing as he asked now and crossing the room to his bed, but out there in the rain, she had decided it was time to be honest, whatever the cost.

"OK. You've got me and you're right: I do want to know. Why did you leave Kate? You did leave her, didn't you—on your wedding day?"

"Who told you that?"

"That doesn't matter. I want to know why you did it."

"I had no reason," he replied, making her wince at his brutal honesty. "I had no reason to leave her."

Gently, he lifted his hand to her face.

"*She* left *me*, Emma. She left me because she didn't love me. She had an affair while I was in New Zealand for six weeks before the wedding. She has a little girl called Alice who was conceived while I was away. But things hadn't been right for a long time, I know that now."

"And you told her to go?"

"No, I begged her to stay."

Emma's eyes widened. She told herself this couldn't be true and that she couldn't believe him, because if she did, it meant…

"I loved her, and I was ready to bring up the baby as mine," Will went on. "I thought we could put it all behind us and start again, but Kate wouldn't have it. I thought she was cruel at the time, but now I know she was so right. She loved Alice's father, not me. It was that simple, but I wouldn't accept it. Not for months—not for years—until…" His fingers brushed her cheek with infinite gentleness, just like a piece of fine porcelain or an exotic flower. "Until I met you."

Emma's stomach went into free fall. This wasn't happening to her. Wonderful things like this didn't happen to her.

A man she loved couldn't care about her.

She snatched her hands away and covered her face to hide from the truth, not daring to believe he could really be saying this, but Will reached up and took away her mask, forcing her to look at him.

"Emma, I need you to understand this. For a long time now, I haven't thought about Kate. When I've woken up in the morning, I've thought about you. In fact, right from the moment I first saw you at the base, then on the mountain, you were driving me wild."

"But that day on the cliff when I kissed you, when you walked away…" she whispered. "You hurt me then and today, when you didn't ask me to stay with you. Will, my world fell apart."

He groaned. "Forgive me, sweetheart. I was scared. Of something much worse than my first rappel." He teased a strand of her hair between his fingers. "I love you. I just needed to take the leap of faith."

She forced her eyes to meet his, finding them bright and dark all at the same time. Full of longing—a longing she didn't dare believe.

"I've been a bastard, Emma, and a coward. To lead you on like that and then pull back was unforgivable. I should have followed my instincts right from the start, and they were telling me to love you."

Emma didn't dare reply. Otherwise, her tight-wound coil of emotion was going to unwind suddenly and spectacularly. She'd come to hear him say goodbye, and instead, he was saying he loved her.

"I love you. Did you hear that?"

"Will—"

"You don't have to say it back. I'll try and understand if you don't feel the same after what I've done to you, but please understand that now, I know what I want. And it's you. It's you, Emma."

She couldn't help herself. She knew she shouldn't do it and they'd be in trouble with the staff, but she had to sit next to him on the bed and put her arms around him. She had to hug him far too hard than was good for him.

"Will, I want to say it back," she murmured against the soft cotton of his hospital gown. "I've wanted to say I love you. I've wanted to trust you for such a long time now, but you've made it hard for me. Why let people think you did that to Kate? Why didn't you tell people she left you?"

His smile was bitter now, just for a moment. "And be laughed at by everyone for fifty miles? When a woman cancels their wedding and rushes off like Kate did, people put two and two together and make five, and the guy usually gets the blame. And it suited me to be the villain." His expression softened again. "I'd rather be hated than pitied, Emma."

She felt one roughened fingertip trace the profile of her cheek and then his thumb rubbing her lip.

"Emma, I take care of things. I'm the one people rely on. I take control of my life, and I keep my private affairs just that. Private. There is no way in the world I was going to apologize or explain what happened between me and Kate to anyone. It hurt, Emma. And you're the only person in the world who'll ever hear me admit that." He kissed the tip of her nose. "I'd like it to stay that way, sweetheart. So you'll have to get used to being seen with the bad guy. You should have known I was never going to be a hero." He smiled.

"I wouldn't mind ending up with the villain, Will," she whispered.

Nothing had ever been so true. She didn't mind ending up with a proud, self-contained man. One who was never going to lie and tell her he agreed with her opinions just to keep her sweet—or to give her spin or slick and honeyed words. She knew she had only the truth now, and she loved him for it.

His arms felt strong around her, almost crushing her. It must have been hurting him to hold her like this, but it felt so good, and even for his sake, she didn't want him to stop.

"For a long time now, sweetheart, you have been the most important thing in my life, and I will understand completely if you don't feel the same. I don't deserve you to feel the same way, but I've spent too long hiding from the truth. I don't ever want to lose you. Stay with me, and wake up with me every morning the way you did today."

The lump in her throat made it impossible to reply.

"You know what I'm asking, don't you? I'd get down on one knee if I could, but that won't be happening anytime soon."

She stopped his words with a kiss and an embrace of such ferocious tenderness that he was left reeling. Pain shot through his leg, but it was drowned by a tidal wave of pleasure, and even through the pain, the agonizing closeness of her body pressing through the thin gown made him dizzy with desire.

"Is that a yes?" he asked, breathless, when she finally released him and he sank back onto the pillows.

"Yes," she whispered, settling beside him, her hand stroking the hair on his chest from where the gown had slipped down his torso. "Are you sure you want to do it—get married again, I mean?"

"More sure than I've ever been about anything, but first, there's something else we need to sort out."

She raised her eyes to him. "What?"

"Your job."

"Will…"

"I can't hold you back, but you know how I feel about you, Emma. I won't lose you. I'm willing to come to London if you want me to. I'll leave Ghyllside and run the business from the city. I can't lose you now, but I also can't ask you to give this chance up for me."

Her heart was racing his to the finish line. Was he really offering to leave his beloved Lakes for her sake? Give up all that for her?

"Leave Bannerdale?" she asked, incredulous. "You live in London?" She shook her head. "Oh, Will, that has to be the most stupid idea you've ever had. You know it would finish you. I don't want to spend the rest of my life with a guy who wants to be somewhere else no matter how much he says he loves me."

Even as the words left her lips, she knew she was saying goodbye forever to all that was waiting for her in the city. The high salary, the party lifestyle, the city bars, the bright lights blocking out the stars that shone over the mountains…

"I'll do it," he was whispering to her. "I'll do it if it means we can be together. Just like you did. You've survived, Emma, up here, away from everything you love."

"Not everything, Will." It was her turn to stroke his face now, her fingertips skittering across the grazes on his cheek. "You won't be leaving Bannerdale because I'm not taking the job. I love you, Will, and though I never thought I'd say this, I love it here. I'm staying." She touched her lips to the graze and whispered, "On strict conditions."

"Anything. Just hit me with it," he murmured.

"Don't ever try and make me go rappelling or climbing or bungee jumping." Hearing him start to protest, she added a twist. "Plus, you agree to be spokesperson for the calendar. An enthusiastic spokesperson, mind, in the press, on TV, radio—the lot."

Will groaned loudly, drawing another disapproving look from the nurses.

"You drive a bloody hard bargain, Emma Tremayne, but I guess you've put me in an impossible position."

"Not with that leg injury," she said. "But in a few weeks maybe… And Will, there's one more thing…"

"Yes?" he whispered, so close now that she could feel his warm breath on her cheek.

"What *is* your middle name?"

"Now that will have to remain my secret—until our wedding day."

She knew he was feeling better when he took her in his arms and kissed her.

Epilogue

WILL FLICKED OFF THE TV REMOTE CONTROL WITH A SIGH. THAT was the third time he'd seen that damn interview this weekend. On the early morning news bulletin too! Good God, everyone in Bannerdale must have seen it by now.

He'd never liked giving speeches, even in business meetings, and to be featured on television talking about his part in a nude calendar was excruciating.

"I'm useless at giving interviews. I always come across as a bit of a cynic." Shivering in the chilly air, he slid back under the duvet, pulling Emma down with him and holding her against his naked body to keep him warm. "I wish you'd do them all."

"We made a bargain, Will, and you know they don't want to see me. They want to see Mr. December in the flesh," she said, resting her cheek on his bare chest. "Look on the bright side. I think every woman in Bannerdale has bought at least one calendar, and we're already into the third print run. I even had an email from a production company the other day. They want to make a documentary about the team."

"No way!"

"It'll wait until we get back," she said, laughing.

"Haven't I got enough to do? Work starts on the outdoor center in a few weeks."

He felt his knee throb. It didn't hurt so much nowadays, but after another night of energetic lovemaking, he could certainly feel it. On the other hand, there were compensations. Cupping one of Emma's breasts in his hand, he wondered if they had time for one more glorious session. He dipped his head to swirl the tip of his tongue around the pink peak of her nipple.

"The answer's no," she whispered, trying to resist the familiar tingle as it spread outward from her breasts through her body. "There isn't time."

Kicking at the duvet, she tried to get up but found his arms around her waist, pulling her back into bed.

"I think there is."

"No. We really have to get up."

She had no chance really. Six feet three inches of hard muscle and power imprisoned her benignly in his arms. Even with his dodgy leg, resistance was futile.

She gave it up as a bad job. And so what if they were late? Let everyone else wait.

Half an hour later, as Will collapsed back against the pillows, Emma reluctantly tore herself out of his embrace and out of their four-poster bed.

She padded naked across the bedroom carpet and threw open the curtains. Out on the frozen lawn, a skittering of snow dusted the frost-spiked grass. In the distance, snow lay on the tops of the fells, softening their jagged peaks against a powder-blue sky. With just a few days to Christmas, the Lake District had obliged with a perfect winter day, and she felt light-headed with happiness.

Will untangled his long limbs from the duvet and came over to the window. She felt his arms encircle her shoulders.

"Beautiful."

She nodded, the breath catching in her throat. Butterflies stirred in her stomach. His touch still and always would have the power to make her ache with anticipation.

"Shame your brother and his family couldn't make it," he observed, touching the back of her neck with his lips.

"Yes," she sighed, trying to hide her disappointment by gazing out the window over the lake. Steve's absence was the only tiny blot on an otherwise perfect day. "It won't be the same without them, but Gina's baby's due next week, and there's no way they'd let her fly. Plus, there are the girls to look after," she added.

The water danced in the winter sunshine as she watched the wavelets break against the jetty. When she turned, Will had gone. She felt a pang of disappointment that he hadn't been listening but smiled when she caught sight of the beautiful ivory gown and matching cloak hung on the closet door. She had to think about getting ready in a moment. Bannerdale church, freshly decorated in holly and ivy, awaited. Soon her parents and Will's mother would be arriving, along with Max and Francine—with baby Olivier of course—the rescue team, her London friends. Just about everyone, in fact, would be there, all waiting for her to walk in on Will's arm.

Under the circumstances, no one had dared question why a bride and groom wanted to spend the night before their wedding together or why they would be walking up the aisle together in an unconventional way.

But Will didn't want to do things the traditional way.

A creak from the bedroom door told her he was back. Then a warm, big hand closed on her shoulder and spun her around to face him. His dark eyes were gleaming as he handed her a stiff white envelope.

"Here. I was going to give you this at the reception, but I think you should open it now."

Never one to savor unwrapping her presents, she ripped open the envelope and pulled out a pair of airline tickets. A slow smile spread across her face. He couldn't have given her a more wonderful present.

"Will..."

His hands were cupping her face now, his head dipping for a sweet, long kiss that drank her in until she felt dizzy with joy.

"It's summer in New Zealand," he was saying. "We can stay for four weeks over Christmas and New Year. I fixed it with your boss. You can see Steve and Gina and the girls. And the new baby."

Her stomach flipped. A brand-new life.

Will's hands moved to her waist again, his eyes glinting with mischief.

"We can even fit in some bungee jumping—tandem."

A small smile curved her lips, and she shook her head.

He lifted an eyebrow. "No?"

"No," she echoed firmly.

"I think you can. You can do anything if you try. Haven't I taught you that?"

"Will. No bungee jumping. Trust me on this."

He was half teasing, half serious as he persisted. "What excuse can you possibly have for not giving it a go? If you don't do it in New Zealand, you never will."

"Maybe one day," she said huskily. "But not this time." She stood on tiptoe and whispered two words in his ear. Two words she hoped would be the best wedding gift she could ever give him.

His sharp intake of breath told her all she needed to know. She found herself enfolded in his arms, the breath almost being squeezed out of her by the ferocity of his love.

"Oh God," he murmured. "Oh, I mean that's wonderful, Emma." He took another deep breath and released his pressure on her body before asking, shakily, "When, sweetheart?"

"The end of June, according to the doctor. So you see, the bungee jumping will have to wait."

"It can wait forever," he replied. "Emma, I love you so much. Both of you."

"*And I love you Will—absolutely.*"

Acknowledgments

Special thanks go to…

Ash Cooper of the Langdale & Ambleside Mountain Rescue Team (lamrt.org.uk) for answering my questions with humor and patience and to Phil Barber for the rappelling advice and instruction. Any errors are entirely my own.

Mum and Dad, Barbara and Charles, Janice Hume, Rosy Thornton, and Julie Haggar for the support and doing the ironing. Claire S. for the great critiques. Annette, Sarah, Clare, Gill, Glenda, Steph, Maggie, and all my friends at C19 for their faith in me.

Catherine Cobain at Headline for the brilliant editing, and Broo Doherty at Wade & Doherty for just being brilliant.

Finally, to John and Charlotte who lived every word of this with me. As Steve Ovett used to say: ILY.

About the Author

Phillipa Ashley studied English language and literature at Oxford University before working as a freelance copywriter and journalist. She lives in an English village with her husband and daughter. Visit phillipa-ashley.com.

12 Men for Christmas has been filmed as *12 Men of Christmas* for the Lifetime channel, starring Kristin Chenoweth, Josh Hopkins, and Anna Chlumsky.

THE TOURIST ATTRACTION

Welcome to Moose Springs, Alaska! A laugh-out-loud romantic comedy series from Sarah Morgenthaler

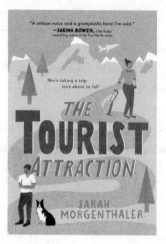

When Graham Barnett named his diner the Tourist Trap, he meant it as a joke. Now he's stuck slinging reindeer dogs to an endless parade of resort visitors who couldn't interest him less. Not even the sweet, enthusiastic tourist in the corner who blushes every time he looks her way...

Two weeks in Alaska isn't just at the top of Zoey Caldwell's bucket list—it's the whole bucket. One look at the mountain town of Moose Springs and she's smitten. But when an act of kindness brings Zoey into Graham's world, she may find there's more to the grumpy local than meets the eye... and more to love in Moose Springs than just the Alaskan wilderness.

"Fresh, fun, and romantic."

—Sarah Morgan, *USA Today* bestselling author

For more Sarah Morgenthaler, visit:
sourcebooks.com

THE KISSING GAME

"I bet you a kiss you can't resist me."
Game on.

Rena Jackson has worked her tail off to open her own hair salon, and she's almost ready to quit her job at the local bar. Rena's also a diehard romantic, and she's had her eye on bar regular Axel Heller for a while. He's got that tall, brooding, and handsome thing going on big-time. Problem is, he's got that buttoned-up ice-man thing going as well. With Valentine's Day just around the corner, Rena's about ready to give up on Axel and find her own Mr. Right. But Axel has a plan of his own when he makes one crazy, desperate play to get her attention…

"Sexy, sweet, and thoroughly satisfying."

—Lauren Layne, *New York Times* bestselling author

For more info about Sourcebooks's
books and authors, visit:
sourcebooks.com

BAD BACHELOR

Everybody's talking about the hot new app reviewing New York's most eligible bachelors. But why focus on prince charming when you can read the latest dirt on the lowest-ranked "Bad Bachelors"—NYC's most notorious bad boys?

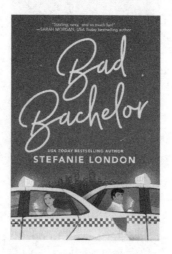

If one more person mentions the Bad Bachelors app to Reed McMahon, someone's gonna get hurt. A PR whiz, Reed is known as an "image fixer," but his womanizing ways have caught up with him. What he needs is a PR miracle of his own.

When Reed strolls into Darcy Greer's workplace offering to help save the struggling library, she isn't buying it. The prickly Brooklynite knows Reed is exactly the kind of guy she should avoid. But the library does need his help…As she reluctantly works with Reed, she realizes there's more to the man than his reputation. Maybe, just maybe, Bad Bachelor #1 is THE one for her.

"Original, witty, and sexy. My #1 romance read of the year!"

—Jennifer Blackwood, *USA Today* bestselling author

For more info about Sourcebooks's books and authors, visit:
sourcebooks.com